Frankly My Dear,

I'M DEAD

Books by Livia J. Washburn

FRANKLY MY DEAR, I'M DEAD

HUCKLEBERRY FINISHED

Published by Kensington Publishing Corporation

Frankly My Dear, I'M DEAD

LIVIA J. WASHBURN

KENSINGTON BOOKS
http://www.kensingtonbooks.com

KENSINGTON BOOKS are published by

Kensington Publishing Corp.
119 West 40th St.
New York, NY 10018

All Kensington titles, imprints and distributed lines are available at special quantity discounts for bulk purchases for sales promotion, premiums, fund-raising, educational or institutional use.

Special book excerpts or customized printings can also be created to fit specific needs. For details, write or phone the office of the Kensington Special Sales Manager: Kensington Publishing Corp., 119 West 40th Street, New York, NY, 10018. Attn. Special Sales Department. Phone: 1-800-221-2647.

Kensington and the K logo Reg. U.S. Pat. & TM Off.

ISBN-13: 978-0-7582-2567-2
ISBN-10: 0-7582-2567-9

First Hardcover Printing: November 2008
First Mass Market Printing: October 2009
10 9 8 7 6 5 4 3 2 1

Printed in the United States of America

This book is dedicated to my agent, Kim Lionetti, and my editor, Gary Goldstein, who were both instrumental in its creation and development, and of course to my husband, James Reasoner, my Rhett Butler.

CHAPTER 1

I didn't mean to lose it. Really, I didn't. It must have been the two squabbling teenagers. Or the two annoying adults. Or the pressure of setting up a new business and knowing that if I couldn't make a go of it, it would be just one more in a long list of failures.

We won't even mention the divorce.

All I wanted was a minute to myself. Just one simple, single minute to sit there in the new office and take a deep breath and look around and say to myself, *This is mine. And it's going to work.*

But I hadn't been there in the chair behind my new desk more than ten seconds when the door burst open and Augusta and Amelia came in snapping at each other over something. They looked at me and said in unison, in the sort of plaintive wail that only teenagers can manage, *"Aunt Deliiiilah!"*

I held up one finger and closed my eyes. If they can do that to me, I can do that to them. They sighed. Together, of course.

Then I heard heavier footsteps, and Luke Edwards, my assistant—and son-in-law—said, "Miz Delilah, the phone's not workin'. Are you sure you called 'em and told 'em we'd be movin' in today?"

"Of course she called them," my daughter Melissa said from behind him. "She wouldn't have forgotten something that important."

I had hired Melissa, too, as secretary/receptionist. It was sort of a package deal. She and Luke hadn't been married for very long, and they thought it would be just darlin' if they could work in the same place and spend all their time together, since they loved each other so much.

I didn't call them poor deluded fools. At least not to their faces. You can't do that to kinfolks.

"Aunt Delilah, she's being totally unreasonable," Amelia said.

"Well, she's stuck in the nineteenth century," Augusta said. "There's nothing wrong with body piercing. It's an ancient custom."

"We can't run the office without the phones," Luke said.

"Will you leave the poor woman alone? She knows that," Melissa said as she crowded into the room along with Luke, Augusta, and Amelia.

"She's going to mutilate herself and embarrass me—"

"Embarrass *you*? It's *my* body—"

"I can call the phone company on my cell—"

"I'll call them. It's my job—"

"Aunt Delilah—"

"Miz D—"

"Aunt Delilah—"

I opened my eyes. I stood up and put my hands

on the desk and said, "Will y'all just *hush up for a minute?*"

Now, I admit I raised my voice a little. But not enough so that all four of them should have stared at me like I just choked a kitten or something. Augusta and Amelia got that little bottom-lip quiver—you know, like they were about to cry because I'd yelled at them—and to tell the truth, so did Luke, whose big ol' country boy, football player looks hid a soul that was a tad on the sensitive side. Melissa had known me the longest, so she recovered first and said, "I think we should all go on and leave her alone for a minute. She's got a lot on her plate these days and we don't need to be bothering her with our petty problems."

"There's nothing petty about tryin' to run a tour business with no phones," Luke grumbled as she shooed him out of the office.

"You, too, girls," Melissa said to her cousins, who, at sixteen, were six years younger than she.

I could tell Augusta and Amelia wanted to argue with her, but they left, too, and Melissa eased the door shut on her way out. I was alone again.

Problem was, I didn't want to be alone anymore. The mood was gone. Like I said, all I'd wanted was a minute. I hadn't gotten it, and now it was time to move on.

But after Melissa had stepped in like that to help me, I couldn't very well act like I didn't want to sit there in the office by myself. I took a deep breath and turned around to look out the window. I had a good view of the office complex parking lot and the big-box discount store across the street and the futuristic skyline of downtown Atlanta rising a couple of miles beyond it. I had worked downtown for several years, in one of the city's biggest travel agencies, and I was glad I didn't have to go down there every day anymore. That was one big reason for starting my own business. I wanted to be able to slow down a little, to take stock of my life, to devote more time to the things that were really important.

Divorce will do that to you, I guess. Make you take a hard look at your life and try to figure out what's working and what isn't, before anything else breaks down beyond repair.

You figure out a way to go on, because you can't just stop.

I stood up, went to the door, and opened it. Luke and Melissa had gone back to their desks in the outer office. Augusta and Amelia were sitting on the sofa, one at each end with as much room between them as they could get.

"Luke, I did forget to call the phone company and make sure they turned the phones on today." I'm sorry. Would you take care of that for me?"

He grinned. "Sure, Miz D."

"Augusta."

She looked at me. I crooked a finger.

"You're going to yell at me? It's not fair. You're not my mother."

"No, but your mama's my little sister, and I promised her I'd look after you girls this summer. I just want to find out what all this fuss is about."

"And you're going to listen to her side of it first?" Amelia said. "It's not fair!"

I could have told her a few things about how fair life is, but I knew she wouldn't want to hear it. So I just said, in as calm and rational a tone as I could manage, "I'll get to you in a minute."

She leaned back against the sofa cushion, crossed her arms, and sulked.

When Augusta and I were back in the office with the door closed, she said, "Aunt Delilah, you've got to talk some sense into her—"

"What's this about body piercing?" I couldn't help but frown as I said the words.

Her response was quick. "It's done by professionals, you know. And I just want to get a belly button ring and maybe a little stud for my eyebrow. It's really no different than having pierced ears. You have pierced ears."

"Yeah, but I don't have a hole in my belly button." I leaned back in my chair. "What do you think your mama would say if I was to call her and ask her if it was all right for you to get these . . . piercings?"

Augusta looked down at the floor and didn't say anything.

"That's what I thought."

"It's still not any of Amelia's business," she muttered. "She's such a little suck-up. And a tattletale."

Inside every sixteen-year-old lurks a twelve-year-old, I guess. Especially when it comes to sisters. Twin sisters, at that.

"Can I at least call myself Gus?"

That took me by surprise. "Augusta is a beautiful name."

"An old-fashioned name."

"Honey, you're talkin' to somebody named Delilah here, you know."

"I still want to be called Gus."

I looked at her through narrowed eyes, or maybe I just squinted at her. "Now *there's* an elegant name."

"There's nothing wrong with Gus."

"Not many sixteen-year-old girls named that, though."

"I don't mind being different. I want to be different, and since you won't let me get my belly button pierced . . ."

I'd lost track of all the pierced, Gothed-up sixteen-year-old girls I'd seen, not that I'd been counting to start with. Augusta's concept of "different" wasn't quite the same as mine.

"You say that now. How are you going to feel about it when school starts again?"

"We'll be back home then, so it won't be any of your business, will it? Anyway, it's got to be better than Augusta."

"Your sister's never minded being called Amelia. You think that's a more modern name?"

I could see her digging in her heels. "All I'm saying is that it ought to be my decision. It's not any of her business what I want to be called."

She had a point there. And calling herself something else wasn't nearly as permanent as getting holes stuck in her.

"Go back out and send your sister in."

"You're not going to make me go by Augusta, are you?"

"Just send your sister in."

I sat down behind the desk and waited. A few seconds later Amelia came in and closed the door behind her a little harder than necessary.

"Augusta is absolutely *immmm*possible. Mama would have a fit if she got her navel and her eyebrows pierced."

"She's not going to. But she's going to change her name to Gus for the summer."

Amelia stared at me in horror for a second before she said, "*Gus?* That's horrible!"

"Your sister's got a right to call herself whatever she wants to."

"But Gus Harris sounds like a boy! An ugly boy, at that."

"Maybe she could call herself Gussie."

Amelia gave me the look. You know, the one that teenagers give adults when they want to say, *Could you be any more ridiculous?*

"You know, she's probably going to change her mind about this whole thing before school starts again. That's still more than two months off."

"But what if she doesn't? I'll be Gus Harris's sister! It's already hard enough being a twin."

"You liked having a twin sister when you were four. You even liked it when you were eight."

"I'm sixteen now." She managed to sound terribly world weary as she said it.

"I know, I know, everything's different now. All I'm sayin' is that if you just let things go for a while, a lot of problems will sort themselves out so they aren't problems anymore."

"Oh? Like the problems you and Uncle Dan had?"

I felt my jaw getting tight. I didn't know if I was more hurt or mad.

She saw that and said quickly, "I'm sorry, Aunt Delilah. I didn't mean that, you know I didn't mean that."

I held up a hand to stop her. "No, you're right," I said. "Sometimes you can't just let things go and hope they'll get better. The trick is knowing when those times are and which battles are worth fighting." I turned my chair so that I was facing the computer and turned it on. "Go on back outside, and we'll talk about this some more at home. For now, you and your sister just try to get along, all right?"

"Yeah." She caught her lower lip between her teeth for a second. "Yeah, sure."

I kept my eyes on the monitor and watched the screens change as the computer booted up. I didn't let myself sigh until Amelia was gone. I didn't let myself cry at all. I'd been there. Done that. A lot.

A knock sounded on the door and Luke opened it without waiting for an answer. "Talked to the phone company," he said. "Phones'll be on by the end of the day."

"Thanks, Luke. Sorry about the mix-up. My bad, as the kids say. If they still say that. I haven't checked lately."

"That's all right. You've got a lot to keep up with these days, Miz D. It's not easy opening your own business, you know. Not to mention taking care of kids, even if they're not yours. I hope by the time Melissa and I have kids, I'm a lot smarter and more grown up than I am now."

I smiled and said, "That's a good way to look at it."

" 'Cause sometimes I think I'm dumb as dirt."

"No, you're a sweet young man, and when the time comes, you'll do just fine." I sat up straighter, trying to be more brisk and businesslike. "Now, let's talk about this *Gone With the Wind* tour."

So that was how things started out on the first-ever day for Delilah Dickinson Literary Tours. A little ragged, maybe, but I had high hopes. We'd get over all these rough patches. Things were going to get better as they went along. I was sure of it.

Of course, folks hadn't started getting killed yet. . . .

CHAPTER 2

Downtown Atlanta was hot and muggy, even at eleven o'clock in the morning. Clouds scudded across the sun every now and then and offered a little relief from its glare, but that didn't affect the humidity.

I was sort of used to it—although anybody who tells you that you can get used to ninety degrees and ninety percent humidity is a flat-out liar—but many of my clients weren't. They were from cooler, drier climates.

The German couple was really sweating; I heard them sigh in relief as we went into the air-conditioned Visitors Center next to the Dump, as Margaret Mitchell had called the house on Peachtree Street, which had been known as the Crescent Apartments when she and her husband, John, moved into it in 1925. They lived there while she was writing a little book called *Gone With the Wind*. I'm sure you've heard of it. It's not such a little book, actually. More of a doorstop. They could've sold it in the bookstores by the pound. It's been read by more people around the world than any other novel ever written.

People love *Gone With the Wind.*

Some of them love it so much they're willing to pay to come to Atlanta and see the apartment where Margaret Mitchell lived while she was writing it, visit the *Gone With the Wind* Movie Museum located in the same house, and have an authentic, genteel Southern lunch at Mary Mac's Tea Room nearby.

The highlight of the tour, though, is the visit to Tara Plantation. It's not the real Tara, of course—not that there ever actually was a real Tara except in the mind of Margaret Mitchell and the imaginations of Hollywood filmmakers. In the first draft of the novel it was called Fontenoy Hall and was based on the farm of Mitchell's maternal grandparents, but the name Tara and the image of the magnificent house were set firmly in the minds of millions of readers and moviegoers. One of the old plantation houses outside of Atlanta, a place originally called Sweet Bay after the magnolia trees that grow there, had been remade into a near-replica of the movie location. It was also a working plantation, producing a good cotton crop most years using only historically accurate methods.

Well, except for the slaves, of course. Historical accuracy only goes so far.

I had a short spiel prepared and went into it as soon as all the tourists were inside, along with Luke, Augusta, and Amelia. Melissa was holding down the fort at the office.

I'd done quite a bit of reading about Margaret Mitchell, from her birth in Atlanta through her early life and her disastrous marriage to Red Upshaw, the man most people believed to be the model for Rhett Butler; her later marriage to John Walsh and the ten years she had spent writing *Gone With the Wind*, with John editing it page by page; her other works (most people didn't know she had ever written anything other than the one book); and her tragic death after being run down by a car on Peachtree Street, not far from here, as she and John tried to cross it to go to a movie theater. I covered that ground pretty fast, because I knew that what people really wanted to do was wander around the house, look at the exhibits, take pictures, and buy stuff in the gift shop: the same things that tourists do at every attraction in the world.

Luke sidled up to me after I turned the tourists loose to sightsee on their own. In a quiet voice, he said, "I think it's goin' pretty well, don't you, Miz Delilah?"

"I hope so. Everybody seems to be having a good time."

He hitched up his pants. "Yep, this here is a fine tour. Gonna be real popular. You'll see."

"It was *my* idea, Luke," I reminded him. "I always thought it would work."

"Yeah, sure, but you had your doubts. I know you."

He wasn't telling me anything I didn't already know. I had doubts about *everything*. That's just part of being a natural-born worrier.

"Believe I'll just circulate," he went on, "in case anybody has any questions, you know."

"Thanks, Luke."

"All part of the job."

He moved off through the Visitors Center and on into the Mitchell house itself. I walked into the gallery, where various historical exhibits that had to do with the South, not necessarily Margaret Mitchell or *Gone With the Wind*, were on display.

Right now it was a series of famous photographs from the Depression. I was glad to see some of the younger members of the tour group studying them. Too many young people don't have much interest in history these days. I think there's a lot of truth in that old saying about those who don't learn from history being doomed to repeat it.

"Mrs. Dickinson?"

I turned to see one of the men from the tour standing there. "It's Ms. Dickinson," I told him, trying to sound nice about it. But I had taken my name back when Dan and I got divorced a few months earlier. I wasn't Delilah Remington anymore and never would be again—although after more than twenty years of marriage I sometimes had a hard time remembering that myself.

"Sorry," he said. "I just wanted to tell you what a fine tour this is. I'm really looking forward to visiting the plantation tomorrow. I hope you'll do me the honor of dancing with me at the ball."

The *Gone With the Wind* tour that I put together with Luke's help lasts three days. One day in Atlanta to see Mitchell's apartment, as well as through the Visitors Center next door and the movie museum. The Tea Room lunch breaks up that part of the tour.

The next day, the group loads onto a bus in the

morning and rides out to Tara—not the movie set, but the other plantation remade into a tourist attraction—where they get not only a tour of the whole place but also an elegant dinner and dance hosted by actors portraying characters from the novel, before staying overnight and having breakfast the next morning, then returning to Atlanta.

It would be more accurate to say that the actors on the plantation were portraying the actors from the movie. They were chosen for their resemblances to Vivien Leigh, Clark Gable, Olivia de Havilland, Thomas Mitchell, Hattie McDaniel, and other cast members. It's quite a show, I tell you. I'd seen it several times myself. Being from Atlanta, when I decided to start my own agency and specialize in Southern-oriented tours, *Gone With the Wind* was a natural. Everybody's read the book. Everybody loves the book. And who wouldn't want to go hang around for an evening with Scarlett and Rhett?

"Oh, I'm not much of a dancer . . ." I said to the man who had come up to me—I was surprised at myself for feeling flustered all of a sudden.

"I have a hard time believing that. Why, a person can tell just by looking at you how graceful you are."

He was flirting with me, I told myself in disbelief.

And I didn't know whether I liked it or not.

He was a nice-enough-looking man, I suppose. About fifty, which made him approximately the same age as me. Medium-sized, with dark hair that I was pretty sure was at least partially a toupee, but a good, expensive one. The smile he gave me was a little smirky. Not too bad, though.

But the important thing was, he was a client, and I don't like to mix business with pleasure. An old-fashioned attitude, I know, but I'm an old-fashioned girl.

How could I be anything else with a name like Delilah Dickinson?

"I'm sorry, Mister . . . ?" I'd heard his name earlier but couldn't remember it.

"Riley. Elliott Riley."

"I'm sorry, Mr. Riley, but I have a policy about not fraternizing with my clients—"

"Fraternizing? What is this, the army? I just want to dance with you tomorrow night at the plantation." He moved closer to me. A little too close. "I got a thing for redheads, you know."

"No, I didn't know that," I told him, and this time I didn't bother trying to keep my voice pleasant. I let it get nice and chilly. He had paid for the tour in advance, after all. But that didn't entitle him to any special privileges, no matter what he appeared to think. "If you'll excuse me . . ."

He took hold of my arm as I started to turn away. "What is this? What happened to that famous Southern hospitality you advertise on your Web site?"

"I'll give you the same sort of hospitality we gave you damn Yankees at Manassas if you don't let go of me."

I know, I shouldn't have said it. You may have guessed that I have this problem with my temper when I'm pushed far enough. Just don't blame it on my red hair. That makes me mad, too.

Mr. Riley's face sort of pinched in. He didn't let go of my arm. I was trying to figure out whether I needed to take a step closer to him before I kneed him or if I could reach the target just fine from where I was, when Luke moved up behind him and said, "Everything all right here, Miz D?"

My fiercely protective son-in-law was three inches taller and probably thirty pounds heavier than Riley, who took one look over his shoulder and then released his grip on my arm.

"Everything's fine, Luke," I said. "Just talking to one of our clients. Isn't that right, Mr. Riley?"

"Uh, yeah." He looked nervous now with Luke looming behind him. He gave me a curt nod and moved on into the gallery. Luke didn't try to stop him.

Instead he asked me in a quiet voice, "Was that guy botherin' you, Miz D?"

"Oh, not too much. Just flirtin' a little, I guess. Nothing I couldn't handle. But I appreciate you stepping in like that, anyway."

He nodded, looked satisfied with himself, and said, "That's my job. I'm a troubleshooter. I see trouble, and I shoot it."

"Didn't Barney Fife originally say that?"

"What?"

"Never mind."

"I hate to say it, but you're gonna have to get used to things like that, Miz D, now that you're single and out on the market again."

"Being single is *not* the same thing as being on the market, Luke."

"Yeah," he said, like he hadn't heard me, "a woman like you who's good-looking in, uh, an older sort of way, you've got to expect to get some attention from those older, desperate kinda guys—"

"Luke," I said, trying not to grit my teeth too hard. "Why don't you go back to circulating, in case any of our clients need anything."

"Oh. Sure, Miz D. But I'll be close by if you need me. Just give a holler."

"I'll do that," I promised, although I wasn't sure I could think of a situation that would make me holler.

Boy, was I wrong about that.

After everyone had had a chance to go through the Visitors Center and have a look at Margaret Mitchell's apartment, which has been restored to look as much as possible like it did during the years she was writing her novel, we all adjourned to Mary Mac's Tea Room for lunch. I kept an eye on Elliott Riley, just to make sure he wasn't bothering any of the other single women. He kept to himself, though, and didn't even talk much to anyone else. Despite what had happened earlier, I felt a little sorry for him, obviously vacationing by himself like that. Had to be pretty lonely.

After lunch, we all returned to the *Gone With the Wind* Movie Museum, which was part of the Mitchell house on Peachtree Street. The exhibits there told the story of how the best-selling, Pulitzer Prize–winning novel became one of the most popular motion pictures of all time, and certainly one of the most eagerly awaited when it was first released in 1939. The lengthy search for the perfect actress to play Scarlett O'Hara, the troublesome production that saw four different directors, including Victor Fleming, George Cukor, and Sam Wood, and the producer, David O. Selznick, work on the movie at one time or another (despite the fact that only

Fleming received screen credit—see, I told you I read up on this stuff), and the controversy over whether or not Clark Gable would utter an uncensored version of Rhett Butler's famous final line from the book. You know the one I'm talking about.

A screening room in the museum showed vintage newsreels about the fabulous world premiere of the film in Atlanta, as well as a documentary about the making of the movie. Let's be honest. As many people as have read the book, a whole lot more have seen the movie. Without Gable and Leigh, de Havilland and Leslie Howard, the story would be a lot less appealing. So most tourists are more interested in the movie museum than anything else. It has plenty to keep people entertained for quite a while.

While the tourists were wandering around the museum and watching the newsreels in the screening room, I found a quiet spot in a corner and caught my breath. Things were going well so far. I hoped that the word would get around about what a nice tour I had put together. We just had to get through the plantation visit the next day without any catastrophes occurring.

I had to rethink that a few minutes later when I heard an angry shout from inside the screening room. It was followed by another yell and then a growing commotion. I muttered, "Oh, Lord, what now?" and looked around for Luke and the girls. But I didn't see them anywhere.

Whatever was going on in there, it wasn't good. I hurried in that direction. A couple of security guards employed by the museum beat me to it. They slapped the door of the screening room open and ran inside. I got there two or three seconds later. My heart was pounding pretty hard, because I didn't know what was going on in there. All I knew was that there was trouble.

And my hopes for a perfect tour were disappearing with every yell.

CHAPTER 3

The lights were still down, the newsreel playing on the big screen that had rows of seats curving in front of it. The glare from the screen was enough for me to see what was going on. A couple of men must have started fighting, and others had stepped in to pull them apart. Luke, in fact, had hold of a man I recognized as one half of the couple that had come all the way from Germany to visit the Southern states.

One of the security guards was hanging on to the other combatant—who was none other than the amorous Elliott Riley, definitely wearing a rug. I could tell that because it was skewed sideways a little on his head from the tussle.

"He is a thief!" the German shouted as he glared at Riley. "A thief, I tell you! He tried to steal my camera!"

"I never touched his blasted camera," Riley insisted. "Let go of me, damn it."

The other members of the group who were in

the room, including Amelia and Augusta, were watching the confrontation like it was more interesting than what was on the screen. I suppose it was. It's not often you see two grown men throwing punches at each other in public.

But all I felt at the moment was anger that something had gone wrong with my tour. My *first* tour. The one that was supposed to be perfect.

This was one instance when having a temper and a loud voice came in handy. I stepped closer and said, "Settle down, both of you. This isn't a bar or a boxing ring."

"He stole—" the German tourist began.

"I never—" Riley began.

"Hush!"

They all looked at me, including Luke and the security guard, and I realized that my voice had been really loud that time.

Amelia and Augusta said in unison, "Whoa."

I tried to tone it down some as I went on. "Look, you're ruining the tour for everybody else. Why don't we step out of the screening room and try to settle this somewhere else, where we won't be disturbing folks?"

"We can go in the security office," the guard suggested.

I nodded. "That's just what I'm talking about. Luke, you take over the tour for a few minutes."

"Hadn't I better go with you?" he asked with a frown.

"No, I want you looking after the clients. I'm sure I'll be fine with—" I looked at the guard.

He supplied his name. "Dave."

"I'm sure I'll be fine with Dave," I went on, "and anyway, Mr. Riley and"—I searched my memory

Livia J. Washburn

for the German's name and came up with it—

"Mr. Riley and Mr. Mueller are going to settle down and behave themselves. Aren't you, boys?"

Both of them looked sullen. Mueller said, "I believe the police should be summoned."

"Fine with me," Riley said. "They can arrest this Kraut for attacking me and making wild accusations."

Mueller's face started to turn red again. "Kraut? Kraut?"

I took hold of Riley's arm and hustled him out of there while Dave followed with Mueller.

I felt a sense of relief when the door of the security office closed behind us. At least this commotion wouldn't be distracting my other clients from the tour anymore. But I still had to deal with Riley and Mueller and try to make peace between them. They glared at each other from opposite sides of the room. I wished the office was a little bigger so they wouldn't be within fist-swinging distance of each other.

"Now," I said, "what happened out there?" They both opened their mouths to yap at me, so I pointed to the German and added, "You first, Mr. Mueller."

"Why does he get to go first?" Riley asked before Mueller could say anything, reminding me of the argument between my nieces a few days earlier. Riley sounded just about as mature as they had.

"Because he's a guest in our country and we're going to be polite."

Riley gave a surly shrug and didn't say anything else.

"This man was sitting behind me and my wife," Mueller said. "I felt my camera move and looked down to see his hand on the case. He was trying to steal it."

"That's not true and you know it," Riley said.

The benches that formed the rows of seating in the screening room had no backs to them, so it would have been easy enough to reach forward and try to sneak something away from whoever was sitting in front of you, I supposed. But Mueller had the strap attached to his camera case looped over his shoulder, so I didn't see how anyone, even the slickest thief in the world, could have hoped to slip it away from him without being noticed.

On the other hand, maybe Riley had intended to open the case and take the camera out of it, leaving the case where it was. That might have worked, although he would have to be pretty daring to attempt that in the middle of a crowd. Some thieves are downright brazen, though.

"Is your camera worth a lot of money, Mr. Mueller?" I asked.

"It is a fine camera. I paid"—he paused to do the math in his head—"what would amount to four hundred of your American dollars for it."

A four-hundred-dollar camera was pretty expensive, all right, but not something that was fabulously valuable. I had no idea how much a thief could have gotten for it, but surely quite a bit less than its retail value. Steal enough stuff, though, and I supposed it would be a living, despite getting only pennies on the dollar for it.

"Did anybody else see Mr. Riley try to take your camera?" I asked.

"Of course not," Riley said, "because I didn't do it."

I shushed him and turned back to Mueller. He frowned and asked, "How would I know what the others saw?"

"Naturally, they would take the side of a fellow countryman over a foreigner."

"Nobody spoke up to say you were right," I pointed out.

I wasn't sure that was true; most folks were still pretty honest, or so I liked to think.

"Look, you've still got your camera, so no harm was done," I said. I took a deep breath, hating to do what came next, but I didn't see any other option. "If you want your money back, I'll be glad to refund it."

Now *that* was a bald-faced lie. I wouldn't be glad to refund what he had paid for the tour at all. But I knew from my years working at one of Atlanta's largest travel agencies that you've got to have a reputation for being honest and trustworthy if you want to succeed in business. I would give Mueller his money back if I had to—but I wouldn't like it.

Mueller sniffed. "My wife is very fond of this *Gone With the Wind* book. I would not deprive her of the enjoyment she gets from this tour."

I looked over at Riley, who had tugged his toupee back into place. "How about you?"

"I'm tempted, believe me, but . . . nah, I'm not going to back out. A deal is a deal, I always say. But I'm going to stay as far away from this guy as I can."

I thought that was a good idea. The more distance between the two men, the better.

I looked at Dave the security guard. "Does that work for you?"

"They didn't damage anything as far as I could see," he said. "Sure, they could be arrested for disturbing the peace, I guess, but what's the point? It's all over, right?"

Mueller nodded, and a second later so did Riley. They had made their peace, such as it was.

"All right," I told them. "Mr. Riley, you go on back to the tour. Mr. Mueller, give him a minute, then you can rejoin the others, too."

"I could sue you for slander, you know," Riley told Mueller. "Making false accusations against me that way."

I made shooing motions at him. "Go on now."

Riley left the office. A minute later, so did Mueller. I looked at Dave and said, "I'm sorry about all the fuss."

"You're going to be bringing more tours here, right?"

"All the time, I hope."

"Maybe the next bunch won't start fighting World War II again. They'd better not."

All I could do was agree with him.

CHAPTER 4

The rest of the tour went smoothly enough that day, with Riley and Mueller staying well apart from each other. The best part of the ruckus was that it got Riley's mind off of flirting with me. He didn't bother me again about dancing with him at the plantation ball the next night.

The bus that would be taking the tour group out to the plantation the next morning would pick them up at their hotels. They were on their own, free to enjoy Atlanta, until then.

By the next morning, I was over being upset with everything that had happened the day before. When you're trying to get a new business off the ground, you can't afford to brood about the past. You have to just charge ahead and do your best.

So that was the plan. The girls and I were at the office early, ready to meet the bus. Luke and Melissa showed up a short time later, and right behind them, the charter bus pulled into the shopping center's parking lot. I walked out to meet it as it rolled to a stop.

The door clattered open as the driver worked the lever. He was a grizzled black man wearing the uniform of the charter bus company. "You Mrs. Dickinson?" he asked as he leaned toward me in the seat.

I didn't bother correcting him about the Mrs. part. "That's right," I said.

"Name's Cobb," he introduced himself. "Wilson Cobb. I'll be your driver today."

"I'm mighty glad to meet you, Mr. Cobb," I told him. I held up a printout and went on, "I've got a list here of all the folks we'll be picking up and where they're stayin'."

"You folks put your bags in the luggage compartment and climb aboard, then," he invited, "and we'll get started. That is, if you're ready to go."

"I'm ready," I said.

The truth was I was more than ready. I was anxious to get the second day of the tour started and anxious for it to go well. I didn't expect it to be otherwise. The folks at the plantation hosted tour groups like mine all the time, so they were experienced at this sort of thing and knew how to make everything go smoothly.

Luke stowed our overnight bags in the compartment that opened on the side of the bus. Melissa wouldn't be going to the plantation, but the rest of us would. We climbed on board and spent the next hour riding around downtown and suburban Atlanta as Mr. Cobb picked up the members of the tour group. Then we headed north out of town. The plantation was less than an hour's drive away.

I watched for any signs of more trouble between

Mr. Riley and Mr. Mueller, but other than a sour glance exchanged between them, each pretended the other didn't exist. They sat at opposite ends of the bus, Mueller and his wife up front, Riley in the back.

We reached the plantation at mid-morning, Mr. Cobb turning the bus from the main road onto a quarter-mile-long driveway lined with magnolia trees, some of which had hydrangea plants climbing them and blooming, in addition to the large, snowy-white magnolia blooms. The plants were just beginning to flower in the fields that flanked the drive. It would still be at least a couple of months before the cotton started to produce fluffy white bolls. Workers hoed weeds out of the field of plants. The men wore overalls and broad-brimmed straw hats. The women were in long dresses and colorful kerchiefs. It was hard work out there in the sun, but they were being paid excellent wages. These folks were actors as much as they were field hands.

The house at the end of the driveway was magnificent, a four-story structure with massive columns supporting a covered portico where the drive curved in front of it. White-painted walls, set off by elegant wooden and wrought-iron trim, shone in the sun. More magnolias, as well as towering cottonwoods, surrounded the house. Well-tended flowerbeds gave the grounds patches of brilliant color. Roses, lilies, gladiolas, and half a dozen other varieties were bursting with blooms. Think of the most beautiful, stately plantation home you can imagine, and that gives you a pretty good idea of what this mock-Tara looked like.

Pretty girls in hoop skirts strolled the grounds,

accompanied by young men in swallowtail coats, silk vests, and fancy cravats with jeweled stickpins in them. A few Confederate officers in spotless gray uniforms were mixed in for good measure. The sun shone on their brass buttons, scabbards, and insignia. The men all had muttonchop whiskers. Some had drooping mustaches and others sported Beauregard beards. The women's hair was done in elaborate arrangements of curls, some of them adorned by flowers.

A burly, middle-aged man in a fancy suit was waiting for the bus. As it came to a stop and the tourists began to get off, this man boomed out, "Welcome to Tara, folks!" He was bigger than Thomas Mitchell but did a passable imitation of that character actor's voice. I thought I heard a hint of a British accent under the Southern drawl that he was putting on. He held out a hand and continued, "Scarlett and I are so glad to see you."

The woman who came forward to take his hand was beautiful, all right, no doubt about that. With her fair skin displayed to advantage in the low-cut gown she wore and ringlets of midnight-dark hair tumbling around her head and over her bare shoulders, she did Scarlett O'Hara proud. She smiled coyly and said, "Why, fiddle-dee-dee, Papa, who are all these nice folks who've come to see us here at Tara?"

Her accent was thick as molasses. I felt a little like groaning because her Southern belle act was so overdone, but the tourists seemed to be eating it up, especially when she turned her head and called, "Rhett, come over here and say howdy to all these nice folks who've come to visit us."

The man who joined them wore a white suit and

a broad-brimmed planter's hat. He had an unlit cigar in his mouth. The strong chin, the narrow mustache, the cocky grin, and the twinkle in his eyes were all just about perfect. He took off his hat, revealing thick black hair, and gave a little bow to the group. Then he put the hat back on, took the cigar out of his mouth, and said, "Hello, everyone. I'm glad you ran the blockade to come see us today."

"We'll be splitting up into three separate groups," the older man explained. "I'll take one group around and explain the workings of the plantation, while Captain Butler will accompany another group to the stables and Scarlett will show a third group through the house. Then we'll switch around later, so everyone will get to see everything, don't worry about that. There'll be a picnic lunch served at one o'clock. After that, we'll finish the tours, and you'll have plenty of time to wander around the plantation on your own before the ball this evening. Are there any questions?"

Mueller looked around and said, "Yes. Where are the slaves?"

Mr. O'Hara—that's how I thought of him, since I didn't know his real name—looked a little surprised and said, "We, ah, don't have any slaves here, sir. Slavery is—"

"Illegal, yes, yes, I know. I meant people portraying slaves. We saw the field hands, but there must be house slaves as well, ja?"

"When you tour the house, you'll see some servants working there," O'Hara explained.

"Good. A plantation should have plenty of slaves."

I didn't like Mueller much to start with, and I

was starting to like him less. I glanced at his wife, a tired-looking woman with red hair. She was supposed to be the *Gone With the Wind* fan in the family, but she didn't look as enthusiastic about seeing all this as her husband did.

You don't have to *like* the people who sign up for your tours, though; you just have to make sure they enjoy themselves. That way, maybe they'll come back sometime, or recommend you to their friends. I put a smile on my face and said, "Let's get started splitting up into groups."

With Luke's help, I got everybody sorted out and on their way. I would have made sure to put Mueller and Riley into different groups if I needed to, but luckily I didn't have to do that. Mueller and his wife went into the house with Scarlett while Riley attached himself to the group following Rhett toward the stables. Augusta and Amelia went with that bunch, too.

I stood beside the bus and said to Luke, "So far, so good."

"Don't worry, Miz D. It'll all be fine."

Wilson Cobb said, "It's air-conditioned inside the house, so I'm going in there to cool off for a while before I head back to town. Going to be a scorcher today."

"That's fine, Mr. Cobb," I told him. "We won't need you until we're ready to start back tomorrow."

He walked off, moving with the caution of the elderly. He didn't want to fall and break a hip or anything like that.

When everyone was gone, I was left by myself standing next to the bus. I looked around at the plantation and thought about how pretty it was.

With my back to the bus, I could almost believe that I had gone back in the past a hundred and fifty years or so. The house and the grounds looked a lot like they must have back in those days. I wasn't foolish enough to believe that things had been better back then for anyone, not just the slaves. The hardships of life were a lot rougher on everyone. Life was shorter, harder, and more brutal.

But, my, the flowers were pretty, and their delicious fragrance filled the air. The sky was a beautiful blue, dotted with fluffy white clouds. The spreading trees around the house provided some welcome shade.

It was only after a few moments of enjoying the solitude and the sense of being transported back in time that I began to notice things like the humming of the central air-conditioning system's round condenser at the side of the house and the whisper of traffic from the nearby highway. I looked up and saw the little satellite dish attached to the fourth-floor balcony. There sure hadn't been anything like that back in the real plantation days. Shoot, the country hadn't even been crossed by telegraph wires back then.

That was proof you couldn't keep the modern world out, even when you tried.

With a shake of my head at that thought, I went into the house to join the group being shown around by the actress playing Scarlett.

The tour went well during the rest of the morning and the afternoon, with the three groups swapping around and, I hoped, learning a lot about life on a Southern plantation in the antebellum days. Luke and I kept ourselves available in the house all afternoon in case anyone had any questions or problems, but everybody seemed to be enjoying themselves. Even Elliott Riley gave me a smile when he ambled by during the time devoted to wandering freely around the grounds and the house.

Dinner was served in a huge dining room lit by glittering crystal chandeliers. I knew there were electric lights concealed here and there, but they weren't in use. The oil lamps and the hundreds of candles provided plenty of illumination. The only real concession to the modern age was the air conditioning, and nobody who was used to modern conveniences could do without that, not even for the sake of authenticity.

Following the banquet, everybody adjourned to an even more vast ballroom with gleaming parquet floors, and walls hung with tapestries and landscape paintings. An orchestra played waltzes and other dance music of the period. The actors who worked there started the dancing, but the tourists were welcome to join in, too, and they did. I kept expecting Riley to show up and ask me for that dance he had mentioned the day before, but he didn't. In fact, I wasn't sure where he was.

But he had to be around somewhere, because the bus wouldn't be back until the next morning.

The phony Scarlett was the belle of the ball, of course. She danced with everyone—Rhett, Ashley Wilkes, the Tarleton twins, and several of the men from the tour group. The actors playing the Tarletons, who looked like real twins, made a point of dancing with Augusta and Amelia, which made the girls smile and laugh and prompted several people to take pictures of them.

I didn't dance at all, although Luke asked me. I knew he didn't really want to and was asking more out of a sense of duty than anything else, so I told him that was all right, not to worry about it.

A little later, I was standing next to the wall, under one of the big paintings, when an unfamiliar voice said from beside me, "Enjoying yourself, Ms. Dickinson?"

I looked over, expecting to see one of the staff from the plantation house, but instead I saw a man wearing a corduroy jacket and jeans, rather than the period costume that the people who worked here wore. He wore glasses and had thinning blond hair touched here and there with gray.

"Have we met?" I asked him.

"No, but I know who you are. Mr. Ralston, who owns the plantation, pointed you out to me." He put out a hand. "I'm Will Burke. Doctor Will Burke."

I shook hands with him and asked, "Doctor as in physician, or professor?"

"Professor, definitely," he said. "My doctorate is in English, and I teach at one of the local colleges. But I do some work on the side as a consultant here on the plantation, as well as at the Center for Southern Literature."

"So you're here because of the *Gone With the Wind* connection?"

"That's right. My thesis was about the interrelationship between literature and history. I've always been interested in the subject."

"Well, no offense, Professor Burke, but I'm not that academically minded."

He smiled. "I try not to be except when I'm teaching a class. Kick me in the shin if I start sounding stuffy, okay?"

"You've got a deal. What do you do here, anyway?"

"It's my job to keep things accurate both from a historical perspective and as they relate to Mitchell's novel."

"I guess you know about other books, too?"

"Some," he said with a shrug and another smile. "Why do you ask?"

"I was thinking about trying to set up some other tours that would be centered around different books and authors. I might just have to pick your brain about that sometime."

"Pick away," he said. "I'd be glad to help if I can."

I chatted for a few more minutes with Dr. Will Burke, then he had to go off to check on some detail. He gave me a wave and a smile as he left, and I smiled back at him. He was a nice-looking, interesting guy, I found myself thinking. Soft spoken, but he was friendly and he obviously knew a lot.

And I knew better than to be thinking such things, with the ink on my divorce papers barely dry, relatively speaking. Keeping my new business going would take all of my time for the foreseeable future.

By late in the evening, I was convinced everything was going to be just fine for the rest of the tour. I'm not superstitious enough to believe I jinxed it by thinking that, but looking back now, I shouldn't have done it anyway. No sense in tempting fate.

Because right about then, somebody screamed and men started to yell in confusion and I looked around for the source of the commotion, halfway expecting that Mueller and Riley had gotten into it again. I was worried about my nieces, too, since I had sort of lost track of them during the evening and I was supposed to be looking out for them.

I found Luke, grabbed his arm, and tugged him along with me. We bulled our way across the crowded ballroom toward the French doors on the far side, which seemed to be where most of the yelling was coming from.

When we got there, I saw that one set of doors was standing open. They led out into an elaborate garden behind the house, which was lit by small colored lamps in the trees. Those lamps *were* electric, not gas, because nobody wanted to take a chance on setting the trees on fire.

I spotted someone standing just outside the doors on the flagstone terrace. It was Elliott Riley, and he was staring down at his hands in horror. I saw the dark red stains on them and felt my insides go hollow. I hadn't seen a lot of freshly spilled blood in my life, but my instincts told me that was what was smeared on Riley's hands.

"He—he's out there," Riley stammered, pointing toward a path that led through the garden. I looked where he was pointing and saw the shape sprawled there on the ground. The crazy thought flashed through my head that Riley and Mueller had been fighting again, and that Riley had killed the German somehow.

But the man on the ground wasn't Mueller at all, because Mueller came up to the French doors, craning his neck to see out.

I started toward the motionless shape, but Luke pulled me back. "You better stay here, Miz D," he said. "Whoever that guy is, you don't want to see him."

"Let go of me, blast it," I told him. "I'm in charge of this group, and if something's happened, it's up to me to see what it is."

Luke let go of my arm, but he stayed stubbornly beside me as I went along the walk. Within a few steps, I recognized the man lying there. He had changed from the white planter's outfit he had worn earlier in the day, donning a tuxedo instead for the ball. Now there was a dark stain spreading on the snowy white front of his frilly shirt, spreading from the knife that was buried in his chest.

Rhett Butler—or the fella playing him, anyway—was dead, as dead as the antebellum South that had been recreated here on this plantation.

CHAPTER 5

Don't ask me how I knew Rhett Butler was dead. I'm not a medical person, and outside of a funeral home or an actual funeral, I'd never even seen a dead body.

But as I looked down at him, there was no doubt in my mind. His eyes were open wide, staring but not seeing anything. His mouth was open and his jaw was slack. His face seemed to be getting paler by the second. I knew from watching crime shows on TV that that meant the blood was pooling in the back half of his body, since that was lower. Lividity, I think they call it. The bloodstain on his shirt was ugly, but it wasn't spreading anymore because the heart had stopped pumping.

All that's logical enough now, looking back on it, but at the moment all I heard was a frantic voice in my brain yammering, *Oh, no, he's dead, he's dead, he's dead!*

I took a step back and bumped into Luke. He jumped a little and I did, too, but both of us managed to keep from yelping. I guess Luke felt like letting out a holler. I know I sure did.

"Holy cow, Miz D! Is that . . . is that . . . "

"Rhett Butler," I said. The strain made Luke's voice sound strange to my ears, but my own voice sounded even more strange.

"Is he——"

I knew what Luke was going to ask, but he didn't get a chance to finish the question. Instead another voice boomed out, "What's going on here?"

We turned to see a bulky, tuxedo-clad figure hurrying along the garden path toward us. The lights out here were bright enough for me to recognize the actor who played Scarlett's father, the man with the faint, underlying British accent who slightly resembled Thomas Mitchell.

He saw the man on the ground and said, "Oh, my dear Lord." His hand went to his pocket and pulled out a bandanna he used to mop away some of the beads of sweat that suddenly popped up on his forehead. The night was warm and humid, but not enough to make a fella look like he was in a steam bath in a matter of seconds. "What happened here?"

"He's dead." Even as the words came out of my mouth, I knew it was a dumb, obvious thing to say.

"He can't be." The man brushed past Luke and me and dropped to one knee on the path beside the corpse. The path was made of flagstones arranged on a bed of gravel, and the gravel crunched a little as the man leaned over and his weight shifted. "Steve! Steve, wake up!"

So the dead man's name was really Steve, not Rhett, I thought. The Thomas Mitchell look-alike reached for him, as if he were going to grab hold of him and try to shake him back to life, and I said, "You better not do that."

He stopped and looked back over his shoulder at me. "Why not?"

"The police won't like it if you disturb the body."

"Police?" His stunned eyes opened even wider.

"Oh, my God. You're right. We have to call the police."

"Got my cell phone right here," Luke said as he pulled it from his shirt pocket. Before anybody could say anything else, he had thumbed in 911 and hit SEND.

The man kneeling next to the body leaped to his feet. "Wait! We don't know . . ." He stopped, his voice trailing off for a second before he went on, "We don't know anything, do we? Only that he's dead."

The police would have to be involved. This was a murder, after all. Unless, of course, Steve/"Rhett" had shoved that knife into his own chest, which didn't seem likely to me. I was starting to get over my own shock to a certain extent, although I was still as horrified and, I admit it, creeped out as any person would be who doesn't deal with violent death all the time.

After he finished telling the 911 operator where we were and that we needed the police and an ambulance right away, Luke said, "You know, I guess we really *should* check his pulse and make sure he's dead . . ."

By now, other people from inside the plantation house had gotten curious enough—and courageous enough—to start edging down the path toward us. I was vaguely aware of lots of whispering going on.

A thought occurred to me, and I turned and called to the crowd, "Is anybody here a doctor or a nurse?"

"Or a paramedic?" Luke added.

The only responses we got were shaking heads and muttered denials.

I turned to look at the man who played the plantation owner. "I guess you can do it, just try not to move him."

The man looked a little queasy. "I don't think I can."

That left it up to me or Luke, since we were the ones standing there, and when I hesitated, he said, "Don't worry, Miz D. I'll do it." He didn't sound real enthusiastic, though, and he swallowed hard as he approached the body and then knelt beside it, the other fellow moving back to give him plenty of room.

Luke grimaced as he felt around on the stabbed man's neck, searching for a pulse. After a minute or two he looked up at me and shook his head.

"He's dead, all right."

Luke made that grim announcement just as a young woman wearing a fancy ball gown with a hoop skirt and lots of petticoats pushed through the crowd and reached a point where she could see the corpse. She screamed, "Steven!" then clapped her hands to her face, and darned if she didn't swoon, just like the character she was supposed to be might have. As she lay there in a faint, I recognized the pretty face and dark curls. She was the actress who played Scarlett O'Hara.

She wasn't the belle of the ball anymore. She was just a crumpled heap on the flagstones. But at least she wasn't dead, like the phony Rhett Butler.

I heard a siren somewhere in the distance. As it began to wail, a couple of men in uniform trotted up to us. They weren't policemen. Logos on their gray shirts identified them as guards from a local security service.

The portly Gerald O'Hara—the Thomas Mitchell character—turned to them and demanded, "How could you let something like this happen?"

The two security guards shook their heads, and one of them said, "Sorry, Mr. Ralston. I checked out here in the garden just a little while ago, and everything was fine then."

"Well, it's not fine now. Mr. Kelley is dead."

The guard nodded. "Yeah, I can kinda see that. The cops're already on the way?"

"That's right, no thanks to you."

Ralston was getting his bluster back. The way he was acting made me wonder if he really did own this plantation, in addition to playing Thomas Mitchell for the tourists. The name Ralston was familiar to me, too, and I recalled that I had seen it on some of the paperwork when I was setting up the tour with the management company that handled business affairs for the plantation.

I took a chance and approached him while we were waiting for the police and the ambulance to arrive. "Mr. Ralston, I'm Delilah Dickinson. . . ."

I saw by the look in his eyes that he recognized my name, too. "Mrs. Dickinson," he said with a grave nod. "I'm sorry we had to meet under such tragic circumstances. I'm Edmond Ralston. This is my plantation."

That confirmed my suspicion. It surprised me a little that a rich man like Ralston would take part in the play-acting, putting on a show for the tourists.

From the way he had been acting earlier, though, he seemed to get a kick out of it.

"Oh! Oh!"

We looked around to see that the woman who had fainted earlier was coming around. Two more ladies in ball gowns hovered over her, helping her sit up. Both were young, a blonde in her early twenties and a brunette who was probably still a teenager. "Scarlett" began to sob as she once again saw the corpse lying a few yards away on the path.

"Maybe we ought to cover him up," Edmond Ralston muttered under his breath.

"The cops wouldn't like it," Luke said, echoing what I had told Ralston a few minutes earlier about messing with the body.

"I just hate for her to have to see him like that." Ralston lowered his voice even more as he added, "She's his wife." He spoke up. "Janice, why don't you and Lindsey take Maura back into the house?"

The brunette teenager nodded. "All right, Dad."

She and the other young woman helped the sobbing Maura to her feet. Maura didn't want to go, though. She tried to pull away, saying, "Let go of me! I have to help Steven!"

Ralston said, "There's nothing you can do for him, my dear. It's a matter for the authorities."

He sounded a little more British now, although his voice still held a trace of the Southern drawl he affected as Thomas Mitchell.

I turned to Luke and said, "Keep an eye on things here. I want to make sure the girls are all right." I had thought about them right away, after Luke and I came out here and saw the body, but I'd seen them dancing in the ballroom only a short time earlier so I wasn't really worried about them. Still, since I'd promised my sister I would take care of them, I knew I'd feel better about it if I saw them with my own eyes.

Luke nodded. "Don't worry, Miz D. I won't let anything happen."

I looked at the corpse and shook my head. "I'd say it's already happened."

CHAPTER 6

I started making my way back through the crowd of onlookers, but I didn't have to go very far before I ran into Augusta and Amelia. Both of them were standing up on tiptoes and craning their necks, trying to see what was so interesting in the garden.

"I heard somebody say there's a dead guy out there," Augusta said.

"Is that true, Aunt Delilah?" Amelia said.

I nodded. "It's true. A man's been stabbed. You girls go on back inside."

"Can't we go and look at him?" Augusta asked.

Before I could tell her that no, they couldn't go and look at him, Amelia made a face and said, "Oh, my God. You *want* to look at a dead guy?"

Augusta shrugged. "I've never seen one before."

"I don't want to see one!"

I made shooing motions at the two of them and said, "Neither of you need to see a dead man. Go on back inside."

"Are the police coming?" Amelia said.

"Will they question us?" Augusta said.

"Yes, they're on the way. Don't you hear the sirens? And no, I don't know if they'll want to question you."

I didn't see any reason why the police would have any questions for my nieces. After all, they'd both been inside when Steven Kelley was killed. But, once again going by what I'd seen on TV and in the movies, I figured there was a chance they'd question everybody who was here tonight, regardless of where they were when the crime was committed.

As I started to herd the girls toward the house, Augusta looked back over her shoulder and said, "At least tell us who it was that got killed, Aunt Delilah. That can't hurt anything, can it?"

I didn't see any reason not to tell them. "It was the man who played Rhett Butler."

They looked at each other.

"Oh," Amelia said.

"Him," Augusta said.

I got the distinct impression that the murdered man's identity meant something to them, but before I could ask them about it, Will Burke came up to me. I introduced him to the girls, then he said, "I heard about what happened, Ms. Dickinson. People are saying that you discovered the body? Are you all right?"

The question took me a little by surprise, both the concern that was evident in his voice and expression and the rumor that I was the one who'd found the murdered man. "I'm fine," I said, "but I'm not the one who found him. That was—" I stopped and looked around for Elliott Riley but didn't see him anywhere. "Now where the heck did he go?"

As I asked the question, I recalled that when I'd first seen Riley just outside the ballroom doors, he'd been upset and had dark stains on his hands—like blood. There was no doubt in my mind now that it was Steven Kelley's blood. Obviously Riley had touched the body. I knew it was selfish of me, but my immediate reaction was dismay that not only had somebody been killed during my first tour, but also that one of my clients had found the body. That couldn't be good for business.

And then a little voice in the back of my head asked, *What if the killer is one of your clients? That's going to be even worse, isn't it?*

I must have groaned at the thought, because Dr. Will Burke leaned closer to me and asked, "Are you *sure* you're all right? Even if you're not the one who found the body, this must still be quite a shock for you."

I held up a hand. "I'll be fine. You're right, Doctor. Murder is just . . . shocking."

"You're sure it's murder?"

I glanced at Augusta and Amelia, who were watching and listening with avid interest, especially Augusta. "The man was stabbed," I said. "It didn't look like an accident or suicide to me."

"Do you know who he was?"

"Mr. Ralston called him Steven Kelley."

I could see that the name meant something to Will. His breath hissed between his teeth.

"I guess you knew him, since you said you work here."

Will nodded. "He and I teach at the same college. He's the head of the drama department there." He stopped and shook his head. "*Taught* at the same college, I should say. It . . . it's hard to believe, hard to grasp when someone you know dies suddenly like this, especially violently. . . ."

"Were you good friends?"

"No, I wouldn't say that. Just colleagues. But I've known him for several years."

Augusta said, "Who'd want to kill him?"

Will looked surprised at the blunt question, but no more surprised than I felt. "I have no idea," he said, at the same time I was telling Augusta, "That's none of our business."

But it might be my business, I reminded myself, if one of my clients turned out to be the killer. This news was going to spread fast through Atlanta's travel agency community. Conventional wisdom says there's no such thing as bad publicity . . . but at the moment I wasn't so sure about that.

The sirens had gotten a lot louder while I was talking to my nieces and to Dr. Will Burke, and now they cut off abruptly. I took that to mean the police and the ambulance had arrived, and sure enough, before I could manage to get Augusta and Amelia back inside, several uniformed officers hurried through the French doors in the ballroom and into the garden. A couple of paramedics carrying emergency kits trotted after them.

The officers were sheriff's deputies, I saw—from the patches on their shirts—as they went past me. The plantation was well outside the Atlanta city limits, so that made sense. They moved the crowd back, telling everyone in brisk, no-nonsense voices to return to the ballroom and stay there. One of the deputies went along with us, I guess to keep an eye on us and make sure nobody tried to sneak off.

Edmond Ralston spoke. to one of the deputies and was allowed to remain in the garden as the paramedics knelt on either side of Steven Kelley and opened their kits. I saw one of them take out a stethoscope and press it to the dead man's chest as he listened for a heartbeat.

He wasn't going to find one.

Luke found me once we all got back into the ballroom. He looked relieved that Amelia and Augusta were all right, as I had been. "I'll bet it won't take very long for the cops to find out who killed the guy. They've got all that forensic stuff now, like on TV. There must be fingerprints on the handle of that knife."

"Will they have to fingerprint everybody here?" Augusta asked.

"They'll get that icky black ink all over our fingers," Amelia said.

"We'll just cooperate, answer all their questions, and do whatever they say," I told them. "It's nothing to worry about."

I *was* worried, though. The more I thought about Elliott Riley discovering the body, the more I wondered about him. He had a temper, as was obvious from that fight he had gotten into with Gerhard Mueller at the *Gone With the Wind* Movie Museum the day before. And he'd had blood on his hands.

That was easily explained. When he found Steven Kelley's body, he could have touched Kelley while trying to see how badly he was hurt and maybe help him if he was still alive. Perfectly innocent.

But where had Riley vanished to after that, and where was he now? That was a little more suspicious, even though Riley's absence might not really mean anything.

I turned to Luke. "Have you seen Elliott Riley?"

"Who?"

"The man who had that trouble with the German tourist at the museum yesterday." I lowered my voice and leaned closer to him. "The one who started yelling tonight when he found the body."

"Oh, yeah, him." Luke looked around the ballroom. "I don't see him anywhere."

The people who'd been told by the deputies to wait in the ballroom had split up into two main groups: the guests from my tour, and the actors and staff who worked here on the plantation, recreating the antebellum lifestyle for the tourists' enjoyment. Within those groups there were smaller bunches, all standing around with shocked expressions on their faces, talking in hushed conversations about how terrible all of this was. At least, that's what I assumed they were talking about. I spotted "Scarlett O'Hara" sitting next to the wall in a white chair with a lot of elaborate scrollwork on the arms and back. She had been married to the murdered man, I recalled Edmond Ralston saying. She was still crying, but she wasn't sobbing loudly and wailing anymore. She dabbed at her eyes with a lacy handkerchief while the two young women who had helped her in from the garden stood by rather awkwardly. From time to time one of them would reach over and pat her on the shoulder in a feeble attempt at comforting her in her grief. The other people who worked here all looked pale and shaken, too. They would have known the dead man pretty well, I thought. My clients were sympathetic, of course, but I got the sense that some of them were also annoyed that something like a murder was threatening to interrupt and possibly ruin their tour.

Nowhere among any of them, though, was Elliott Riley, and that was downright odd.

I couldn't very well go looking for him; the deputies had told us all to stay put in the ballroom. I wasn't sure I wanted to find him, anyway. I hadn't liked him to start with, and I liked him even less now.

A stocky, gray-haired man in a brown suit came into the ballroom. His tie was loosened, and he had a weary expression on his face, as if this were a long day that was about to get even longer. He was followed by a couple of men and a woman, all wearing polo shirts that had the sheriff's department logo on the front and the words CRIME SCENE on the back.

The people with all that forensic stuff Luke had been talking about earlier had shown up.

The gray-haired man, who must have been a detective, led the investigators through the ballroom and into the garden. He closed the doors firmly behind them, making it clear that he didn't want any interruptions. That left the rest of us cooling our heels inside as time dragged. Within fifteen minutes, both Augusta and Amelia were whining about wanting to go to their rooms. I made an effort to hold on to my temper, even though it wasn't long before they were getting on my last nerve.

The wait stretched to forty-five minutes. Even though a couple of deputies were standing in front of the French doors now, from time to time I caught a glimpse of camera flashes going off in the garden as the crime scene folks photographed the body and its surroundings.

Finally, the paramedics came out through the ballroom, were gone for a couple of minutes, and came back wheeling a gurney between them. That quieted down the buzz of conversation in the big room, but absolute silence fell a short time later when they reappeared. A long, motionless shape shrouded in a black body bag lay on the gurney now.

Rhett Butler would never run the blockade or return to Tara again.

CHAPTER 7

The gray-haired man came back into the ballroom a few minutes after the paramedics removed the body of Steven Kelley. He was trailed by a couple of deputies, one of whom asked in a loud voice for everyone's attention. When he had it, the gray-haired man stepped forward and spoke.

"My name is Timothy Farraday. I'm an investigator for the sheriff's department."

That confirmed my guess about him being a detective.

"I'm sorry for any inconvenience, but my men and I will be taking statements from all of you before you'll be allowed to return to your rooms this evening."

One of the actors—I think he was supposed to be a Tarleton twin—said, "That's fine for *them*." He gestured toward the guests who had come there on the tour. "But what about the ones who just work here? Can't we go home?"

Timothy Farraday shook his head. "Not yet. Sorry."

He didn't sound particularly apologetic. The irritated, impatient muttering that greeted his answer didn't appear to bother him, either.

"Everyone just be patient, and we'll get to you as soon as we can."

Farraday headed for Maura Kelley, the murdered man's wife, and led her out of the ballroom. Her face was pale and her eyes were red, but she appeared to have stopped crying. In fact, she had that overly calm look that said the shock was really beginning to settle in on her. While Farraday was doing that, two of the other deputies picked someone else to question, and the others kept an eye on the rest of us.

"They're going to fingerprint us," Amelia said.

"I just know they are."

"It'll be fun," Augusta said.

"If that's your idea of fun—"

"That's enough," I said. I had already decided that I wasn't going to let either of the girls be interrogated unless I was there. They were minors, after all.

Luke whispered to me, "I bet they do fingerprint us. You know they got some latents off that knife."

I looked at him. "Latents?" I knew what he meant, but his use of the technical term surprised me.

"Yeah . . . Hey, I watch TV, Miz D. I know all about that kind of stuff."

He wasn't the only one. I'd read that, because of the popularity of forensics-based police procedural series, people thought they knew so much that it was making life difficult for real-life detectives and prosecutors. Juries expected a ton of forensic evidence, all of it as conclusive as what they saw on TV, and when they didn't get it, they were less inclined to convict a defendant.

One thing about TV, though: no matter how realistic they make the corpses look these days—and they're usually pretty dad-gummed gruesome—when you're watching it there's a part of your brain that always knows it's just a TV show. You can tell yourself it's not real, that it's just make-believe, an actor made up to look dead.

Well, Steven Kelley had been an actor, but there was nothing make-believe about the blood on his clothes or the pasty, fish-belly look of his skin or the sightless, staring eyes. The real thing always looks different from what you see on the screen.

The angry muttering in the ballroom grew louder as more time went by. The hour was getting kind of late. The fancy dress ball would have been over by now, and the guests would have all retired to their rooms for the night. The people who actually lived here, like Edmond Ralston and possibly his daughter, would have gone to their own quarters, and the actors would be on their way home.

Instead, the burly deputies made sure that no one left the ballroom, even the people who had already given statements. Timothy Farraday obviously thought there was a good chance the killer was still here—a reasonable assumption, I suppose—and he wanted to make sure that he didn't let a murderer slip through his fingers.

Eventually, he got around to me, coming across the ballroom and saying as he walked up, "Ms. Dickinson?"

"I'm Delilah Dickinson," I told him. "Would you come with me, please?"

I hesitated and made a motion toward Augusta and Amelia. "These are my nieces."

Farraday smiled, but the expression didn't reach his eyes. "And they're lovely young ladies. Would you come with me, please?"

"They're minors. I don't want any of your men questioning them while I'm not there."

His eyebrows rose. "And why is *that*?"

"Yeah, Aunt Delilah," Augusta said. "Why's *that*?"

I suddenly realized that I'd made it sound to Farraday like the girls might have something to hide. That was ridiculous, of course. They couldn't have possibly had anything to do with Steven Kelley's murder, and since they'd been inside when it happened, they couldn't even be of any value as witnesses.

I guess I've always been just a wee bit too stubborn for my own good, though, because I said, "I just don't think it would be right. They're not of legal age."

"And they're not being charged with anything." Farraday's voice had a patient tone to it, as if he were explaining something to a child—or somebody too dumb to understand what he was talking about. "We're just taking statements, Ms. Dickinson, not officially questioning anyone yet." He paused, then with weary patience asked for the third time, "Would you come with me, please?"

I didn't see any way around it. I turned to Luke and said, "Keep an eye on the girls."

He nodded. "Will do, Miz D."

I followed Farraday out of the ballroom and

down a hall to another room. He stood by the open door and ushered me through it.

"Right in here, please."

This was an office with a couple of good-sized desks and some filing cabinets. I figured Edmond Ralston ran the business of the plantation from here, or rather, employees of the management company he used did.

Farraday motioned me into a leather chair in front of one of the desks and took the chair in front of the other desk, rather than sitting behind either of them. As he slipped a notebook and a pen from his jacket pocket, he said, "Mr. Ralston is being kind enough to let us use this office."

I nodded toward the notebook and pen in his hands. "Sort of low tech, isn't it?"

He chuckled, and for the first time this evening he seemed genuinely amused. "I'm a low-tech sort of guy." That moment of good humor lasted only a second, and then he was all business again. "Now, if you would, tell me everything you remember about what happened tonight."

"You mean after the body was discovered?" I was anxious in one way to tell him about Elliott Riley finding the body, reluctant in another. I *was* running a business after all.

Farraday shook his head. "No, start before that. In fact, since you're in charge of the tour, why don't you back up all the way to the time you and your clients arrived here at the plantation and take it from there."

I stared at him. "That was this morning."

He nodded. "I know."

I had already figured out that he wasn't the sort

of fella who could be talked out of anything very easily, so I took a deep breath and then launched into as detailed an account as I could remember of the day's activities. I actually went back further than he had asked, explaining how the tourists at their hotels and motels to bring them out here. Farraday wrote something down, and I figured it was Mr. Cobb's name. That probably meant he'd be questioned, too, the poor man, and I felt bad about dragging him into this.

From there I went over the details of the tour, and after a few minutes I started to feel like I was giving a sales pitch, not being questioned by the authorities. Farraday didn't seem to mind, though. He kept taking notes, occasionally interrupting me to ask a question and get something straight. I reached the part where the ball started, but I didn't say anything about the conversation I'd had with Dr. Will Burke. It didn't seem the least bit relevant.

"Then I heard some sort of commotion going on and went to see what it was all about. Mr. Riley was yelling and pointing out into the garden. He said, 'He's out there,' or something like that."

"What did you think he meant by that?"

I took a deep breath. "Well, Mr. Riley had something on his hands, and it looked like blood to me, so the first thing I thought . . . I thought he'd got-ten into a fight with Mr. Mueller again."

Farraday's eyebrows were a little more than normal. They climbed up his forehead now.

"Who's Mr. Mueller?"

That opened up a whole new can of worms, as the old saying goes, so I had to explain about the trouble at the museum the day before. "There was bad blood between those two, so I thought they'd been tusslin' again. I was afraid that maybe this time Mr. Riley had really hurt Mr. Mueller, because of the blood and all, you know. So Luke and I hurried out there to see what had happened."

Farraday consulted his notebook. "That would be Luke Edwards, your assistant?"

I smiled. "He's my son-in-law, too."

"Okay. So you thought you'd find this man Mueller out in the garden, maybe hurt. How'd you feel about that?"

How did I feel about that? Was I a detective or a psychologist? Either way, I had to answer the question.

"I was so mad I was about ready to spit. This is my *first* tour since I opened my own agency, Mr. Farraday. I was afraid two of my clients had gone and messed it all up."

He grunted. "It's messed up, all right, but this guy Mueller doesn't appear to have had anything to do with it."

"What about Riley?"

He looked surprised that I was asking a question, instead of answering one. He was noncommittal in his reply. "We'll be talking to him."

Even though I didn't like Riley, and even though I was the one who had brought up his name, I felt compelled to defend him. "There could be a perfectly innocent explanation for how he got the blood on his hands. He could have found the body and tried to see if the man was still alive, or something like that."

"We'll ask him. He'll have a chance to tell his story."

Farraday wasn't going to give me anything else. Instead he had me go over what had happened in the garden after Luke and I walked out to where Steven Kelley's body lay, and then I told him about Edmond Ralston joining us, and Maura Kelley's reaction when she saw her husband, and that was about it. He nodded, thanked me, and told me I could go back to the ballroom.

I stood up. "How long are we going to have to stay here?"

He closed his notebook and looked up at me. "I was under the impression that you and your assistant and the rest of the tour group were going to spend the night here anyway."

"That's right."

"So you already have rooms assigned to you."

I nodded.

"It shouldn't be too much longer before you're allowed to go to your rooms for the night."

"What about tomorrow?" I asked. "The bus will be here in the morning to take everybody back to wherever they're staying."

Farraday shook his head slowly. "We'll have to wait and see about that."

"You mean we may not be able to leave the plantation tomorrow morning?" I knew that would really upset some of my clients.

He got to his feet, and the lumbering motion reminded me a little of a bear. "We'll have to wait and see," he said again.

I had figured out by now that I'd run into somebody who was just as stubborn as me. When somebody challenged him, Timothy Farraday fell back on repeating what he had said before, refusing to be budged from his position. I didn't like him very much, I didn't like the possibility that we were all going to be stuck here on the plantation while Farraday carried out his investigation, and I especially didn't like the chance that before this was all over, some of my clients might be thinking about suing me.

And the chances that some or all of them would be asking for refunds were just, well, astronomical.

My business was going to go bust before it even had a good start. As I went back to the ballroom I felt a little like murdering somebody myself. Problem was, I didn't know who to kill, because I didn't know who was responsible for what had happened.

If I did know, though, I wouldn't have stabbed him.

I'd have strangled the son of a gun.

CHAPTER 8

If going through a relatively amicable but still painful divorce had taught me one thing, it was that no matter how bad the situation is, it can always get worse.

That was what I found when I returned to the ballroom. Luke was standing where I'd left him, all alone now with a frantic look in his eyes.

"I couldn't help it, Miz D," he said as soon as I walked up, before I could even ask him where Augusta and Amelia were. "The deputies came and got 'em, and when I said that you didn't want them questioned unless you were there, they told me to back off or they'd arrest me for interfering with an investigation." He shook his head. "I thought about sluggin' one of them, figured that would distract them from the girls, but then I thought about what Melissa would say if she had to come and bail me out of jail. . . ."

I was upset, but I managed to pat him on the arm. "That's all right, Luke. Your getting arrested wouldn't really help anything. Did they take the girls somewhere together?"

He shook his head. "No, ma'am. They separated 'em . . . I guess to see if they told the same story when they were apart."

That was what the deputies would do, all right. I suspected that Farraday had given them instructions to handle it that way, as well.

"Did you see where the deputies took them?"

He shook his head again, still looking miserable. "Nope. I followed them all the way to the ballroom doors and told them again you didn't want it this way, but the deputy there stopped me."

"There was nothing you could do, Luke. Don't worry about it."

"You're sure?"

"I'm sure," I told him.

There hadn't been anything Luke could do . . . but that didn't mean I couldn't.

I went to the ballroom doors and the deputy there stopped me, just as I expected he would.

"Some of your men took my nieces away to question them," I said. "They're minors. I want those interrogations stopped right now."

"You'd have to talk to Lieutenant Farraday about that, ma'am."

"I was just with the lieutenant. He knows how I feel about this."

The deputy shrugged. "If you're not the legal guardian of the girls, I don't imagine there's much you can do. Are you the legal guardian?"

"Well . . . no. But I know their mama wouldn't want them being questioned about a murder they didn't have anything to do with!"

The man just shook his head, and I knew it wasn't

going to do any good to keep arguing with him. I knew what Luke meant about wanting to slug one of them, but that wouldn't help, either. I settled for glaring and muttering under my breath as I turned away from the doors.

To take my mind off the girls and what they might be going through, I made my way across the ballroom to where Edmond Ralston was standing with his daughter Janice. Ralston still looked upset, naturally enough. The tourist trade was important to him, and once the word got around that a murder had taken place here on the plantation—during one of the tours, even—that might cut into his business.

Or, depending on how morbid people were, I told myself, it might even *increase* the number of tourists who wanted to come out here.

Even though Ralston was still shaken, he was back in master-of-the-plantation mode, at least to a certain extent. He gave me a little half-bow and said, "Ms. Dickinson, I simply cannot begin to express my regret at the pall these circumstances have cast over the evening's festivities."

His daughter gave a quiet, hollow laugh. "Dad, you're not really Thomas Mitchell, you know. You just look a little like him."

Ralston sighed. "I know. Would that this was a movie, because the director would have yelled 'cut' before now."

"Poor Steven was the one who got cut," Janice said. "Or rather, stabbed." A shiver went through her.

"Had you known him for very long?" I asked.

"He's been our creative director for the past couple of years," Ralston said. "He supervises all the actors, and he's in charge of the costuming and things like that. And of course he supplies most of the performers. They're students of his."

I recalled Will Burke saying earlier in the evening that Kelley was the head of the drama department at a nearby college.

"I don't know what we'll do without him," Ralston went on. "We'll have to find someone else to take charge, I suppose."

"What about Dr. Burke?"

Ralston looked surprised. "You know Will?"

"Not until tonight. We met earlier during the evening, before . . ."

I didn't have to finish. They both knew what I meant.

"Dr. Burke's areas are history and literature," Janice said. "He doesn't know anything about theater and things like that."

She looked to be about the right age to be in college, so I asked, "Were you in Mr. Kelley's classes?"

"Oh, yes. Steven was a wonderful teacher. Perry can tell you."

She turned to a young man standing near us and reached over to tug on the sleeve of his brown swallowtail coat. He was one of the actors, dressed in swallowtail coat, tight, tan whipcord trousers, high-topped brown boots, white frilly shirt, and a gray silk cravat. He was tall and lean and had sleek, dark blond hair, and I realized he was the actor who played Ashley Wilkes. He even bore a slight resemblance to Leslie Howard, the movie Ashley, just as Edmond Ralston looked a little like Thomas Mitchell. I looked at Janice, with her rounded face and wholesome prettiness, and realized she was supposed to be Melanie Hamilton, or rather, Olivia de Havilland. She was a little young for the part, but I thought she could probably carry it off.

"Perry works with Steven," Janice continued. She caught her breath as she realized what she'd just said, and with that catch in her voice she added, "I mean . . . worked with him."

The young, blond Leslie Howard look-alike gave me the same sort of half-bow that Ralston had. Obviously it was a common mannerism among these folks. "Perry Newton, ma'am, at your service," he introduced himself. "I was Steven's teaching assistant."

I managed a smile and a nod for him, but before I could say anything, Ralston spoke up again. "Perry, it just occurred to me that you're the natural candidate to take over Steven's job, since you were his assistant. Are you interested?"

"Dad!" Janice said. "You shouldn't be . . . it's too soon after . . . after what happened . . ."

"Nonsense. Business is business, and it doesn't stop for anyone's death. How about it, Perry?"

Stiffly, Perry Newton answered, "I think Janice is right, sir. This discussion isn't very seemly at the moment."

"Seemly be damned. I have tours to put on, and I need someone to run them. You're the best qualified."

Perry shrugged his narrow shoulders. "I suppose I ought to do what I can to help out, for the time being, anyway."

"That's good." Ralston slapped him on the back. "Thanks, son." Perry Newton still didn't look very happy about it, though. Ralston sighed and went on, "Of course, we don't know when we'll get to go ahead with the tours. That detective from the sheriff's office is acting like he's going to shut us down until he solves this murder. He'll be hearing from my lawyer if he tries a stunt like that."

"Finding out who killed Steven is more important than keeping the tours going, isn't it?" Janice said.

Ralston smiled humorlessly and put a hand on his daughter's shoulder. "Ah, spoken like someone who doesn't have to pay the bills."

She looked a little resentful at his attitude, as well she should have, I thought. She was upset about Kelley's murder, and he seemed to be concerned only with how it was going to affect the bottom line. I understood how someone could worry about a business—I was sure as heck worried about mine right about now—but ultimately, human life is more important.

Before father and daughter could get into an argument, the blonde who had helped Janice earlier with Maura Kelley came over to us. She slipped her arm through Perry Newton's, and the way she stood next to him told me that they were a couple. It's an indefinable something, but most people know that connectedness when they see it.

"Have any of you seen Maura recently?" she asked, directing her question to the Ralstons and Perry, not me. Even though I was standing there, I wasn't part of their little circle.

"She hasn't come back since the detective took her away to question her," Ralston said. "He either let her go on up to her room, or he's holding her somewhere else with a deputy guarding her."

"Why would he have a deputy guarding her?" Janice asked. "Do you think she's in danger, too, Dad?"

Ralston shrugged his heavy shoulders. "There's that," he said, "but you also have to remember: anytime someone is killed, the person who's married to them is the most likely suspect."

Janice, Perry, and the blonde all stared at him. After a few seconds of stunned silence, Perry said, "You can't believe that Maura would kill Steven! It's impossible."

"I'm just saying what the police are thinking. And they're probably not the only ones."

I thought about what he'd just said, and even though I didn't really know the people involved, I knew that the statistics were on Ralston's side. Most people who are murdered are killed by somebody they know, and the closer the relationship, the more likely the suspect. That's just common knowledge.

But I had witnessed first-hand Maura Kelley's reaction when she saw her husband's body with the knife sticking out of his bloody chest. She had been so shocked that she fainted right on the spot. On the other hand, she *was* an actress, I reminded myself.

The question might well be, just how good of an actress was she?

While I was pondering that, the blonde turned to me and put out her hand. "We haven't met. I'm Lindsey Hoffman. I'm one of the performers here."

That last bit of information wasn't really necessary, what with the elaborate upswept hairdo, the low-cut ball gown that left her shoulders bare and a considerable amount of cleavage showing, and the big hoop skirt with numerous petticoats under it that rustled every time she moved. She sure as heck wasn't dressed for the mall.

I shook hands with her and said, "I'm Delilah

Dickinson. I arranged this tour. Which of the *Gone With the Wind* characters do you play?"

She laughed. "Oh, I'm not one of the main characters. I guess you could say I'm just a generic Southern belle. Window dressing for the ball."

"You're not being fair to yourself, Lindsey," Perry protested. "You're a fine actress. It's only a matter of time until you move up to a better role. That is, if the performances continue." He glanced at Edmond Ralston.

The plantation owner jerked his head in a gruff nod. "They'll continue . . . as soon as the blasted detectives tell us that we can get back to business as usual."

Perry turned back to Lindsey. "You know, with everything that's happened, I'm sure Maura's not going to want to play Scarlett again any time soon, if ever. With a dark wig, you could play that part, Lindsey. Mr. Ralston wants me to take over temporarily as the creative director, so . . ."

A big smile lit up Lindsey's face, making her even prettier. "You think so? You really think I could do it?" Then, abruptly, she covered her mouth with her hand for a second and looked shocked. "What am I saying? I can't be happy about anything that happens because . . . because of a tragedy like this . . ."

"Like I've been saying, life goes on," Ralston said, "and so does our work. There's nothing disrespectful about thinking ahead, my dear."

I wasn't quite as sure about that as he was. While everyone seemed to be shocked and saddened by Steven Kelley's murder, they were also thinking about how it was going to affect *them*. I supposed that was just human nature; I'd had several moments this evening, after all, when I had done the same thing, going all the way back to the commotion at the French doors leading into the garden. When I'd hurried toward them, all I'd been worried about was how whatever was going on was going to affect the tour and my business. Then I'd seen Elliott Riley with blood on his hands.

And I'd *still* thought more about the tour than anything else, right up until the moment I had seen the corpse sprawled on the flagstone path.

And speaking of Elliott Riley . . .

There he was again, the rascal.

CHAPTER 9

He was standing by himself on the other side of the ballroom, a sour look on his face. I excused myself to Ralston and the others I'd been talking to and started making my way across the room toward Riley.

He saw me coming and for a second looked like he wanted to run away and hide. I guess he figured I was mad, and he was right about that. At the same time, unless he'd killed Steven Kelley, none of this was his fault just because he had discovered the body. If he hadn't stumbled over it, somebody else would have. But everybody has a tendency to blame the messenger at times, and I'm no different from anyone else in that respect.

He gave me a curt nod as I came up to him.

"Ms. Dickinson."

"Mr. Riley. Where have you been?"

"What do you mean? I've been in here with the rest of this mob ever since the cops got here."

I knew that wasn't true, because I'd looked for

him. I suppose it was possible that I had just missed seeing him in the crowd, but I didn't think that was the case. I couldn't help glancing down at his hands.

No bloodstains. They were clean, and the nails were cut short, I noticed.

"You sneaked off somewhere to wash the blood off your hands," I said.

"I don't know what you're talking about."

"It was a waste of time. Plenty of people saw you after you found Kelley's body. I already told Lieutenant Farraday about the blood on your hands, and I'll bet I'm not the only one. Anyway," I added, thinking about those TV crime shows, "you can't wash blood off well enough so that the police can't find it. They've got those special lights that make it show up."

His jaw tightened, and he said through clenched teeth, "All right, already. I didn't want to stand around with the guy's blood on my hands. Do you have any idea how *creepy* that is? So before the cops got here, I slipped upstairs to one of the bathrooms and scrubbed it off. Damn near took the hide off, too, but it didn't really help." He held his hands open in front of him and looked down at them. "I can still feel it on there."

My anger at him eased a little. "How'd you get back down here without the deputies seeing you?"

"I didn't. One of them collared me as I was trying to sneak back into the ballroom. I thought that would be better than hiding in the bathroom and letting them find me there. I gave him some story about being sick to my stomach and looking for a place to throw up." He grunted. "It wasn't that far from the truth, either. I keep thinking about the way that guy looked."

"You mean Steven Kelley?"

"Was that his name?" Riley shook his head. "I didn't even know that much. I don't know anything about the guy, or what happened to him. I told the deputies that when they questioned me."

"Why don't you tell me what you did and saw out there in the garden?"

"Why would I do that? You're not a cop."

"No, but this is my tour that's gotten all flummoxed up, so I'm makin' it my business to find out what happened."

I didn't really think about what I was saying. It just sort of came out in a burst of anger and frustration and determination. And other than feelings of natural curiosity, it had never occurred to me that I ought to try to figure out who killed Steven Kelley. But even as the words came out, they felt right to me.

Riley looked convinced. "All right, all right," he muttered. "I'll cooperate, but only because I've got this thing for—"

"Redheads, I know. What were you doing out in the garden instead of dancing in here?"

"Why bother dancing when the prettiest woman in the room already made it clear that she didn't want anything to do with me?" Even under the circumstances, he managed to leer.

I suppressed the urge to give him a quick slap to the back of the head. "Just tell me what happened?"

He shrugged. "I got bored. Decided to take in a little of that moonlight and magnolias stuff I've heard so much about, so I went out into the garden. I gotta tell you, the whole Southern charm bit is overrated. The moonlight was nice, but the smell of all those flowers was a little overwhelming. Almost sickening."

"Get to the part where you found Kelley's body."

He looked offended. "Hey, you're the one who said you wanted to hear all about it. I'm tellin' you. I wandered around in the garden for a while and then started back in on the main path. If the moonlight hadn't been so bright, I probably would've tripped over the body."

"But you saw it before you stumbled over it?"

"Yeah. I thought at first somebody'd had a few too many mint juleps, if you know what I mean. I said, 'Hey, buddy, you better get up from there before somebody falls over you.' But he didn't budge, and then when I got closer I saw why. You couldn't miss that stain messing up his fancy shirt, and then I realized there was a knife sticking up in the middle of it."

Riley frowned and sighed, and I knew that going over the story again had rattled him.

"Look, I'm not the nicest guy around, you know. I'm not just overflowing with the milk of human kindness, if you get my drift. But the guy was hurt, and I'm not some kind of ogre. I got down on one knee beside him and shook him to see if he was still alive. Then I thought I ought to take the knife out of his chest. I even put a hand on his chest to brace myself while I grabbed the knife with my other hand, before I realized I ought to leave it alone."

"That's how you got the blood on your hands. . . ."

"Yeah."

"And your fingerprints on the knife."

He rolled his eyes. "You don't have to tell me

how stupid that was. I know. Believe me, I know. I gave the cops a tailor-made suspect, didn't I? But I never thought about that at the time. When you nearly trip over a dead body, you don't think very straight, lemme tell you."

I'd have to take his word for it because I'd never tripped over a body and didn't want to, thank you very much. And it occurred to me that his whole story might be a clever concoction, a way of explaining away his fingerprints on the murder weapon if he was the one who'd killed Steven Kelley.

But if that possibility was so obvious to me, then surely it would be even more so to the authorities, and if Riley was the killer, he'd try to come up with something better. Unless he was counting on everybody feeling that way . . . .

I shoved those tangled thoughts out of my head. That was a good reason right there why I was a travel agent, not a detective. I could sort out a lot of complicated things, but a murder wasn't one of them.

"Anyway," Riley continued, "I had a pretty good idea the guy was dead and I knew I couldn't do anything to help him, so I ran inside and started looking for somebody in charge so I could tell them what happened. Then some of the people saw the blood on my hands and started yelling, and you and Li'l Abner came up, and since you're the one who put on the tour, I tried to tell you what I'd found. I still wasn't thinking any too good, though. All I could do was point and say that he was out there."

Now that Riley reminded me of it, I knew he was right. He hadn't been the one doing the yelling;

that was other people who had seen the blood on his hands. He was shaken up when Luke and I reached the doors into the garden, of course, but he was still relatively calm.

"Did you see anybody else out in the garden?"

"You mean besides the dead guy?" Riley shook his head. "Not a soul. Everybody else was in here, I guess, doing the waltz or the polka or whatever the hell dance it was."

I found it hard to believe that Riley didn't know the difference between a waltz and a polka, but maybe he didn't. Some people just don't have any appreciation for music.

Elliott Riley didn't seem to have much of an appreciation for anything, come to think of it. He'd made disparaging comments about moonlight and magnolias and hadn't been impressed with the plantation, the movie museum, or any other part of the tour.

So why had he booked it in the first place? I could understand if his wife or girlfriend was a big *Gone With the Wind* fan and had dragged him along. But he was traveling by himself, as far as I knew. His reservation had definitely been a single, and he hadn't acted like he knew anybody else in the group.

I couldn't answer the question, and I knew it was going to nag at me.

"Nobody else was around the body when you first saw it?"

"You mean like the killer bending over it, cackling fiendishly? No, sorry."

"You just make people want to slap you, don't you?"

He smirked at me. "Only women. It's a gift."

I ignored that and said, "You've already told all of this to the deputies?"

"Yeah. I didn't see any point in lying. They would have just found out the truth anyway."

"But you haven't talked to Lieutenant Farraday yet?"

"Nope. I'm sure he'll get around to me soon enough, though."

I suspected he was right about that. Farraday might have been tired, but his determined nature would keep him going, all night if necessary. Don't ask me how I knew that, I just did. Stubborn knows stubborn.

I might have kept on talking to Riley, even though I had a feeling he had already told me everything he had to tell—about his discovery of the body, anyway—but right then Luke came up to me. I could tell that he'd been looking for me, and that something was wrong.

"Miz D.," he said, "the deputies are through with Augusta and Amelia."

"Thank God," I breathed.

But I had spoken too soon, because Luke went on, "Now that detective who's in charge wants to talk to them, and to you, too."

I stiffened. What in the world could the girls have told the deputies that made Lieutenant Farraday interested in them? I was glad he wanted to see me, too, because that meant Augusta and Amelia wouldn't have to face him alone, but at the same time that seemed to indicate it was something fairly serious.

He had said earlier that it didn't matter whether

the girls were minors because they weren't being charged with anything or even officially questioned.

Was he going to question them now—or charge them with something?

"Where are they?"

"Right over there, Miz D. One of the deputies was gonna come looking for you, but I said I'd find you."

I followed him across the ballroom toward the main door. A small, grim-faced group stood there, consisting of Timothy Farraday and three deputies. They encircled Augusta and Amelia, who looked young and frightened now.

Before Farraday could say anything, I lashed out at him. "You ought to be ashamed of yourself. Does it take four big strong men to surround a couple of scared little girls?"

Even under the circumstances, Augusta said, "We're not little girls, Aunt Delilah."

"Close enough," I snapped. I glared at Farraday. "Well?"

He didn't lose his temper. He said, "I just thought that you might like to be present while I talk to your nieces some more, Ms. Dickinson."

"Do they need a lawyer?"

"I don't think so."

I relaxed, but only for a second before I remembered how tricky police detectives could be. I didn't know that from personal experience, of course, but I was pretty sure it was true.

"We'll just see," I told Farraday. "If I think they shouldn't answer your questions, I'm gonna tell 'em so."

"That's fine."

He and the deputies escorted the girls and me out of the ballroom. Luke would have come with us, but one of the deputies put a big hand on his chest and shook his head. Luke gave me a helpless look, and that was the last thing I saw before the ballroom doors swung shut, leaving us in the hall with Farraday and the deputies. We started toward the office where Farraday had questioned me earlier.

"You're sure about that lawyer?" I asked him again.

"Yes. Your nieces aren't suspects in Steven Kelley's murder, at least right now."

Then he smiled and said something that knocked me back on my heels.

"On the other hand, before this night is over, *you* may want to be represented by legal counsel, Ms. Dickinson."

CHAPTER 10

I might have stopped short in surprise at the implication of his words, but one of the deputies was walking behind me and put a hand on my shoulder to keep me going. You've heard about the heavy hand of doom falling on a person? Well, that's what it felt like . . . even though I knew darned well I hadn't done a thing to feel guilty about.

"*Me?* What in the world are you talkin' about?" I demanded of Farraday as we reached the door of Edmond Ralston's office.

Farraday opened the door. "Let's just all go inside and talk about it, shall we?"

The room was more crowded this time with me, Augusta and Amelia, Lieutenant Farraday, and the three deputies in it. In fact, Farraday sent two of the deputies back to the ballroom, saying, "I think Perkins and I can handle this all right."

He went behind one of the desks and sat down this time, so I had the girls take the two chairs in front of the desks. I stood between them, my left hand on Amelia's shoulder, my right on Augusta's. Perkins, the deputy who had remained behind, leaned against the closed door.

"All right now," Farraday began as he took a couple of folded sheets of paper from inside his coat. As he unfolded them I saw that they had been torn from notebooks like the one he carried. "These are the statements the young ladies made to Perkins and Renfro. I'd like for them to look them over and see if there's anything they'd like to change or add."

He stood up and started to hand the papers to the girls, then stopped and looked a little sheepish. "I don't, ah, know which one of you ladies is which . . ."

"I'm Amelia," Augusta said. Even scared like she was, she couldn't resist trying to stir things up.

"No, she's not," Amelia said. "I am."

"Girls, this isn't the right time for this," I said. "Lieutenant Farraday, this is Augusta"—I pointed—"and that's Amelia."

"I don't see how you tell 'em apart. No offense, ladies," Farraday added as he handed over the written statements.

Amelia and Augusta nearly always dressed differently, but their physical features were so similar that it *was* difficult for most people to tell them apart. Augusta had a tiny mole near the right corner of her mouth, but it was hard to see if you didn't know it was there. Amelia's eyes were a little more gray than blue, but it was only a slight difference. Once you got to know them, though, the easiest way to tell them apart was their personalities. Augusta had always been the tomboy of the two when they were little, and even though she had lost that quality as she grew older, she was still the more daring. More of a hell-raiser, I guess you'd say. She gets that from my side of the family."

Farraday continued, "Later on, these notes will be typed up into formal statements, and you'll be asked to sign them. So it's a good idea to be sure that they're complete and correct."

Augusta thrust her paper toward him. "That's what I told the deputy. I don't have anything else to add."

"This looks correct, too," Amelia said. "Other than some spelling and grammatical errors I can correct for you if you'd like."

Farraday shook his head. "No, that's all right, but thank you."

I put out my hand. "Can I see those?"

He put them on the desk behind him. "No, I'd rather you didn't right now, Ms. Dickinson. But I can tell you what they say, and if I get anything wrong, your nieces are right here to correct me." He smiled. "As I'm sure they will."

Augusta made a noise in her throat, as if to say, *Darn right we will, buster.*

Instead of going behind the desks to sit down again, Farraday leaned back and propped a hip against one of them. He said, "Earlier today, when the bus carrying the tour group arrived, everyone split up into three different bunches."

I nodded. "That's right. I was there, remember?"

"Of course you were. But you didn't go with any of the groups, did you?"

"Well . . . no, not really. I sort of wandered around, keeping an eye on things and making sure that all the tours were going all right. I guess I spent most of my time in the house."

"You didn't go to the stables with Steven Kelley and his group." It was a statement, not a question.

"No. And at the time, I didn't know he was Steven Kelley. He was just the actor playing Rhett Butler. Doing a Clark Gable impersonation, actually."

"And a pretty good one, too," Farraday commented. "With that fake mustache, he actually looked quite a bit like Gable."

I hadn't known the mustache was fake and didn't see what that had to do with anything. When I said as much, Farraday agreed with me.

"You're right, Ms. Dickinson, that's not important. The reason we're here is because while the group of tourists with Steven Kelley was touring the stables, Kelley managed to get your nieces alone and suggested to them that they both have sex with him—at the same time."

I was so shocked by his blunt statement that all I could do for a moment was stare at him, speechless. Then my mouth started working again, and I yelled, *"What!"*

"I'm sorry to have to tell you like that—"

"The hell you are! You did it that way just to see how I'd react!" I glared at him. "Satisfied?" Then I turned to Augusta and Amelia, who didn't seem to want to look at me. "Is this true?"

"It's true that he asked us," Augusta said.

"Well, actually, he *implied* it more so than actually came right out and asked us," Amelia said.

"But we didn't do it."

"Of course not."

"I mean, he was like twenty-five or thirty years old. Ooh."

If there had been a chair handy, I would have

sat down. My knees felt weak, and the room was trying to spin. "Did he touch you?"

"No," Amelia said. "I would have screamed."

Augusta said, "I would've kicked him right in the—"

I held up a hand to stop her. "That's enough."

She smiled. "Right there in the stable, that's what I was going to say."

I still felt a little dizzy. I said, "I may be sorry I asked this, but what exactly did he do?"

The girls looked at Farraday, who shrugged as if telling them to go ahead.

"He asked us . . ." Amelia began, but then she stopped and blushed.

Augusta didn't have any trouble carrying on with the story. "He wanted to know how experienced we were. He said that if we hooked up with a guy together it would be a lot of fun. Then he offered to show us."

"Where the heck was this? And where was everybody else when it was going on?"

"In a little room behind the tack room in the stables. Everybody else was looking at the horses. There's a little racetrack down there, and the grooms were working out some of the horses."

"What in the world were you doing in there alone with him?"

"He said there were some things stored in there that he needed for the tour, and he asked us to help him bring them out. Of course, that was a lie."

"What did you do when he . . . when he said those awful things?" I saw Farraday watching the girls closely, and I supposed he was interested in their answers because he wanted to know if they would match what had been told to the deputies earlier.

"We told him we weren't interested," Amelia said.

"I called him a perv," Augusta said.

"Then he begged us not to tell anyone what had happened," Amelia said.

"We told him we wouldn't, and then we got out of there," Augusta said.

I could only stare at them and sigh. "Why didn't you tell me? Or Luke?"

"We promised we wouldn't," Amelia said.

"And it's not the first time a guy ever hit on us like that," Augusta said. She nodded knowingly. "Things have probably changed since your day, Aunt Delilah, but there are a lot of horny high school boys today, not to mention sleazy older guys. And look at us. We're twins. We're hot. What do you *think* is going to happen?"

I looked over at the wall of the office and wondered how it would feel to pound my head against it. Then I glanced at Lieutenant Farraday and saw that he at least had the decency to look a little embarrassed.

"It hasn't been *that* long since my day," I said, "and things haven't changed all that much. But you should have told somebody."

Augusta shrugged. "He's dead now, so we figured we didn't have to worry about keeping the promise we made to him."

"He was really rather pathetic, actually," Amelia said. "Like it was a compulsion of some sort that he couldn't help." She lowered her voice to a whisper. "I think he might have been a sex addict."

Farraday cleared his throat, and the girls looked

at him. "All right, ladies. I know talking about that wasn't pleasant for you . . ."

Augusta gave her no-big-deal shrug. Farraday continued, "But what I need to know now is whether or not you told anyone about Kelley's actions before my deputies questioned you."

"Who would we have told?" Amelia asked.

Farraday nodded toward me. "What about your aunt? She's the one taking care of you this summer, isn't she?"

"We can take care of ourselves," Augusta said. "Besides, like we just said, we promised the guy we wouldn't tell anybody."

I was starting to get the idea, and I thought I understood why Farraday had made that comment earlier about how I might need a lawyer. I said to him, "You think I killed Kelley because I found out about him propositioning my nieces?"

Augusta and Amelia both looked around sharply at me, and Augusta said, "Uh-uh! That's crazy!"

"Aunt Delilah would never kill anybody," Amelia said. "Anyway, she didn't know about what Mr. Kelley said to us in the stable. We've explained over and over that we didn't tell her."

"And I'm sure you wouldn't lie to protect your aunt," Farraday said.

But he didn't sound convinced of that at all.

I took a deep breath, uncertain just how much trouble I was really in here. Farraday sure looked and sounded like he considered me a legitimate suspect in the murder, but maybe that was just his way, I told myself. Maybe he just wanted me to go ahead and clear myself so he could concentrate his deductive efforts elsewhere.

"You saw how I reacted when I heard about what

happened to the girls, Lieutenant," I said. "Unlike some of the folks on this plantation, I'm *not* an actor. That was genuine surprise. This was the first I'd heard of the incident with Kelley."

"Can you prove that?"

"Well, nobody was with me all the time during the day, so I suppose not, but *I'm* telling you I didn't know about it, and the girls have confirmed that."

"Their testimony could be biased."

"I was in the ballroom when Kelley was killed. There were people all around."

"And is there anyone who can swear that you never left the ballroom during the evening, even for a few minutes?"

I thought about it for a second and realized that there wasn't. In fact, the size of the crowd sort of worked against me. I had been circulating, making sure everything was going all right, and I don't suppose there was anyone who could *swear* that I was in there the whole time. With that many people around, I could have slipped out and back in without being noticed.

I could see how Farraday could make a case against me. But it would be purely circumstantial. There couldn't be any physical evidence against me, for the simple reason that I hadn't killed Steven Kelley. And with the girls and me all testifying that I hadn't known about the incident at the stables, I wouldn't have had any motive for wanting to murder him.

I looked at Farraday and shook my head. "No one can swear I didn't leave the ballroom, Lieutenant, but even so, you don't have a case. You'd have to prove that I knew about what happened and that I did slip out of the ballroom, and you can't prove either of those things because they didn't happen."

"That's telling him, Aunt Delilah," Augusta said.

I wasn't through, though. "If you ask me," I went on, "you ought to find out if Kelley's wife knew he was the sort of man to make indecent advances to teenage girls."

"His wife?" Amelia said. "He was married?"

"Double ooh," Augusta said.

"Don't worry, we'll be looking into that," Farraday said. "I think we're done here."

"That's it?" I said. "You're not going to arrest me?"

"You didn't do anything wrong, did you?" he asked, his face and voice bland.

My eyes narrowed. "This whole thing was just a test to see what I'd do when I heard about what Kelley said to my nieces. You knew I didn't kill him, but you had to be sure."

He didn't admit to anything. "Thank you for your cooperation. The three of you can go back to the ballroom."

I couldn't let it go. "Are you convinced now?"

A little flare of anger appeared briefly in his eyes before he banished it. "To tell you the truth, Ms. Dickinson," he said, "I'm not convinced of anything right now . . . except that this is probably going to be a long night for all of us."

CHAPTER 11

So I wasn't completely out of the woods yet, I thought as Deputy Perkins escorted Augusta, Amelia, and me back to the ballroom. I didn't believe that Farraday seriously considered me a suspect in Steven Kelley's murder, but he hadn't ruled me out completely, either.

And I was willing to bet that he still considered the girls to be suspects, too, no matter how remote the possibility. They came closer than I did to having legitimate alibis, because they had been busy dancing most of the evening. It was true what Augusta had said: the fact that they were good-looking twins meant that they drew a lot of attention. I supposed that was sometimes a good thing, like when it meant that there were witnesses to swear that you couldn't have committed a murder.

Luke must have been watching the door, waiting for us to come back, because he showed up as soon as we entered the ballroom. His face wore an anxious expression. "Thank God," he said.

"Did you think they hauled us off to the slammer?" Augusta asked him.

"I didn't know what was going on. I'm just glad to see that you're all okay."

"That detective practically accused Aunt Delilah of murder," Amelia said, sounding properly outraged.

"What?" Luke stared at me. "Miz D, a murderer? That's just crazy! She couldn't hurt anybody."

I said, "I wouldn't be so sure about that, Luke. If anything else goes wrong with this tour, I might start to feelin' like killin' somebody."

"Yeah, but you'd never do it. You're harmless. Wouldn't hurt a fly. I never heard a sillier idea in all my life."

"That's enough, Luke."

"Why, they might as well accuse *me* of murdering that guy. That's how far fetched it is. Why did the detective think you'd want to kill that actor, anyway?"

Augusta answered before I could. "Because he hit on Amelia and me. At the same time."

Luke's eyes widened, and his nostrils flared like those of an angry bull. "He what?"

"It's a sordid story," Amelia said. "Do we have to tell it again?"

"Darn right you have to tell it!" Luke said. "Why, if I'd known about this, I would have—"

"What?" I broke in. "Punched him out?"

"I might have. And he'd've had it comin'."

"Or would you have been so upset you might have stabbed him?"

Luke stared at me. "Miz D! How can you think such a thing?"

"Not me, you big goof. But that's what Lieutenant Farraday would be asking you if he heard you carryin' on like that. Now just settle down, and I'll tell you what happened."

"We're gonna go mingle," Augusta said. "I don't want to listen to all this again."

"You'll do no such thing," I told her. "I don't want any more wandering around tonight. Go over there and sit down." I pointed to a couple of chairs next to the wall nearby.

"Just sit? That's boring."

"I think we've had enough excitement for one night. I could use a little boredom."

The girls grumbled about it, but that was nothing new. They nearly always grumbled about whatever I told them to do. They went to the chairs and sat down. I knew I'd have to keep an eye on them, though, if I wanted them to stay put.

While I was doing that, I told Luke what had happened, both in the stables that morning and in the office as Farraday interrogated the three of us a few minutes earlier.

"I guess it's a good thing I didn't know about it," Luke admitted when I was finished. "If I had, I don't know what I might have done."

From behind him, Lt. Farraday said, "That's interesting, Mr. Edwards."

I hadn't seen him come up. As Luke and I turned toward him, I said, "Don't tell me you suspect Luke now? He was here in the ballroom all evening, just like me."

Farraday looked steadily at him. "Is that true, son?"

I punched my son-in-law on the arm. "Tell him, Luke."

Instead, Luke grimaced and said, "Wellllll . . ."

"You were in here," I insisted. "I saw you."

"Not . . . exactly . . . the *whole* time, Miz D. I had to step out for a little while . . ."

"But for a good reason, right?" I prodded. "And somebody must've seen you."

Luke didn't say anything.

Farraday filled the silence, though, by saying, "Why don't you come with me, Mr. Edwards? We need to talk."

I grabbed the sleeve of Luke's coat. "You don't need to drag him off to your interrogation chamber. He didn't know about what happened with Kelley and the girls, either. We just told him, and he was just as shocked to hear about it as I was."

"Actually, Ms. Dickinson, I wasn't planning to ask him about that . . . not that I need your advice on how to conduct a murder investigation."

"Well, then, how could Luke possibly have anything to do with it?" I demanded.

Quietly, Farraday said, "I thought maybe Mr. Edwards would like to tell me about Lauren Holcomb."

At that moment, Luke turned paler than I had ever seen him in the time I'd known him. He looked shaken, too, even more so than when we'd gone out into the garden and seen Steven Kelley's body. In fact, he looked more scared and pale than he had the day he married Melissa, and I'd thought then that he was fixing to faint as he watched her father walk her up the aisle of the church.

"Luke?" I said. "What's he talking about? Luke?"

He ignored me and stared at Farraday. "He can't be the same one," he muttered. "He didn't look anything like him."

Farraday took Luke's arm. "Come on, son." His

voice was gentle, but I could tell by the way his fingers dug in that the grip was a tight one.

Luke went with him, but he shook himself out of his stunned state long enough to glance back at me as Farraday led him out of the ballroom. "I'm sorry, Miz D," he said, and then they were gone.

Leaving me there to wonder what in blue blazes was going on.

And who was Lauren Holcomb?

I went over to where Augusta and Amelia were sitting. They had seen Farraday take Luke out of the ballroom, and both of them wore anxious expressions.

"What happened, Aunt Delilah?" Amelia asked.

"That detective looked like he was ready to arrest Luke," Augusta said.

"I think Lieutenant Farraday is just questioning Luke like he's been questioning everybody else," I said, even though I knew from Farraday's attitude that it was more serious than that. "Do either of you girls know who Lauren Holcomb is?"

"Never heard of her," Augusta said without hesitation, and Amelia shook her head. "Who's she supposed to be?"

"I don't know, but Luke recognized the name."

I cast my memory back to when Melissa had met Luke when they were both in college. He was from a small town in southern Georgia, had gone to school on a football scholarship, and then had injured his knee in the first practice. He wasn't hurt so badly that he could never play again, but he lost his starting safety job while he was laid up and couldn't get it back from the player who had stepped in for him. Eventually, tired of sitting on the bench, he had quit the team, given up his scholarship, and finished his business degree on his own. By then he'd met Melissa and they had started dating. They got engaged during their senior year and then married as soon as they both graduated. During that time I had gotten to know Luke pretty well. I had figured out quickly that he was going to be my future son-in-law, so I made it a point to take an interest in him.

But I didn't recall him ever mentioning anybody named Lauren Holcomb.

I pulled over another chair and sat down with Augusta and Amelia to wait for Luke to come back . . . if the police let him go. While we were sitting there I looked around the room. The animation that had gripped the place after the discovery of Kelley's body was long gone by now. It had been replaced by boredom, impatience, and anger. The dance floor was empty because everyone was sitting around the tables, and of course there was no music anyway. Deputies stood guard at all the doors leading out of the big room, including the ones that went to the garden. I could see through those doors, and the view included the crime scene, illuminated now by powerful lights set up by the crime scene technicians as they went over it, searching for evidence.

"Ms. Dickinson."

The tightly controlled but still obviously angry voice made me look around. Gerhard Mueller stood there.

"What can I do for you, Mr. Mueller?"

"How much longer will we be forced to endure

these indignities, Ms. Dickinson? My wife is tired and wishes to go to bed."

"I'm sure she's not the only one," I told him.

"Lieutenant Farraday will let us know when we can go up to our rooms. I'm sure it won't be too much longer."

I wasn't sure of any such thing, but I hoped that would satisfy Mueller and he would go away. He stayed where he was, glaring down at me.

I sighed. "Is there something else?"

"This high-handed treatment by the police is unconscionable."

I wanted to make some comment about the Gestapo, but that would just make a bad situation worse, I decided. "Well, they *do* have a murder to investigate."

"Murder is not the only crime that has taken place here tonight."

I frowned. "What do you mean by that?"

"I have overheard people talking. Wallets and jewelry have been stolen."

That made me sit up straighter. In fact, it made me get to my feet. "What?"

"You heard me. There is a thief in the group." He sneered. "And I think we both know who it is."

"Riley," I breathed.

"Ja. *Herr* Riley. Yesterday he tried to steal my camera. Tonight he has, how do you say it, picked the pockets of these people."

"Why hasn't anybody said anything to me about it?"

"No one wanted to interfere with the police investigation, for fear that we would be here even longer."

That seemed a little far fetched to me, and I wondered suddenly if Mueller was just trying to stir up more trouble for Riley because of the grudge he held against him from the day before. Elliott Riley was so unlikable that even he knew it, but I hadn't seen any evidence that he was a thief.

"Look, everybody's still here," I said. "I'll talk to one of the deputies. If there are any items missing, the deputies can search everyone. That's bound to turn up anything that was stolen."

"Unless the thief has already hidden it somewhere for safekeeping until he can retrieve it later. Or perhaps Herr Riley has a confederate, so to speak, among the people who work here and has already passed along the things he stole."

Now Mueller was just looking for conspiracies where none were likely to exist, I told myself. But considering everything that had already happened on this tour, maybe nothing was too crazy to rule out completely.

"Tell the people who have lost things to come talk to me about it," I said. "I'll make a list of everything that's missing, and then I'll talk to Lieutenant Farraday. If somebody's really stealing stuff, we don't need to ignore it."

"Very well. But if this results in a longer incarceration for the entire group, people will not be happy."

"We're not incarcerated."

"We are being detained against our will. I fail to see the difference."

Mueller turned around and stalked away. I closed my eyes and rubbed my temples for a moment, wondering what else could go wrong.

A word of advice: never ask yourself what else could go wrong.

Because it was right then that a vaguely familiar voice called out loudly, "Let go of me, blast it! I haven't done anything!"

CHAPTER 12

It took me a few seconds to place that cranky tone, but then I recalled who it belonged to. I swung around and saw an elderly man struggling in the grip of one of the deputies by the ballroom's main door. I was surprised because I hadn't expected to see him again until the next day.

But I hadn't expected a lot of things that had happened since the bus pulled away that morning, so I wasn't sure why anything still surprised me. I told Augusta and Amelia to stay where they were and hurried toward the door.

"Mr. Cobb," I said, "what are you doing here?"

The deputy who was holding Wilson Cobb by the left arm turned to look at me. "You know this old guy, ma'am?" he asked.

"Of course I do. He's Mr. Cobb. He drove the tour bus out here this morning."

"You sure about that?"

"I'm not blind," I said. "He's Mr. Wilson Cobb,

and I reckon he's old enough to be your grandfather. Now show a little respect and let go of him."

I could tell that the deputy was thinking of telling me that he didn't take orders from me, but then he thought better of it. He shrugged and let go of Mr. Cobb's arm.

With an offended sniff, Mr. Cobb straightened his jacket. "Old enough to be your *great*-grandfather," he said to the deputy, then turned to me. "Thank you, Ms. Dickinson."

"Mr. Cobb," I said again, "what in the world are you doing here? You weren't supposed to bring the bus back until in the morning."

"I'll tell you what he was doing," the deputy said. "He was sneakin' around like a burglar. That's why I grabbed him. I figured Lieutenant Farraday would want to talk to him."

"I wasn't sneaking around like a burglar," Mr. Cobb insisted. "The front door was open. I came in to see if I could find anybody, and when I opened *this* door to look in, this bruiser pounced on me. Like to broke my arm. Haven't you ever heard that old bones are brittle, boy?"

"Why did you come back out here to the plantation?" I asked him. His story about the front door being open sounded unlikely to me. There should have been at least one deputy watching it. But that was just part of what I wanted to know. "You didn't bring the bus back tonight, did you?"

He drew himself up. "Of course not. The tour's not over until tomorrow. But when I heard about the trouble out here, I figured I'd better find out for sure what you wanted me to do. Thought maybe you'd want me to pick you folks up tonight."

"You could have called me on my cell phone."

"Tried. Didn't get an answer."

That didn't make any sense. I reached in the pocket of my blazer where I keep my phone.

It was gone.

While I was gone.

While I was trying to digest that startling bit of information, something else occurred to me. "Wait a minute. You said you heard there was some sort of trouble out here?"

He nodded. "That's right. It's all over the news-breaks on the TV tonight. 'Murder on the Planta-tion,' some of them are calling it."

"How did the TV people find out?"

"You're asking me? I don't work for TV, I just watch it." He chuckled. "But a lot more people are going to know pretty soon. I must've passed half a dozen news trucks on the way out here."

I had a feeling Lieutenant Farraday wasn't going to be too happy when he found out about that. But then, he hadn't been happy about any of this so far, so why should things be different now?

One of the main double doors leading into the ballroom from the hallway was partially open; it must have been left that way when the deputy nabbed Mr. Cobb. Now, through that open door, I heard a commotion from the front of the house. I couldn't make out all the words, but male and fe-male voices were yelling what sounded like ques-tions, and angry male voices were responding.

Mr. Cobb smiled. "Reckon those TV news folks have gotten here."

I knew he was right. Those were reporters shouting the questions, and deputies telling them to get back and be quiet. Edmond Ralston came up and demanded, "What's going on here?"

"The story's gotten out," I told him. "The media's arrived."

Ralston paled. "Lord, no. They'll make a circus out of it. Everybody will know that someone was killed in my garden."

"People would have found out anyway. You can't keep something like this quiet."

He rubbed a weary hand over his face and then sighed. "I suppose not. I just wish it would have taken a little longer."

I didn't see what difference it made if the story broke tonight, tomorrow, or the next day. The end result was going to be the same, whether it was for better or worse.

Those of us near the ballroom doors weren't the only ones who heard the commotion. A familiar voice called, "What the devil! Get those people and those cameras out of here! There's an investigation going on!"

That was Lieutenant Farraday. I didn't know if he was finished with questioning Luke or if the arrival of the media horde had interrupted the interrogation. But a moment later Luke appeared in the doorway, accompanied by Deputy Perkins. Luke still looked pale and shaken as he came into the ballroom. Perkins shut the door behind him, cutting off the sound of Farraday's angry voice. I could still hear the lieutenant, but his words were too muffled to understand.

Anyway, I was more worried about Luke at the moment. "Are you all right?" I asked him.

"Yeah. Yeah, I guess." He glanced over at Mr. Cobb, and a look of surprise appeared on his face. "Hey. What are you doing back here, Mr. Cobb?"

I took Luke's arm and said, "It's a long story,

and right now I want to hear about what Lieutenant Farraday said to you."

Luke hesitated. "I dunno if he wants me to talk about it. I dunno if I want to talk about it."

"Luke, you better ask yourself just who you're more afraid of here . . . him or me?"

I knew I was being too rough on him, and I felt bad about it. But I had the feeling that things were spiraling out of control and that this tour was going to turn into even more of a catastrophe than it already was unless I could do something to stop it. So I had to know what was going on to have any hope of figuring out a solution.

"All right," Luke said after a moment. "I guess you've got a right to hear about it, Miz D. But let's find someplace quieter than this."

Ralston was arguing with the deputy at the door. He wanted to go out and issue a statement to the media. "This is my house, damn it!" he argued. "I have a right to talk to the press."

I knew he wanted to put the best spin he could on the story, but the deputy was equally determined to follow the orders Farraday had given him and not let anybody out of the ballroom. I took Luke's arm and left them wrangling. Luke and I went over to the wall where Augusta and Amelia still sat, avidly watching everything that was going on. They looked glad to see Luke, too. I noticed that the deputy was distracted by the argument with Edmond Ralston. I let him come along, figuring that it wasn't going to hurt anything. I had just met him earlier that day, but somehow I thought of him as an ally.

"Luke!" Augusta said as we came up. "You're all right?"

He frowned. "Why wouldn't I be? The detective just wanted to ask me some questions."

Amelia said, "She thought maybe they were going to work you over with a rubber hose."

"I did not!" Augusta protested. "I just said it would be terrible if they did."

"Yeah, I think so, too," Luke agreed, "but nothing like that happened." He got a faraway look in his eyes. "I almost wish it had. That might not have been as bad as all the questions Farraday asked about me and Steven Kelley."

"You and Kelley?" I echoed. "How can there be a you and Kelley? You never saw him before today, did you?"

Keeping his voice pitched low, Luke rubbed his chin and said, "I, uh, sort of . . . went to 'high school with him."

All I could do for a moment was stare at him. When I got my voice back, I said, "You didn't recognize him?"

Luke spread his hands. "He looked like Clark Gable! That's all I saw."

"But you've heard his name probably two dozen times this evening. It didn't occur to you that it was the same fella you went to school with?"

He shook his head. "I just figured it was somebody with the same name. Steven Kelley's not that odd a name, you know. And he grew up a long way from here, like I did, and I hadn't seen him in years, and . . . and he looked like Clark Gable!"

When I thought about it, I supposed that what Luke was saying made sense. Steven Kelley wasn't as common a name as, say, John Smith . . . although how many John Smiths do you actually run into these days, I asked myself. And the Steven Kelley who had gotten himself murdered in the garden was years older than when Luke had known him, as well as looking completely different.

"When I first heard the name," Luke went on, "I thought, huh, I went to school with a Steven Kelley. But that brought back a lot of bad memories, so I tried not to think about it anymore."

"What sort of bad memories?" Augusta asked.

"Was this guy, like, your nemesis in high school or something?"

Luke sank onto one of the empty chairs. "Yeah, I guess you could say that. We were rivals all the way back to grade school and Little League. He was always just a little bit faster than me, a little bit smarter than me, a little bit better than me at anything we both tried to do. You know how there's always somebody that you just can't quite catch up to?"

"I have the highest grade average in my class," Amelia said.

"I'm head cheerleader," Augusta said.

"You're both wonderful," I said. "Luke, go on." I made a guess. "Does this have anything to do with Lauren Holcomb?"

Luke didn't look shocked by the name anymore. He just looked sad. Incredibly sad.

"I've got a confession to make, Miz D," he said.

"You'd better not say that too loud, boy," Wilson Cobb advised. "Not with all these badge-wearin' fellas standin' around."

I thought that, too, but at the same time I had to know what Luke was talking about. "Go on," I told him as I glanced around to make sure that none of the deputies were nearby eavesdropping. "Just be careful."

"Well . . . I hate to say it, Miz D, since she's your daughter and all . . . but Melissa wasn't my first love."

Augusta leaned forward and asked breathlessly, "You mean you and this Lauren chick hooked up back in high school?"

"It wasn't like that. Lauren and I started dating when we were in eighth grade. We gave each other promise rings when we were juniors. We were gonna get engaged as soon as we graduated from high school."

"Wait a minute," I said. "Have you told Melissa about this?"

"Of course. We don't have any secrets from each other."

"But neither of you ever saw fit to tell *me?*"

"Well, no offense, Miz D, but it's sort of . . . none of your business."

I didn't like it, but I knew he was right. So I reined in my temper and told him, "All right, keep going. You and this girl Lauren were in love."

He nodded somberly. "I thought so. And then at the beginning of senior year, she . . . she broke up with me."

"Dumped," Augusta said. "Always tragic."

"And I'll bet Steven Kelley had something to do with it," Amelia said.

"Yeah," Luke said. "They had gotten together somehow over the summer between junior and senior year. And of course he took her away from me. Was there ever any doubt? He'd had his eye on her ever since we started going together. If I had something, he always wanted to take it away from me. It just took him longer this time than it usually did. But in the end, he wore down her resistance and . . . he got what he wanted."

I thought about Lt. Farraday's attitude earlier. "This doesn't make sense, Luke," I said. "Are you tryin' to tell us that Farraday thinks you killed Kelley over a high school break-up? I know it must've hurt, but that was years ago. And you're happily married now. At least, you'd better be."

"Of course I am. Melissa and I are happy as we can be. But you're right. Lieutenant Farraday does think I'm a suspect in the murder."

"Because of an old girlfriend Kelley took away from you?" I shook my head. "That's crazy. Anyway, how did he even know about what happened years ago in another town? He couldn't have found out about it tonight, in the time since he got here."

Luke took a deep breath. "That's not all the story. You see, Kelley did more than just take Lauren Holcomb away from me." His eyes were more haunted than I'd ever seen them. "He killed her, too."

CHAPTER 13

All of us stared at him this time, obviously finding it difficult to grasp what he had just said. Augusta was the one who spoke up first.

"You mean, the guy who got murdered tonight murdered your old high school girlfriend?"

"The one who tragically broke up with you because of him?" Amelia added. "It's like a novel by one of the Brontë sisters!"

"He didn't *murder* her," Luke said. "They were in a car wreck a few weeks later. Kelley was driving, going too fast like he always did. And Lauren was killed, while he walked away with hardly a scratch."

"Wait a minute," I said. "If he was driving too fast and somebody was killed, shouldn't he have gotten in trouble with the law?"

Luke nodded. "He did. I'm sure that's how Lieutenant Farraday was able to find out about it so quickly. He probably had a couple of his deputies runnin' everybody through the computers as soon as he got our names. Kelley was arrested and charged with vehicular manslaughter. But his parents had a lot of money and got him a hot-shot lawyer, and the lawyer got him off. He even walked on the stage at graduation. The principal wanted to keep him from doing that, but his folks threatened to file a lawsuit if he tried it."

"And this is the fella who wound up playing Rhett Butler for a bunch of tourists?"

"He was in the drama club at school, always had the lead in the plays they put on, of course. And I heard he got his doctor's degree in theater from one of those Ivy League schools. My guess is that he worked here because he liked it."

"And so that he could hit on hot teenage tourists," Augusta put in.

I thought she might have something there. Plenty of attractive women would pass through during the tours of the plantation, and if Kelley had really been a sex addict, as Amelia speculated, he would have had plenty of chances to approach some of them with a proposition.

Of course, he was married and his wife worked right here on the plantation with him, I reminded myself. She even played Scarlett to his Rhett. But clearly, based on what had happened with Augusta and Amelia, that didn't stop Kelley. Carrying on right under his wife's nose might even make it better for him.

I was making a lot of assumptions and jumping to a lot of conclusions about the man, considering that I had never seen him before today and hadn't spoken to him even once. But Luke knew him, and I believed my son-in-law. I believed my nieces, too, at least about Kelley's behavior in the stables. I thought I had enough evidence to reach some of those conclusions in a logical manner.

But I had no evidence whatsoever about who might have killed Steven Kelley. As far as I could see, that was still completely up in the air. Lieutenant Farraday had his suspicions about me, Augusta, and Amelia, but right now, based on the grudge that Luke had held against the dead man, he had to be the leading candidate for the role of murderer.

"You said you weren't here in the ballroom all evening, Luke. Where did you go?"

He looked up at me. "Miz D! Don't tell me you think I killed him, too?"

"Oh, of course not." I stopped myself before I called him a lunkhead. "I just want to know if you've got an alibi."

"Not really." He glanced at Augusta and Amelia and then lowered his voice. "I was indisposed."

Mr. Cobb said, "Boy must mean he had the trots."

Luke glared at him. "I have a delicate stomach sometimes."

I happened to know that was true. Luke was a big strong boy with the stomach of a little girl. "So you were in the bathroom."

"Yeah. And since I was in there by myself . . ."

"No alibi."

"That's right. I could have slipped out of the ballroom, stabbed Kelley, and gotten back in without anybody noticing because there were so many people around and there was so much going on." Luke grunted and shook his head. "That's the way the lieutenant sees it, anyway."

And I had to admit that it was a fairly strong theory, especially to somebody like Lieutenant Farraday who didn't know Luke. Who didn't know that he couldn't possibly murder somebody, even a sorry son of a gun like Steven Kelley. Like Luke had said when he found out what Kelley had pulled with the girls, he might take a swing at somebody who deserved it, but that was as far as he would ever go. I believed that with all my heart.

On the other hand—and I hated myself for thinking this way—all I really knew about Luke Edwards was how he had been the past few years, since he'd met and married my daughter. I didn't want to believe that Melissa could have married a murderer.

And I *wasn't* going to believe it.

"Dad gummit," I said, "it doesn't matter what Lieutenant Farraday thinks, Luke. We know good and well you didn't do it. Don't we, girls?"

"Sure," Augusta said, and Amelia nodded.

"I don't think you did it either, son," Mr. Cobb said. I didn't point out that he barely knew Luke. At the moment, any voice of support was welcome.

"At least he didn't go ahead and arrest me," Luke said. "And it's not like I'm the only one he's holding here, either."

I looked around the ballroom, which was still crowded with tired, impatient, frustrated people, and said, "Not hardly."

"You know," Augusta said, "if the guy was such a sleaze that he hit on innocent teenage girls, there could be a lot of people here who were mad at him. He's bound to have done other things he shouldn't have."

That made a lot of sense, I thought. And then Amelia brought up something else that was worth thinking about.

"Where'd the knife come from?"

I had no idea, and somehow I didn't think that Farraday would tell me what they'd found out about the murder weapon, even if I asked nicely. But I was going to keep it in mind and keep my eyes and ears open for a possible answer. The idea was taking root in my brain that if I could figure out who killed Steven Kelley, this whole crazy nightmare would be over.

The murder wasn't the only mystery, though, I recalled abruptly. I checked my pockets again. My cell phone was definitely gone. I hadn't used it since I'd checked in with Melissa at the office during the afternoon, and I was sure I'd had it after that. So I didn't think I had laid it down anywhere and accidentally walked off and left it.

Thinking of the call to Melissa reminded me that by now she might have heard that there was trouble here at the plantation, especially if it was all over the TV news like Mr. Cobb said. The media didn't have the full story yet, but they might know that there had been a murder. The way they reported it might range all the way from "one person suspected to be dead" to "an alleged bloodbath among the magnolias." Melissa hadn't been expecting us back until the next day, but if she heard that sort of report on TV, she would probably be scared out of her wits.

"You have your cell phone?" I said to Luke.

"What?" He was still distracted by being suspected of murdering somebody. "Oh. Yeah, sure, it's right here." He reached into his jacket pocket. "Or here." He slapped his trouser pockets, then frowned. "That's funny. I was sure I had it."

I turned to Augusta and Amelia. "Girls?" I knew at least one of them would have a phone. Even though we had all put our bags in the rooms we'd been assigned earlier for the overnight stay, no teenage girl was going to be without a phone.

Both of them looked completely aghast, though, as they searched their pockets and didn't find their phones. "It's gone!" Augusta announced in a shocked voice.

"That does it," I said. It looked like there was some truth to Gerhard Mueller's story about things disappearing.

I told Luke, Mr. Cobb, and the girls to stay put, then went looking for Elliott Riley.

Even though I had no proof that Riley was a pickpocket and a thief, *he* was where I was going to start. It was bad enough that somebody had gotten murdered on my first tour; I sure didn't want the word getting around that my clients got robbed, too.

I spotted Riley standing by himself—that was no surprise—and was making my way toward him when the doors into the ballroom opened and an angry-looking Lieutenant Farraday came in, followed by a couple of deputies. Farraday raised his voice and called, "Everyone give me your attention, please!"

It didn't take much to quiet the place down since all the conversations in the room were pretty subdued by now. In fact, things got noisier as people turned toward the lieutenant and started calling out questions, all of which could be summed up as "When the heck do we get out of here?"

Farraday had to lift his hands over his head and call for quiet several more times before the room settled down again. Then he turned to gesture at his deputies and said, "My men are going to confiscate your cell phones. I hoped that it wouldn't come to this, but I have no choice."

That brought more protests. Farraday let them run their course, then went on, "I should have done this as soon as I arrived on the scene, but I thought it might be a good idea to let you people contact your loved ones if you needed to, since you're going to be stuck here for a while. Unfortunately, several of you decided to contact the news media instead." His expression was as dark as a thundercloud. "In fact, some of you even sent video footage of the crime scene to local TV stations. I suppose your fifteen minutes of fame was more important to you than allowing the authorities to do their job and catch a killer," he added bitterly.

That answered the question of how the TV news crews had come to show up at the door of the plantation house. And Farraday was right, of course: these days everybody with a camera phone has the potential to be as famous as that Zapruder fella with his JFK film, or whomever it was who shot the Rodney King video. All you needed was to be on hand for a big enough news story. Heck, Larry King might even call and want you to appear on his show.

One of the tourists asked, "If we give up our phones, how do we know we'll ever get them back?"

"Yeah!" another man said. "What if you keep all of them as evidence?"

"The likelihood of that is remote," Farraday answered, "and you'll all get receipts for the phones."

He didn't bother trying to keep the disgust out of his voice as he added, "Believe me, people, we have more important things to do than try to steal your cell phones."

The police might have had more important things to do, but somebody sure as heck didn't, because over the next couple of minutes all sorts of commotion broke loose in the ballroom as people reached for their phones and found them gone, just like Luke and the girls and I had done. As the angry outbursts spread, it took Farraday several minutes to restore order.

People weren't just yelling about their phones being gone, either. Wallets and jewelry were missing, too, as Mueller had told me earlier. Once Farraday realized that he was dealing with widespread robbery as well as murder, he looked like he was torn between the urge to shoot us all or sit down and cry.

What he wound up doing was ordering his men to search us. "Each and every one," he said. "Call for more female deputies if you need to. But it's past time we find out what everybody in this room is hiding."

Lindsey Hoffman, the good-looking blonde in the low-cut Southern belle outfit who seemed to be Perry Newton's girlfriend, said in an outraged voice, "Do I look like I could be hiding anything in this outfit, Lieutenant?"

"Lady," Farraday said, "you could have an elephant under those hoop skirts for all I know!"

CHAPTER 14

Lindsey was outraged by Farraday's comment, of course. I would have been, too, if I'd been wearing hoop skirts. Not that I ever would. And because Lindsey was mad, Perry was, too, and the feeling spread quickly among the other performers from the plantation, which added to the already prevalent ill-feeling in the ballroom.

But there was nothing anybody could do except submit to the patdown that Farraday's deputies carried out with brisk efficiency. Searching the men went quicker that it did with the women, because Farraday had brought only two female deputies with him. They led the women one by one into a small cloakroom just off the ballroom and conducted the searches there. The men were frisked out in the open.

Most of them didn't like it. I could tell they felt humiliated and angry, and despite the fact that Lieutenant Farraday wasn't one of my favorite people, I felt a little sorry for the guy. There were going to be plenty of formal complaints lodged about this investigation, and maybe even some lawsuits. But all Farraday was really trying to do was find out who killed Steven Kelley, and that was something I wanted, too. It was too late to salvage any sort of success out of this tour, but I wanted the damage minimized as much as possible. That was all I could hope for at this point.

While I was standing in line with Augusta and Amelia, waiting to be searched, I kept an eye on Elliott Riley. By now I hoped that he really was the thief, as Mueller had claimed, and that the deputies would find the stolen items on him. That would put an end to this part of the debacle.

But from the usual smirk Riley wore as one of the deputies patted him down, I knew that the search wouldn't find anything on him. Of course not. He couldn't hide dozens of cell phones and wallets in his suit, even though it *was* a little baggy.

No, Mueller was right. If Riley was the pickpocket, he had already stashed everything he'd taken or passed it on to someone who was working with him. It seemed unlikely that he could have done that with so many deputies around.

But maybe he did it *before* the murder was discovered, I thought. I hadn't missed my phone until later; it was possible that was the case with most of the other victims, too. They could have had their pockets picked during the dance. It would have been easy for somebody who knew what he was doing.

I had no proof that somebody was Riley. I told Farraday about the dispute between Riley and Mueller the day before, but that wouldn't prove anything.

Especially since Mueller was braying like a jackass about being searched and making comments about America being a police state while his long-suffering wife just stood in the women's line and ignored him. He was just about as unlikable as Riley was; given the choice, most folks wouldn't want to believe him or Riley.

The girls and I were getting closer to the head of the line. They were in front of me. Amelia looked over her shoulder and said, "I don't like this very much, Aunt Delilah."

"Neither do I," Augusta said. "It's creepy."

"I know," I told them, "but there's nothing we can do about it except wait for it to be over."

Amelia frowned. "It's not like you to be so passive, Aunt Delilah."

"Yeah," Augusta agreed. "You usually don't put up with something if you don't like it."

They were right. I'd never been the sort of person who kept my mouth shut if I thought something wasn't right. I spoke up instead, and raised my voice if I had to.

But everything that had happened this evening—the murder; the things I had learned about Augusta, Amelia, and Luke; falling under suspicion of being a killer myself—had all combined to beat my spirits down, I supposed. I thought that I had dealt with some hard times in my life, including that recent divorce, but never anything like this.

I was about to tell the girls that I was sorry when I realized it didn't have to be this way. I felt my backbone stiffening as I said, "Wait here."

"Uh-oh," Augusta said. "We shouldn't have said anything. I know that look."

"Please, Aunt Delilah," Amelia said. "Don't get into trouble on our behalf."

"This doesn't have anything to do with you girls," I told them. "This is all me."

I left the line and stalked toward Lieutenant Farraday, who was standing by as some of his deputies searched the men. One of the deputies keeping the women in line called out to me as I made my move, but I ignored him.

I had barely gotten started, though, when a hand grasped my arm, not roughly by any means, but firmly enough that I had to pause and see who it belonged to.

I was a little surprised to find Dr. Will Burke beside me. "I need to talk to you, Ms. Dickinson," he said, and his voice carried a note of urgency to it.

I still wanted to go chew out Lieutenant Farraday, but Will Burke looked like he had something serious on his mind, so I nodded and stepped to the side. He came with me.

"All right, Dr. Burke, what is it?"

He still wore the grim expression, but I suddenly noticed humor twinkling in his eyes. "I thought we were going to call each other Will and Delilah."

I curbed my impatience and said, "All right, Will, what's so important?"

"Keeping you from getting shot."

My eyes widened. I couldn't help it. "Shot?"

"Well . . . Tasered, more likely. That deputy who was trying to stop you from leaving the line was reaching for his hip. He probably would have gone for the Taser instead of the service revolver, since you don't look *too* dangerous."

I looked around and saw the deputy he was talking about glaring at me. "Oh, Lord. He thought I'd gone nuts and was charging Farraday, didn't he?"

Will chuckled. "To tell you the truth, that's sort of the way it looked to me, too."

I shook my head. "My temper gets the best of me sometimes, I guess. I was gonna give the lieutenant a good talkin' to, but I wasn't about to attack him or anything like that."

"I thought I'd better step in anyway. Maybe distract you a little."

He was right. Whether it was my nature or not, it wasn't going to do any good to lambaste Lieutenant Farraday. I had already seen how stubborn the man was, and I didn't think he'd change now.

Besides, while I didn't think this search was going to turn up the missing items, maybe it would find something else.

Like a motive for murder, maybe. It didn't hurt to hope.

"What about you?" I said to Will. "Won't you get in trouble for leaving the line?"

He shook his head. "They've already searched me." A grin broke across his face. "I'm not the thief. Or the murderer."

Now that was something that had never occurred to me. But if what Augusta had said about other people who worked on the plantation having grudges against Steven Kelley was true, then I supposed Will Burke would have to be considered a suspect, too. My instincts told me he wasn't a killer . . . but again, I had never met him before this evening and didn't really know him at all.

"I guess I'd better get back in line before that deputy gets trigger happy," I said. "Want to come along and keep me company?"

Will was still smiling as he nodded. "I guess I could do that."

I moved back into my place just behind Augusta and Amelia. Augusta said, "I was afraid you were gonna rip that cop a new one, Aunt Delilah."

I frowned at her. "I don't think your mama would like you talkin' that way, Augusta."

"Call me Gussie." She turned her high-voltage smile on Will Burke. "Hi, Dr. Burke."

She wasn't flirting with him, at least not any more than she flirted with every male she met. Both girls seemed to be a little taken with him, Amelia because of his smarts, Augusta because he wasn't hard to look at.

That combination sort of appealed to me, too, or at least it would have if I hadn't still been hurting a little from the divorce and stressed out over starting my own business, which was on the verge of getting ruined by that blasted murder. This was no time for me to be thinking about some man being smart and good-looking, whether he was or not.

I figured it might be a good idea to distract the girls from Will; I didn't have to worry about distracting *him*, because he was being polite to them but that was all. I said, "Since you work here and at the college, you must've known the murdered man pretty well."

Will's smile went away. "I knew him. Like I said earlier, we were just colleagues, though."

"I've heard some things about Kelley since we talked then," I said. "Things that make him sound like he wasn't . . . well, wasn't a very good person, even though I hate to speak ill of the dead."

Will suddenly frowned. "Did Kelley make a pass at you, Delilah?"

"Me? No, I never even talked to him."

Will looked at Augusta and Amelia. "Did he try something with you girls?"

"Oh, wow," Augusta said. "How did you know that?"

"Because Mr. Kelley must have done things like that before," Amelia said. "Isn't that right, Dr. Burke?"

Will hesitated for a second, then shrugged. "Kelley had a reputation among the faculty. Some of his more attractive female students occasionally got better grades than they seemed to deserve. He wasn't too blatant about it, though, and I never heard any rumors that students who turned him down had their grades lowered. That wouldn't have been tolerated. University administrators are very sensitive to charges of sexual harassment these days. Nobody wants their school to be the target of a lawsuit."

"But some professor/student hanky-panky still goes on anyway," I guessed.

Will inclined his head in agreement. "Some of it still goes on. As long as everybody keeps it low-key, and as long as the students who are involved are willing, blind eyes get turned."

"I reckon Kelley had a pretty good idea what he could get away with and what he couldn't."

"I suppose, because like I said, I never heard about him getting into any official trouble over it. There were just rumors, and vague ones at that."

"And he had to be careful because he was married, too," I pointed out.

"To a former student."

"Really? Maura Kelley was a student of his?"

Will nodded. "Several years ago."

"So she must've known what he was like."

Will's shoulders rose and fell. "I wouldn't hazard a guess what she knew or didn't know. Maybe he convinced her that he'd changed his ways." He glanced at Augusta and Amelia. "Although from what I'm hearing now, it sounds like he actually might've gotten worse. He didn't hurt either of you girls, did he?"

Amelia said, "No, he just made some suggestive comments . . . after he had gotten us alone under false pretenses."

"But we shot him down pretty quick," Augusta said. "No harm, no foul."

I hadn't seen Maura Kelley since right after the discovery of her husband's body. I asked Will, "Do you know what's happened to Kelley's wife?"

Will's face grew more solemn as he nodded. "I heard that since she collapsed, she's been held under guard in one of the rooms upstairs. Lieutenant Farraday has a deputy outside the door. That's what Ralston said, anyway."

"If she knew that her husband was carrying on with other women and had been ever since she was his student, she either accepted his behavior or finally got so sick of it that she couldn't stand it anymore."

Will frowned at me. "Are you saying you think Maura killed him?"

"I don't have any idea," I answered honestly. "But it seems to me she'd have as good a motive as anybody."

Will nodded slowly as he thought it over. "I suppose you're right. Maura never struck me as the violent type, but she *does* play Scarlett O'Hara, and Scarlett was capable of doing just about anything she thought she had to do."

I wasn't sure that the role Maura Kelley played

had any bearing on this case, but for all I knew, Will was right.

Before I could think about it anymore, Luke came up to us. He had already been searched, too, he explained, and so had Wilson Cobb, who trailed after him.

I was introducing Luke and Mr. Cobb to Will when Augusta's turn came to be searched. Making a face, she went into the cloakroom with the two female deputies. When she came back out a few minutes later, her features were red. I knew it must have been a bad experience, because it took a lot to make Augusta blush.

Looking nervous, Amelia went in next. She was blushing even more than her sister when she emerged from the cloakroom. "Watch out for that brunette deputy, Aunt Delilah," she whispered to me. "I think she may have Sapphic tendencies."

I thought Amelia was probably overreacting, and after being searched myself, I knew that was true. Both deputies were professional about it. Brusque, uncomfortably thorough, and a mite humiliating, but not unprofessional.

I came out of the cloakroom and rejoined my little group, which was drifting off toward one of the walls now that the deputies were through with us. The girls and I had been toward the rear of the women's line, and it took only a few more minutes for the deputies to wrap everything up. As far as I could tell, they hadn't found any of the missing items, although they had confiscated all the cell phones that the thief, whomever he was, hadn't gotten around to stealing before all hell broke loose.

A disgusted Lieutenant Farraday faced the crowd

in the ballroom and said, "I'm sorry to report that we didn't find any of the stolen property, but we'll keep looking. I'll be honest with you, though, that's not as high a priority as catching whoever murdered Steven Kelley."

Edmond Ralston spoke up. "It's nearly midnight, Lieutenant. How much longer are you going to keep us penned up like cattle in this ballroom?"

"I think the furnishings here are a little more comfortable than in a corral, Mr. Ralston . . . but I know what you mean. You already had rooms arranged for the guests who were taking Ms. Dickinson's tour, correct?"

Ralston nodded. "That's right."

"Are there enough bedrooms to accommodate the actors who put on the show, too?"

Ralston rubbed his chin and frowned in thought. After a moment he said, "We can probably crowd everybody in, especially if some people are willing to double up."

Farraday nodded. "That's what we'll do, then. Figure out the arrangements and let me know the details. I'll want a list of who's in which room."

"You mean you're *still* not going to allow anyone to leave?" Ralston sounded flabbergasted, and the angry mutters from some people in the crowd showed that the reaction was widespread.

"There's an excellent chance that the person who murdered Steven Kelley is still in this house. Until I'm certain that's not the case, I'd prefer to have everyone stay here."

Farraday left unsaid the fact that it wasn't just a preference on his part; it was an order.

"So we're stuck here," Augusta said.

"Cut off from the outside world," Amelia said.

"Like the people in an English country house mystery. Like something out of Agatha Christie."

"But we're not in England," Augusta said. "And this is a plantation. I thought Margaret Mitchell wrote *Gone With the Wind*, not Agatha Christie."

"Margaret Mitchell never wrote anything like this," I said.

CHAPTER 15

Accompanied by Lieutenant Farraday, Ralston went upstairs to try to figure out the sleeping arrangements. A few minutes later, one of the deputies came over to me and said, "The lieutenant wants you upstairs, ma'am."

"Me?"

"You're Ms. Dickinson, aren't you?"

"Yeah, but what does Lieutenant Farraday want with me?"

"I dunno, ma'am, he just called down on the radio and said to get you and bring you upstairs."

That didn't bode well. I looked at the girls, Luke, Will, and Mr. Cobb and shrugged, then followed the deputy. There wasn't anything else I could do.

The deputy took me out of the ballroom and down the hall to the main entrance of the plantation house, where a grand curving staircase led from the foyer to the upper floors. As we started up the stairs, I had the wild idea that maybe Farraday and Ralston had found another body. Will had said that Maura Kelley was being held in one of the bedrooms. Maybe the killer had struck again, getting to her some way and murdering her, too, just like her husband. Maybe there was a knife-wielding maniac on the loose in the house. . . .

And maybe I was letting my imagination get the best of me, I told myself. As we reached the second-floor landing and I saw Lieutenant Farraday and Edmond Ralston standing in the long corridor that had bedrooms on either side of it, I took a couple of deep breaths to setle myself down. Neither man looked like he had just discovered a second corpse.

"Thanks for coming up, Ms. Dickinson," Farraday said—like I'd had any choice in the matter. "We need your help with something. You have a list of all the guests on your tour, correct?"

"That's right."

"Maybe you can help us work out who can double up in a room so that we can fit everybody in."

I managed not to heave a sigh of relief. Administrative details like that, I could handle, as long as I didn't remind myself that the only reason there was a shortage of rooms was because everybody was a suspect in Steven Kelley's murder and had to stay at the plantation tonight.

At *least* for tonight, I reminded myself. I'd heard that most murders are solved in the first twenty-four to forty-eight hours, if they're ever going to be solved. The cops break cold cases every now and then, but those occurrences are rare. What if Farraday *didn't* find the killer tonight or tomorrow? I had this sudden wild vision of all of us being stuck here from now on as Farraday conducted a never-ending investigation. The men would all have long white beards, and I'd be a little old lady.

A tiny shiver went through me, and I shook my head to banish those thoughts. Farraday *couldn't* keep us all locked up here indefinitely. It wasn't even legally possible.

I nodded and told Farraday, "That list is in my briefcase, which is in the room where I was supposed to stay. I can get it for you."

"Thanks. Deputy Morton will go with you."

The deputy who had brought me upstairs walked down the hall beside me to my room. Like in a hotel, the bedroom doors all locked, and each guest had a key to his or her room. My key was in my pocket.

At least, I hoped it was. As I reached for it, I was reminded of my missing cell phone. Maybe my room key was gone, too.

But it wasn't. I used the key to unlock the door, went into the room, and retrieved the client list from my briefcase. Out of habit, I turned the case so that Deputy Morton couldn't see as I worked the combination locks to open it. When I closed the lid, I reset the locks.

We rejoined Farraday and Ralston, and I handed over the list. "I can make a suggestion to start with," I said. "There are two queen-size beds in my nieces' room. I can move in there with them. That'll free up my room."

Farraday nodded. "All right. I hope everyone is as cooperative as you're being, Ms. Dickinson."

"I wouldn't count on that," I warned him. "And I'm not known for bein' all that cooperative myself. I guess this is just your lucky night, Lieutenant."

He sighed, obviously thinking about the murder and a killer being on the loose. "Yeah. Lucky."

It took close to an hour to get everything sorted out so that everyone could be accommodated in the bedrooms on the second and third floors of the plantation house. That meant it was well after midnight before deputies began escorting small groups of people upstairs, either to the rooms where they'd originally been assigned to stay, or to the new rooms they'd be sharing with other guests.

Nobody felt like a guest anymore, though. They all felt like prisoners, and I couldn't blame them for that. Even though the rooms here in the plantation house were comfortable, bordering on luxurious, everyone was aware that they couldn't leave. That made them nervous, angry, and frustrated.

I was moving my stuff into the room I'd be sharing with Augusta and Amelia when Wilson Cobb called my name from down the hallway. He came toward me with one of the deputies following him.

"Miz Dickinson, this young fella says I can't go home," Mr. Cobb complained. "I wasn't even here when that killin' took place. I don't see why I should have to stay."

"Because the lieutenant says you got to," the deputy explained in a tone of strained patience.

"He's not holdin' all those TV reporters who showed up not long after I did," Mr. Cobb pointed out.

That was true, but the TV reporters weren't leaving, anyway. Farraday had succeeded in banishing them from the inside of the house, but their news trucks with the satellite dishes on their roofs were still parked out front. Some of the cameramen had tried to sneak around to the garden to get live shots of the murder scene itself, but Farraday had put a stop to that, too. Pretty much everything except the long, tree-lined drive was off limits to the TV people. Farraday considered the whole plantation to be a crime scene.

"I'll see what I can do, Mr. Cobb," I said. "I wouldn't get your hopes up, though. I don't have any more influence with the lieutenant than anybody else."

That was true, too. I had a feeling that, to Lieutenant Farraday, I was just another murder suspect. He would feel that way about everybody until he nabbed the real killer.

I finished putting my bags in the girls' room. Augusta and Amelia were already there, getting ready for bed. They had the resilience of youth, but even they looked tired. It had been a long day, and I guess falling under suspicion of being a killer is enough to wear anybody out, even teenagers.

"I'll be right back," I told them. "I have to go talk to Lieutenant Farraday."

"Something about the murder?" Amelia asked.

I shook my head. "No. He won't let Mr. Cobb go home, and I thought I'd see if I could convince him he ought to. After all, Mr. Cobb wasn't even here when Kelley was killed."

"I like him," Augusta said. "He's kind of grumpy, but in that lovable-old-man sort of way."

I knew what she meant. I felt the same way about Wilson Cobb.

I stepped back out into the hall and looked both ways along it. People were going in and out of their rooms, getting situated so that they could settle down for the night. A lot of grumbling and complaining was still going on. A couple of deputies were posted in the hallway to keep an eye on things. I figured that Farraday would have guards on duty all night to make sure that nobody tried to slip out.

I approached one of the deputies and asked if he knew where Lieutenant Farraday was. He nodded toward the landing and the curving staircase and said, "Downstairs in the command post, ma'am."

"And where's that?"

"The ballroom."

"Thanks." I turned and started toward the stairs.

"Wait a minute, ma'am." The deputy's voice was sharp and commanding.

I paused and looked back over my shoulder, halfway expecting to see him reaching for a Taser—or a gun.

Instead he just looked worried. "The lieutenant said nobody was supposed to leave this floor until he gave the word, ma'am."

"You know I worked with the lieutenant and Mr. Ralston arranging rooms for everybody, don't you?" I didn't figure that would confer any special status on me, but it wouldn't hurt to try.

"Yes, ma'am, but that, uh, doesn't really have anything to do with my orders."

"And I really need to talk to the lieutenant." I pointed at the little walkie-talkie clipped to the deputy's belt. "Can you raise him on the radio and ask him if it's all right for me to come down there and see him?"

He nodded. "I suppose so. He didn't give me any orders not to do that."

He took the radio off his belt and pushed whatever button it was that connected him with Farraday. "Lieutenant, Ms. Dickinson wants to come down to the command post and talk to you."

Farraday's voice crackled back. "What? What does she want?" He sounded annoyed.

"I don't know, sir, but the lady's right here if you'd like for me to ask her."

"No, no, that's all right. Let her come on down. Straight to the command post, though. No wandering around."

"Thanks, Lieutenant." The deputy broke the connection, hooked the radio to his belt again, and told me, "You heard the man, ma'am. Please do like he said so I won't get in trouble."

The deputy was young, probably no more than twenty-two. Just a kid, really. Young enough to be *my* kid. So I smiled at him and said, "Don't worry, Deputy. Straight to the command post it is."

I knew my way around the plantation house pretty well, so when I reached the bottom of the stairs I was able to turn toward the ballroom without any hesitation. The double doors stood open, I saw as I approached. The brilliant crystal chandeliers were still lit up, as if the room were filled with men in tailcoats and hoop-skirted ladies twirling gracefully around the dance floor.

Instead the big room was empty except for Lieutenant Farraday, who sat at one of the tables with stacks of papers in front of him. I guessed that they were the statements that had been given earlier in the evening by everyone who had been questioned.

He looked up at me and grunted. "What can I do for you, Ms. Dickinson?"

I didn't answer him right away. Instead I waved a

hand toward all the papers and asked, "Sorted out who the killer is yet?"

He grimaced. "If I had, we'd all be going home by now."

I pulled back one of the chairs at the table and sat down. It was a deliberate move in a way, an attempt to put things on a more equal, informal basis between us, like we were allies instead of adversaries. And it was just my nature, too, the sort of friendliness that even under bad conditions comes naturally to anybody who was raised in the South.

"Sorry, Lieutenant," I said. "I reckon I knew you hadn't found the killer. Can't blame a girl for hopping, though."

He shook his head. "No, I suppose not. What can I do for you?"

Lord, the man was a bulldog. If you didn't answer a question, he waited a minute or two and then asked it again. I said, "I need to talk to you about Mr. Wilson Cobb."

"The bus driver? What about him?"

"He says you won't let him go home. There's no reason to keep him here, Lieutenant. He didn't know Steven Kelley, doesn't have anything to do with anybody on the plantation, and he wasn't even here when Kelley was murdered. He drove us here this morning and then went back home to Atlanta. He didn't come back until after the murder."

"How do you know that?"

The question made me blink. "Well . . . he told me so."

Farraday nodded. "I'm sure he did."

Something about his attitude set me off again. I leaned forward in my chair and said, "Now wait just a doggone minute. It almost sounds like you consider Mr. Cobb a suspect now, and that's just crazy!"

"Why?"

"Why what?"

"Why is it crazy?"

"Because it is!" I couldn't keep myself from waving my hands around a little. "Why in the world would you think that a nice old man like Wilson Cobb would kill anybody?"

"Because he has before," Lieutenant Farraday said.

CHAPTER 16

There had been too many of these unexpected revelations since the discovery of the murder. I was getting jaded, I supposed, because although I stared at Lieutenant Farraday, I wasn't as shocked as I had been a couple of times earlier in the evening.

"Wait a minute," I said. "You're telling me that sweet old man is a murderer?"

Farraday shrugged. "I don't know how sweet he is. And I didn't say that he was a murderer, just that he'd killed somebody."

"Same thing, isn't it?"

"Not always."

He was right, of course; and if I'd been thinking straight I would have realized that right away. There are all kinds of situations where you might wind up being responsible for another person's death and still not have committed an actual homicide. Like a car wreck, or self-defense, or involuntary manslaughter . . .

"Cobb was convicted of voluntary manslaughter twenty-five years ago," Farraday went on. "He was sentenced to ten to twenty years in the penitentiary, but he was released after six years. Then the governor pardoned him. That's why he was able to get a commercial driver's license and be bonded by the bus company, because his record was wiped clean. All the records of the case are still available to law enforcement agencies, though. I have a laptop that's connected to the computer network back in the sheriff's office, and Cobb's history popped right up when I ran his name."

"Why would you do that?"

"What, run him through the computer?" Farraday shrugged. "I've been doing that for everybody. Well, one of the deputies has handled most of the actual computer work, not me personally."

That was exactly what Luke had said earlier, so I wasn't surprised. I was still mighty curious about Mr. Wilson Cobb, though.

"You said Mr. Cobb was pardoned. That means he didn't do it, right?"

Farraday shook his head. "No, that means the governor felt there were enough mitigating circumstances to set aside the conviction."

"So he actually did kill somebody?"

"No doubt about it."

"And he meant to, because you said it was voluntary manslaughter."

"Not much doubt about that, either."

"Enough so that the governor pardoned him."

"Yeah. I didn't say I agreed with the pardon, though." Farraday's mouth twisted. "It made for some nice publicity for the guy who was governor at the time. Maybe I'm being too cynical about it, but it didn't hurt him with the civil rights people or the federal government, either, since Cobb's black and his victim was white."

Twenty-five years ago, Farraday had said. I tried to remember any high-profile criminal cases from that time period but came up blank. I'd been a young mother with a baby at the time, so I'd had other things to occupy my mind . . . not to mention the fact that I hadn't been sleeping much then and was in sort of a daze most of the time like all parents of infants, especially cranky ones. And Melissa had been cranky.

Mr. Cobb had served six years of his sentence, which meant it had been nineteen years since he'd been released and pardoned. From the way Farraday talked, the pardon had received quite a bit of press, but again, nothing jumped out at me as I searched my memory. By that time Melissa had started school and I'd been busy juggling those responsibilities along with work and being married to Dan. I was trying to be SuperMom, in other words—a common ailment among my generation. It didn't leave much time for paying attention to what was going on in the rest of the world, outside of home, school, dance lessons, soccer practice, and the like.

"All right," I said to Farraday. "You're gonna have to tell me the rest of the story, like Paul Harvey."

He hesitated, a frown creasing his forehead. "That wouldn't be proper. You're a civilian, not law enforcement personnel."

"Oh, come on. If you weren't going to tell me all of it, you shouldn't have brought it up, especially makin' a dramatic pronouncement of it like you did."

"I didn't do that."

I just crossed my arms and gave him a caustic look.

After a second he sighed. "All right, maybe I did. I still can't share official information with you. For God's sake, you're still a suspect in this murder, to put it bluntly."

"That's blunt, all right. Allow me to be equally blunt, Lieutenant. We both know there's not a chance on God's green earth that I killed Steven Kelley."

"He made improper advances to your nieces—"

"For which I might've slapped him upside the head if I'd known about it at the time, but I didn't."

"You're the mother-in-law of another leading suspect."

"Who didn't do it, either." I was tired of arguing with Farraday, so I played my trump card. "Anyway, you already told me enough so that five minutes on the Internet would get me the whole story. You said the governor got some nice publicity out of it, so I'm sure there were newspaper stories galore, stories that are now archived online."

He looked at me for a long moment and then nodded. "You're right about that. I suppose it wouldn't do any harm. Might be a good idea for you to know the sort of man you're attempting to defend."

"I believe in Mr. Cobb."

That was *my* stubbornness talking. I didn't know Wilson Cobb, didn't know what he was capable of doing. But I wanted to find out, and Farraday was the one who could tell me.

"I won't sugarcoat it," he warned me. "Cobb

beat a man to death with a piece of iron pipe. I've seen the crime scene photos—which you *can't* get on the Internet—and they're not pretty."

I didn't think they would be, when I heard that about the iron pipe. It would be hard to beat anybody to death with anything and leave a pretty picture, I thought.

"Twenty-five years ago, someone was attacking teenage girls in the neighborhood where Cobb lived," Farraday went on. "The Atlanta police tried to catch him, but they hadn't had any luck."

That rang a bell in my brain. "I remember a case where some little boys were killed. . . ."

"The Wayne Williams case." Farraday shook his head. "This one was completely unconnected to Williams. He was never a suspect in the rapes, because he was already in custody at the time. The cops didn't really *have* a suspect . . . until Cobb caught the guy attacking a girl who lived in the same apartment building as he did."

"It was just luck, then?"

Farraday nodded. "Good luck for the girl, because Cobb heard her cries from a stairwell and got there before the rapist could hurt her. Bad luck for the guy, because Cobb took that pipe to his head. And the worst luck of all for Cobb, I guess, because he went to prison for saving a girl and killing a worthless piece of trash."

"How in the world does something that unfair happen?"

"An ambitious prosecutor and a certain ambiguity in the facts of the case. Also the fact that Cobb hit the rapist in the head thirty-seven times. If he'd clipped him once and killed him, there might not have been any charges filed. But thirty-seven times? That shows that he really wanted the guy dead."

"You said something about a certain ambiguity in the case?"

Farraday leaned forward. "Yeah. You see, the girl could testify that the man attacked her, and Cobb could testify to what he'd seen before he started swinging that pipe—namely that the girl was struggling and the man was hitting her and trying to tear her clothes off—but there was no direct evidence linking him to the other rapes."

"DNA," I said.

"It was twenty-five years ago," Farraday said heavily. "Using DNA evidence in criminal cases was in its infancy then. None of the other victims were able to make a positive identification, because the man always wore a ski mask when he attacked his targets. There weren't any credible eyewitnesses to the crimes, because until he slipped up and went after the girl in Cobb's apartment building, he always struck when his victims were isolated and alone. He was a bad actor, let me tell you." Farraday paused. "And I mean that literally."

"You mean he was an actor?"

"Yep." The informality took me by surprise. I supposed that the lieutenant was getting more comfortable talking to me. "Mostly dinner theater stuff, local TV commercials, things like that."

"So his face *might* have been easily recognized. That's another reason he wore the mask."

"Right. It concealed his features. Didn't do a thing to stop that iron pipe from crushing his skull, though."

I shuddered. I could see it in my head: the dimly

lit stairwell, the terrified girl, the sinister ski-masked figure, and Mr. Cobb with that pipe in his hand, rising and falling, rising and falling, with more blood on it each time. . . .

Farraday wasn't the only one who had gotten a mite dramatic, I told myself as I forced my thoughts back to what the lieutenant was saying.

"The rapist came from a fairly good family, and of course they didn't want to believe that he was the monster he really was. They denied that he'd had anything to do with the other attacks. They said that the girl was a prostitute and had lured the guy into the building. They even hinted that she and Cobb were working together in some sort of robbery scheme that had gone wrong and turned into murder. Enough people believed it so that the district attorney presented the case to the grand jury, got an indictment, and then took it to trial. He couldn't prove that Cobb and the girl were planning to rob the man, but those thirty-seven blows with the iron pipe . . ." Farraday shook his head. "The jury just couldn't get past that. They wouldn't bite on murder one, but they did go for voluntary manslaughter."

"What changed six years later to make the governor pardon Mr. Cobb?"

"New evidence. Cobb still had his defenders, and they kept pushing to have the investigation reopened. The political climate changed, too. There was a different district attorney, a different chief of police, more media pressure. . . . Eventually, the investigation *was* reopened, and the detectives found a witness who had seen the man Cobb killed taking off a ski mask after one of the earlier attacks. He had alibis for some of the attacks but not all of them; he was smart enough to know that if he had alibis for *all* of them, that would look a little suspicious, too, like he'd set them up. The investigators were able to break down some of the alibis and place him near the scenes of the earlier crimes. Cobb had been a model prisoner, so after all this came out, the parole board recommended that he be released early. That wasn't enough, though. The governor pardoned him. That was showboating, in my opinion. I mean, Cobb *did* kill the guy, and to hit him thirty-seven times . . . Anyway, that's the story."

I had taken it all in, listening carefully, and now I said, "It's not a pretty story, but there's not a dad-gummed thing in it to make you think that Mr. Cobb might've killed Steven Kelley."

"You mean other than the fact that Kelley had a thing for teenage girls, like your nieces?"

And some of his students, I thought. I didn't know if Farraday was aware of that yet.

I didn't have to wonder about it for long, though, because the lieutenant went on, "He had a reputation on the campus where he taught, too. Supposedly he liked some of his female students a little too much." He paused, then asked, "You know who goes to the same college where Kelley taught?"

I had to shake my head. A bad feeling started to dog me.

"Wilson Cobb's granddaughter," Farraday said.

"Oh, now, come on!" I said. I couldn't hold in the reaction. "You really think that Kelley might've made a pass at Mr. Cobb's granddaughter, so Mr. Cobb got the job of driving the bus out here for my tour group so he could murder him? That doesn't make any sense. Anyway, he drove the bus back to Atlanta! Surely you can check with the bus company and find out if it's where it's supposed to be."

Farraday nodded. "It is. I already checked. Cobb returned to the city on schedule and turned in the bus. I don't know what he did after that, though. He could have driven back out here, parked somewhere in the area, and walked onto the plantation grounds after dark. He could have hidden in the garden and waited for a chance to kill another actor who liked to take advantage of young women."

I supposed the logistics of it were possible, and there was that link of Kelley being an actor to consider, too.

While I was pondering that, Farraday continued, "Then after he killed Kelley, he went back to his car, waited a little while, and drove up here openly, making sure one of my men grabbed him so he could establish that he didn't arrive on the scene until well *after* Kelley was killed."

I didn't want to believe it for a second, but it made sense. Too much sense. Except for one thing.

"Why would Mr. Cobb wait in the garden for Kelley? How could he know that Kelley would even come out there during the dance?"

Farraday shrugged. "He probably didn't know. He was just lurking around the place, waiting for a chance, and Kelley handed it to him."

"Where did he get the knife?"

"It's just a regular kitchen knife. He could've brought it with him."

"Isn't it more likely it came from the kitchen here in the house?"

"We're looking into that," Farraday said. "Nothing's been established conclusively yet."

But I knew more now about the murder weapon

than I had before, which was a good thing. At least I thought so. The more I could find out about everything, the better. That would mean I was closer to figuring out who the killer was, so I could bring this disastrous tour to a close. Of course, it would have been just fine with me if Farraday had found the murderer and gotten a confession. That was his job, after all. I didn't care who solved the case, as long as it got solved. Soon.

"So you can see why I don't want to let Cobb go right now," Farraday went on. "I plan to question him and see if he can account for his whereabouts after he left here with the bus this morning." He grunted as he looked at his watch. "I mean yesterday morning. Midnight was a long time ago."

That was true. And it was going to be even longer because I had to go back upstairs and tell a sweet old man that he couldn't go home yet.

A sweet old man who, years earlier, had taken an iron pipe and bashed a man in the head with it . . . thirty-seven times.

CHAPTER 17

Mr. Cobb was sitting on a spindly legged antique chair under a big landscape painting as I approached him in the second-floor hallway. A deputy stood nearby, close enough to make it obvious that he was keeping an eye on Mr. Cobb, not so close as to be overbearing. When Mr. Cobb saw me coming, an eager, anxious expression appeared on his face.

"What about it?" he asked as he got to his feet. "Is that lieutenant friend of yours gonna let me go home, Miz Dickinson?"

I don't know where he'd gotten the crazy idea that Farraday was a friend of mine. I mean, only a few minutes earlier downstairs the lieutenant had made it plain that he still considered me a suspect, at least officially, whether he really believed I might have killed Steven Kelley or not.

But I let that go and said, "I'm sorry, Mr. Cobb. I'm afraid I didn't do a lick of good. Lieutenant Farraday says you have to stay here tonight."

Mr. Cobb shook his head and let out a little groan of despair. "Lord have mercy. That ain't right. It just ain't right."

"It'll be okay," I told him, trying to reassure him. "I'm sure everything will be cleared up by tomorrow—or later on today, however you want to look at it—and then we'll all be able to go home."

"You don't understand. I need to get back tonight. I can't wait until morning."

I couldn't help but frown. The desperate edge I heard in Mr. Cobb's voice and the frightened look on his face suddenly made me wonder if there might be something to the lieutenant's suspicions after all. Mr. Cobb wanted out of here mighty bad, there was no doubt about that.

"Whatever it is that's got you so worried, I'm sure it'll be all right. . . ." I let my voice trail away. I admit that I was fishing for information, rather than coming right out and asking him what was so important about him needing to leave the plantation.

He sank back onto the fragile-looking chair. "I got somebody waitin' for me at home," he said. "There's liable to be trouble if I don't get back there until sometime tomorrow."

"Oh. Well, maybe Lieutenant Farraday will let you use the phone long enough to call your wife and let her know that you won't be home tonight."

He shook his head. "It's not a wife I'm worried about. I'm not married."

"You could still call."

"Wouldn't do any good. She wouldn't understand."

"I'm sure if you explained about what's happened—"

"Wouldn't do any good, I tell you. She doesn't speak English."

"Maybe somebody here could translate for you," I suggested.

A grunt of humorless laughter came from him.

"Only if one o' these folks speaks Schnauzer."

Now I understood at last. "You have a dog!"

"That's right. Sweet little miniature Schnauzer named Betsy Blue. I need to be there to feed her and take her for her walks. If I'm not . . ." He shook his head. "Well, it's not gonna be pretty, that's all I can say. And if she makes a big mess in the apartment, the landlord's liable to kick me out or tell me I got to get rid o' Betsy if I want to stay there."

I saw his problem, but I didn't have any sort of solution to offer him. After listening to the story Lieutenant Farraday had told me, I knew the lieutenant wasn't going to let Mr. Cobb leave the plantation because of a dog. Like the rest of us, Cobb was stuck here until Farraday found the murderer.

"I'm sorry, Mr. Cobb. I'm afraid you're just gonna have to hope for the best. Maybe you'll get home before Betsy causes any problems."

"I sure hope so. Don't have a family. That dog's about all I got."

"That's not true. You have a granddaughter."

Mr. Cobb had been gazing gloomily at the floor. When I said that, though, his head came up in a sharp movement, and his eyes narrowed as he stared at me.

"How do you know I have a granddaughter?" he asked.

I realized my mistake. "You must have mentioned her sometime—"

"I didn't. It's true I have a son and a daughter-in-law and a granddaughter, but I wouldn't have said anything about them because they don't have anything to do with me." His face hardened. "You found out some way about what happened, all those years ago, didn't you?"

I didn't see any way out of admitting it. "The lieutenant told me some things when I went to talk to him, to see if he'd let you go home."

"And I'm guessin'" he told you the real reason he said no. He figures since I killed once, I must've done it again."

I didn't say anything. I knew that Farraday wouldn't want me to share his theory about how Mr. Cobb could have committed the murder and then tried to make it look as if he didn't arrive at the plantation until after Steven Kelley's death.

"That son of a bitch had it comin'. Pardon my French, ma'am, but he surely did."

"You mean Steven Kelley?"

"I mean Jerome Chantry."

"The fella you . . ." I couldn't bring myself to say it.

Mr. Cobb didn't have that problem. "Yeah, the fella I hit with that pipe. He had it comin'. The way he was fightin' with Shondra, he would've hurt her bad for sure, maybe even killed her, if I hadn't heard the commotion and stopped him."

"Shondra was the girl who lived in your apartment building?" Lieutenant Farraday hadn't mentioned the names of either the rapist or the victim.

Mr. Cobb nodded. "That's right. And Chantry was the piece o' scum who attacked her and a dozen other girls. Maybe more that never came forward. I'm a Christian, Miz Dickinson, and I believe in forgiveness . . . but Jerome Chantry didn't deserve to be forgiven. He deserved just what he got."

"All thirty-seven times?"

He grimaced, and I regretted saying it. But the words were already out. He nodded and said, "Maybe I got a mite carried away. But let me tell you, he was a big, strong man. I was a lot younger then, but I was older than he was, and not as big. I was afraid he'd get back up again, after I knocked him down. I was afraid he'd get back up and hurt me, and then he'd go after Shondra again, and so while I could, I kept hittin' him. I never knew it was no thirty-seven times. I didn't keep count. I just kept hittin' him until I was sure he wasn't gonna get back up and hurt anybody else. I didn't even think about the fact that he was dead."

Chantry had probably been dead for most of those thirty-seven wallops with the iron pipe, I thought. But Mr. Cobb hadn't known that. And I could understand the fear he must have felt. He had performed a heroic action by going to the girl's rescue, but that didn't mean he wasn't scared out of his wits at the same time.

"I told folks at the trial I didn't mean to kill him," Mr. Cobb went on. "If I'd stopped to think, I would've known what hitting him like that was gonna do . . . but I didn't stop to think. I'll bet most folks wouldn't at a time like that."

He was probably right. I don't know what I would have done if I'd found myself in the same situation. I'd like to think I'd be clear-headed enough not to lose control, but deep down, I don't *know* that. I don't reckon anybody can be really sure what they'll do until the time comes, if it ever does.

Mr. Cobb heaved a sigh. "But that didn't mean

anything to the folks on the jury. Not enough to keep 'em from convictin' me, anyway. Didn't make my boy feel any better about havin' a jailbird for a father, either. He turned his back on me, wouldn't even come see me while I was in prison. My wife was dead by then, so didn't anybody come to see me. My son got married while I was behind bars. I didn't get to go to the wedding, not that I would've been invited anyway. And my first and only grandchild was born before I got out, too, and I missed that."

"You must've seen her since then."

He shrugged. "A few times when she was little. But even though I'd been paroled and then pardoned, my son still didn't want anything to do with me and didn't want me around his family. He was still ashamed o' me. Reckon he still is, since he never calls or comes around and won't return my calls."

"Why, dad gummit, he should've been proud of you! You saved that girl's life."

"Yeah, but all he saw was a jailbird who beat a man to death. Never could get that outta his head. Reckon he still can't, to this day. I haven't seen or talked to any of them in more'n ten years, Miz Dickinson. So you can see why I said the only family I got is that sweet little dog o' mine. She doesn't judge me by the past. Not ever."

My heart went out to him. His story was tragic. And more than that, it shot holes in Lieutenant Farraday's theory. If Mr. Cobb hadn't had any contact with his granddaughter in over a decade, then it didn't matter if she went to the same college where Steven Kelley had taught. It didn't matter if Kelley had made advances toward her or if she had just heard rumors about him. Either way, she couldn't have told her grandfather about it.

At least, according to Mr. Cobb's story . . . which Lieutenant Farraday would probably say was uncorroborated, since all anybody had to go on at the moment was what Mr. Cobb said. It was just his word.

That was good enough for me, I decided, but I understood that it wouldn't be for the law. And even if I went back downstairs and talked to Farraday again, told him everything that Mr. Cobb had just told me, it wouldn't accomplish anything. Farraday would just shake his head and, as unbending as ever, refuse to let Mr. Cobb leave the plantation.

"I'm sorry," I told him. "If I could fix things, I sure would, Mr. Cobb, but I don't know of anything else I can do, except hope that things work out for you and Betsy Blue."

He smiled faintly. "I appreciate that." Resting his hands on his knees, he got ready to push himself to his feet. "Reckon I'd better figure out where I'm gonna stay tonight, if I can't go home."

"I've got that worked out already," I said. "You can double up with Luke. I asked him about it earlier, and he said that would be fine."

Mr. Cobb nodded. "He seems like a decent young fella. I suppose that would be all right."

I took his arm and helped him to his feet. "I'll show you your room."

We walked down the hall, followed by the deputy, until we reached the door of the room where Luke was staying. I rapped on the door, and when it swung open Luke smiled out at us. He was already in his pajamas.

"Howdy, Mr. Cobb," he said with a welcoming smile. "Come on in."

"Thanks, son. I appreciate you bein' willin' to put up with an old reprobate like me."

"Oh, it's nothing," Luke assured him. "I put up with Miz D all the time, and I don't reckon you could possibly be any crankier than . . ." He saw me frowning at him. "I mean, uh, nicer than . . . uh . . ."

"Oh, give it up, Luke," I said. "Nobody expects a fella to get along that well with his mother-in-law, anyway."

"But I do," he protested. "I think you're great, Miz D. You know that. But you can be a little . . . I mean, what's that old sayin' about sufferin' fools gladly? Not doing it, I mean. Not suffering. Fools. Gladly."

"Good night, Luke," I said, reaching for the door to pull it closed. "Get some rest. You're babblin'."

I shut the door.

Quiet had pretty much descended on the plantation by now. Folks were in their rooms, guests from the tour as well as the actors who'd been forced to stay here. I had a feeling that Farraday and his men would be up all night, trying to find the evidence they needed to nail a killer, but everybody else, at least, could get some sleep.

Except for maybe the killer. As I walked back toward the room I'd be sharing with Augusta and Amelia, I wondered if the person who had murdered Steven Kelley was lying in bed wide awake, perhaps even tossing and turning restlessly as he or she remembered what it had felt like to drive the blade of that knife through flesh, deep into

Kelley's chest. Were they recalling the hot spurt of blood, the gasp of pain that must have come from Kelley's lips, the look of shock and agony in his eyes?

Or did the killer think that Kelley had deserved it, and now whomever it was slept the sleep of the just?

I wondered if Mr. Cobb had ever lost any sleep over the death of Jerome Chantry. I would have been willing to bet that he had, even though he'd said that Chantry had it coming. He didn't strike me as the sort of man who could take a human life and never have it prey on him. That was just one more reason I was convinced Mr. Cobb hadn't killed Steven Kelley.

But it wouldn't be enough for Lieutenant Farraday. Nothing would except evidence. Concrete proof.

And so far there wasn't any of that, just theories and speculation about Mr. Cobb, Luke, Amelia and Augusta, me, and who knew who else? As far as the lieutenant was concerned, this plantation was just full of suspects.

Maybe things would all be clearer in the morning, I told myself. It seemed to be worth hoping for, anyway.

CHAPTER 18

I thought maybe Augusta and Amelia would be asleep by the time I got back to the room I was now sharing with them, but I should have known better. They were teenagers, which meant it was difficult for them to go to sleep until the wee hours of the morning and well-nigh impossible to rouse them before noon. So they were still wide awake, sitting up in the queen-size bed they'd be sharing tonight.

"What happened with Mr. Cobb?" Augusta asked.

"He's such a sweet old man," Amelia said. "I really like him."

I wondered for a second if she would feel the same way about Mr. Cobb if she knew what he had done a quarter century earlier. I wasn't going to tell her. It wasn't any of her business, and I felt bad enough already that I had wound up prying into his tragic background.

"Lieutenant Farraday isn't going to let him go

home," I told the girls. "He says Mr. Cobb has to stay here tonight like the rest of us."

"That's crazy," Augusta said. "He can't think Mr. Cobb had anything to do with the murder."

"He suspected Aunt Delilah and Luke, remember?" Amelia reminded her sister. "Not to mention you and me."

"He didn't really think we killed that guy."

"I'm not so sure about that."

"I'd like to know when we could have. We were dancing all evening, remember? My feet even hurt a little."

"Mine, too."

"But those Tarleton twins were kinda cute. If *they* had asked us to go out into the garden—"

Amelia shushed her sister before Augusta could say anything else. I took the opportunity to get a word in edgewise.

"Girls, you'd better go ahead and try to get some sleep. I don't know when we'll be going home."

"They'll let us go tomorrow," Augusta said, as if there was no doubt in her mind. "They have to. I only brought enough clothes to stay one night. If we can't go home I'd have to wear the same outfit more than once."

I wanted to say *Heaven forbid*, but I managed not to. I sure as heck wouldn't want to go back and be a teenager again, but there are times when I wouldn't mind having some of the simple concerns of youth instead of the problems of adulthood. Not that it's easy being a kid these days. When you come right down to it, it probably never was.

I went into the bathroom and got into the pair of pajamas I'd brought along, and by the time I came back out the girls had at least settled down and were trying to sleep. I climbed into the other bed and turned off the lamp. As I lay back I was aware of just how tired I was.

But when my head hit the pillow, my eyes were still wide open and my brain was racing a mile a minute.

I suppose it was too much to expect that after everything that had happened, I would drop off to sleep right away. My mind started replaying the entire tour, starting at the *Gone With the Wind* Movie Museum the day before. The trouble between Elliott Riley and Gerhard Mueller had indeed been a bad omen, although I never would have dreamed that it would be followed by murder. Maybe another fight between those two troublemakers, but not a fatal stabbing.

Thinking about Riley made me wonder again about all the things that had been stolen during the tour, including my cell phone. Since searching everyone in the ballroom hadn't turned up any of the missing items, it seemed logical that the thief had hidden them somewhere. That was the only answer that made sense. If Riley was the thief, as Mueller insisted, then where could he have hidden all the things he had lifted?

In the garden, of course.

That had to be the answer. I'd been on the verge of figuring that out earlier, I realized now, but then I'd gotten distracted by some other uproar. There had been plenty of distractions during the evening. But Riley's answer about why he had been in the garden hadn't satisfied me. It made a lot more sense that he had gone out there to stash his loot. If not for Kelley's murder, Riley could have returned to the garden later, after everyone had settled down for the night, and retrieved the stolen items. He could have brought them back to his room, hidden them in his bags, and then walked out the next day with no one being the wiser. The more I thought about it, the more I was convinced that the theory was plausible.

More than plausible. Heck, I was convinced I was right.

The only thing wrong with Riley's plan was that he had practically tripped over Steven Kelley's body. Once that happened, all bets were off. The plantation was crawling with sheriff's deputies, and he couldn't get back to the garden to get his loot. The smart thing would be to write off the loss of his ill-gotten gains, keep a low profile, and get the heck out of here so he could move on to his next job. I didn't know if Riley was smart enough to do that, but I suspected that self-preservation was more important to him than anything else, even his loot.

Still, I wondered if I should share my ideas with Farraday. He could have his deputies conduct a thorough search of the garden, and if the stolen items were found, I would know I was right about Riley's plan.

Of course, it was still just an assumption that Riley was the thief. But he'd been out there in the garden for no good reason. Maybe it was time the lieutenant questioned him some more about that.

And maybe, I thought suddenly, maybe Riley had been hiding the loot when Steven Kelley discovered him at his dirty work. Then Riley could have reacted without thinking and plunged that knife into Kelley's chest.

What was Riley doing with a kitchen knife, though?

I didn't have an answer for that question, and as I thought about it, my pulse, which had started to race, slowed down again. For a second there I'd had visions of being able to present Lieutenant Farraday with the solution to the whole thing, so that the rest of us could get the heck out of here.

Still, I didn't think it would hurt to tell Farraday my idea about the thief hiding the stuff in the garden, so I slipped out of bed and stood up in the darkened room. By now exhaustion had caught up with Augusta and Amelia. Two sets of soft snores came from the other bed. I felt around on mine and found the robe I had tossed on the foot of it. I put it on, tied the belt around my waist, and went to the door, figuring that I would step out into the hall and tell one of the deputies standing guard there that I wanted to talk to the lieutenant.

When I opened the door I saw that the lights in the hallway had been dimmed. They were set in wall sconces and most of the bulbs were turned off. The only lights burning were at the ends of the hall and the landing.

And there wasn't a deputy in sight.

That surprised me. I turned my head back and forth, checking in both directions. The corridor was empty of deputies and everybody else. All the doors were closed, and everything was quiet.

Farraday didn't have unlimited manpower, I wondered if he had pulled the deputies who had been up here back downstairs to help search the garden or some other chore. Farraday wanted everybody to stay in the house, but he could post a few men outside to make sure that nobody left. People were tired and scared and angry, and it made sense that once they were settled down, they would stay in their rooms until morning . . . especially if they *thought* that a deputy might be right outside their door.

The lack of guards in the hall surprised me, but it didn't really change anything. I still wanted to talk to Farraday again, and I figured he was probably still down in the ballroom. I started to open the door wider so that I could step out into the hall.

That was when another door, somewhere down the hall, opened with a faint click. As soon as I heard it I froze for a second, then eased my door up so that it was almost closed.

I left enough of a gap that I could put my eye to it and have a narrow view of the hallway. I wasn't sure I could see what was happening from this angle, but I intended to try.

Don't ask me why I reacted like that. I guess by now I was so caught up in the whole thing that the natural-born snoop in me was coming out more than ever before. But if somebody else was about to slip out into the hall, I wanted to see who it was.

Sure enough, I caught a glimpse in the dim light of a woman leaving one of the rooms and slipping along the corridor. She wore a long gray T-shirt that came down over the tops of her thighs, and apparently not much else. Blond hair fell around her shoulders and down her back. It took a moment for me to recognize Lindsey Hoffman without her Southern belle outfit and with her hair loose and down instead of swept up and pinned in an elaborate arrangement of curls.

Lindsey must have peeked out and discovered that there were no deputies in the hall, just as I had. I had a suspicion why she had taken this opportunity to sneak out of her room, but I wasn't sure. Since she had her back turned toward me, I risked opening the door of my room a little more and leaning out to watch her as she moved stealthily along the corridor.

She went to a room near the other end and tapped on the door, so lightly that even though I could see what she was doing, I couldn't hear her knuckles striking against the panel. The door opened a moment later. From where I was, I couldn't see who was inside, and I was afraid I wouldn't be able to tell for sure whose room Lindsey was visiting, even though I had a pretty good idea.

A second later, though, my hunch was confirmed as Perry Newton came out into the hall just enough for me to recognize him. He wasn't dressed as Ashley Wilkes anymore, of course, any more than Lindsey was wearing her costume. He was in a T-shirt and a pair of boxers. Most of the actors hadn't come prepared to spend the night, so they had to sleep in their underwear or whatever else they could scrounge.

Perry also wore a big grin on his face as he reached for Lindsey and took her into his arms. As they kissed, Perry tugged up the hem of Lindsey's T-shirt in the back and revealed that I'd been wrong.

She wasn't wearing *anything* under it.

Feeling my face start to get warm, I looked away and was glad when Perry pulled Lindsey on into his room and closed the door behind them. Obviously he wasn't sharing the room with anybody. I couldn't remember if he was supposed to be doubling up with one of the other actors or not, but I supposed he wasn't—because he was doubling up with Lindsey now, so to speak.

I sighed to myself and shook my head. For a second there, as I'd seen the door of the other room opening, I had thought that I might witness the murderer skulking out to kill again, like in one of those movies where there's an old dark house and secret passages and hidden dumbwaiters and stuff like that.

Instead it was just a couple of horny college kids taking advantage of the opportunity to get together. So much for sinister.

Augusta and Amelia were still sleeping soundly, so I returned to my original plan. I'd go downstairs, find Lieutenant Farraday, and tell him to look in the garden for the stolen loot, just in case he hadn't already thought of that himself. Now that some of my initial enthusiasm had had a chance to wear off, I wondered if I was wasting my time. Farraday wasn't an idiot. Surely he had realized by now that the missing items might be hidden in the garden. Maybe what I ought to do, I told myself, was go back to bed and try to get some sleep.

At the moment, though, I wasn't sure I'd ever sleep again. And I can be stubborn, too, as anybody who knows me very well will tell you.

So I stepped into the hall, closed the door quietly behind me, and started toward the staircase.

I hadn't yet reached it when somebody came up behind me, grabbed my shoulder with one hand, and reached around me to clamp the other hand over my mouth.

CHAPTER 19

Okay, so I've exaggerated a little bit. He didn't exactly grab my shoulder. But he definitely put his hand on it to stop me. And the hand over my mouth was too gentle and careful to say that it clamped. My nerves were stretched so tight, though, that both of those things felt like that, and I would have let out a holler they could have heard back in Atlanta if I *hadn't* had a hand over my mouth. I jerked free and whirled around, ready to fight.

"Don't, Delilah," Will Burke said in an urgent whisper. "It's just me."

My heart was hammering like John Henry on steroids. I stared at Will and opened and closed my mouth without saying anything several times until I realized that I probably looked like a fish. With an effort, I got my breathing under control and managed to stop staring bug-eyed at him. That whole fight-or-flight thing was right; when I spun around I'd been ready to either start throwing punches or run for my life.

When I was able to talk again I leaned closer to him and hissed, "What in the Sam Hill are you doin' out here?"

Will smiled, which made me want to smack him all over again. "I could ask you the same question. We're fellow skulkers."

"Yeah, well, I was about to go talk to Lieutenant Farraday."

"What happened to the deputies?"

"I figure he's got them all downstairs, searching for clues. Telling us that they were going to stand guard up here all night was just a bluff so folks would stay put in their rooms."

He thought it over and then nodded, evidently agreeing with my logic. "Yeah, that's probably right." He paused. "Or maybe the lieutenant's trying to lure the killer back out into the open."

I frowned. "Are you sayin'—"

"No, of course not. I don't think you're the killer. I'm just not sure it's a good idea for either of us to be out wandering around in the hall, under the circumstances."

"You haven't told me yet what you're doing here," I pointed out.

He chuckled. "I don't suppose you'd believe me if I told you I was looking for a midnight snack."

The look I gave him was all the answer he needed.

"This is an old house," Will whispered. "No matter how quiet you try to be, the floor makes some noises now and then. I thought I heard someone go by in the hall, and something about it seemed more . . . stealthy, I guess you'd say . . . than if it was just one of the deputies. So I decided to take a look, and sure enough, I saw that red hair of yours."

"I didn't hear you come out of your room."

He shrugged. "I'm light on my feet."

I didn't know whether to believe him or not, but one of the nearby doors stood open, which seemed to back up his story. I supposed I was willing to accept it.

Like me, Will was wearing pajamas and a robe. His weren't silk and didn't have any lace around the collar, of course, but still, the nightclothes and the fact that we were standing out in the hall whispering in the middle of the night gave the whole situation a definite feeling of intimacy. I liked that in a way—it had been a while since I'd had any sort of middle-of-the-night conversation with a man—but it made me nervous, too. I had met Will Burke less than twelve hours earlier; we sure as heck shouldn't have been to the pajama buddies stage yet.

"Well, now that you know what's going on, you can go back to bed," I told him, "and I'll go find the lieutenant."

"I'll come with you," Will suggested.

"There's no need for that."

"Don't forget there was a murder here tonight. Even with all the cops nearby, I'd feel better if you weren't walking around by yourself."

"I appreciate the concern, but I don't need you to protect me. I can take care of myself just fine."

"I'm sure you can, but there's such a thing as being too stubbornly independent."

My eyes widened again, but with anger this time,

not surprise and fear. "Are you callin' me stubborn?" I demanded.

"Well . . . aren't you?"

I jabbed a finger at him. "Yeah, but that's not the point. You and I barely know each other. But like all the rest of you Southern men, you figure that I'm just a fragile little female who needs lookin' after by some big strong redneck—"

"I'm not your ex-husband, Delilah," he broke in. "I don't know if that's the way he treated you or not, but either way, I'm not him."

I stood there taking deep breaths, trying to bring my anger under control. "How'd you know I was divorced?" I asked after a moment. "I don't recall mentioning that."

"You didn't. But you said that Luke is your son-in-law, which means you have a grown daughter. You don't wear a wedding ring, which you probably still would if you were widowed. I can see the untanned line on your finger where one used to be, though. It was just a guess that you were divorced, but I thought it was a pretty good one."

"Who the heck are you, Sherlock Holmes?"

A smile lurked around the corners of his mouth again. "I'm right, though, aren't I?"

"Yeah, yeah, but for your information, Dan didn't treat me the way I was talkin' about. Not often, anyway, even though he might've liked to."

"I can understand why he wouldn't, with your temper. That red hair—"

I lifted a finger again. "Don't you say it. Just don't you say it."

Will held up both hands, palms out in surrender. "Sorry. I'll make a note of that for future reference. Don't equate hair color with temper."

"I reckon you *are* smart enough to be a professor. Maybe."

"But I still think I ought to go with you. Just in case."

With a sigh, I gave up. I didn't want to stand around in the hall arguing with him all night, not when Elliot Riley was looking better and better to me as the killer, especially if I could figure out why he'd had that knife with him.

Or maybe Kelley had had the knife, and the murderer had taken it away from him. . . .

That would bear some thinking about, too. I whispered to Will, "All right, if you're gonna insist, then come on."

I halfway expected either Lieutenant Farraday or one of the deputies to show up anytime and shoo us back into our rooms, but we reached the stairs without running into anybody. Looking down the grand, curving staircase with its elaborately carved banister and the portraits of previous generations of Ralstons on the wall, I didn't see anybody.

Will and I were about to start down when I heard the sound of angry voices somewhere above us. I couldn't make out the words, but I thought there were two voices and that they belonged to a man and a woman.

Will must have heard them, too, and realized why I stopped short at the top of the stairs, because he put his mouth close to my ear and asked, "Who's that?"

I shook my head to indicate that I didn't know.

"Should we find out?"

He was asking if I thought we should play detective. I had already been leaning in that direction because I wanted this mess cleared up before it did too much damage to my fledgling business. And, to be honest, because I was curious. Like I said, I guess I'm just a natural-born snoop. Maybe all mothers are, to a certain extent. When our kids reach a certain age, they make us work like detectives to find out what's going on in their lives, and some of us never get out of the habit, I suppose.

So I hesitated only a moment before I nodded in response to Will's question and inclined my head toward the stairs that led up instead of down.

As we climbed them, staying close to the wall so that the steps were less likely to squeak under our weight, I felt nervousness tingling along my veins. I didn't know what we'd find up there on the third floor. Some of the tour guests were staying there, and the Ralston family quarters were on that floor, too. And just because there were no deputies in the hall on the second floor, it didn't mean there wouldn't be any upstairs. If Will and I kept this up, we ran the risk of getting into trouble with Lieutenant Farraday.

Of course, the man already considered me a murder suspect, and he had the whole lot of us under house arrest, pretty much, so how much more trouble could I get into, I asked myself.

As we followed the curving staircase and neared the third-floor landing, the voices became more distinct. "I tell you, it's none of your business," I heard a woman say. Her voice was just familiar enough so that I knew I'd heard it before, but I couldn't place whom it belonged to.

That wasn't the case with the voice that replied, "And I tell you, it most certainly *is* my business," I would have known those plummy, slightly British tones anywhere.

Recognizing Edmond Ralston's voice tipped me off that the other one belonged to his daughter Janice. I motioned for Will to stay where he was and went up another step, craning my neck to try to see down the third-floor corridor.

Ralston's quarters were on the left at the far end of the hall; his daughter's were across the hall. Both of them had spacious suites. I had discovered that earlier when I was working with Ralston and Farraday, figuring out the accommodations. Ralston had said nothing about a wife and I hadn't seen any evidence of one, so I assumed he was either divorced or a widower. And Janice was either an only child or the only one still living here on the plantation, because there were no siblings around.

The hall was empty except for Ralston, who stood in front of the door to his daughter's suite. Janice faced him in the open doorway, with one hand on the edge of the door itself. She had changed into a nightgown, but Ralston still wore the costume he'd had on earlier, during the ball.

Even at this distance, I could tell that Janice's eyes were red and puffy, like she'd been crying. And I could hear the strain in her voice as she told her father, "Just go away and leave me alone."

"It's just that I hate to see you suffering so over that . . . that disreputable . . . weasel!"

Janice took a step toward him. "Don't call him that! You have no right to judge him. You don't know what he was really like."

"I know he was married," Ralston said coldly. "And so do you."

I became aware that Will Burke had edged up beside me, even though I had told him to stay back. That came as no surprise, since I didn't really have the right to boss him around. He gave me a look of surprise as we both digested Ralston's comment.

"As far as I'm concerned, you're well rid of him," Ralston went on. "Whoever killed that bastard did you a favor, my dear."

Janice's hand flashed up and cracked across her father's face in an angry slap. Ralston didn't hesitate. He slapped her. Janice gasped in pain and shock and put a hand to her face as she took a step backward.

Ralston reached out to her. "Janice, I'm sorry. I didn't mean to do that. It was just a reaction—"

She closed the door in his face, hard enough so that it was just short of a slam. Ralston stood there staring at the door for a long moment, then shook his head heavily and turned away toward his own rooms across the hallway.

Will and I both sunk down quickly, sitting on the steps, as Ralston started to turn. It would have been pretty embarrassing if he had caught us spying on him—which was exactly what we'd been doing, of course. We sat there listening to his footsteps, and I don't know about Will but I was sure hoping that Ralston wouldn't come this way and start down the stairs. If he did, there was no place for us to hide.

He went into his suite instead, closing the door behind him. I breathed a sigh of relief and relaxed slightly. As I did, I became aware of how closely Will and I were huddled together on the step. My leg was pressed against his. I didn't figure I could move it without being too obvious about what I was doing, so I left it where it was for the time being.

"Kelley was carryin' on with Janice Ralston,

too," I whispered. "Were there any women on this plantation he *wasn't* foolin' around with?"

"I don't know, but from the sound of it, Mr. Ralston wasn't happy about the situation."

"Did you know about Kelley and Janice?"

Will shook his head. "No. They must have been pretty discreet. And you saw Janice earlier, after the murder. She didn't act like somebody who was all broken up about Kelley's death." He grunted. "She's an even better actress than I thought she was, but she could only keep up the façade for so long. Once she was alone, it was too much for her."

"Her daddy knew about it, though, and he didn't like it."

Will looked intently at me. "What are you thinking, Delilah?"

I said, "I'm just wonderin' how far Edmond Ralston would go to break up a romance between his teenage daughter and a married man with the habit of sleepin' with everything in a hoop skirt."

CHAPTER 20

Will continued looking at me with an intensity just short of a stare. After a moment he said, "Do you really think Ralston could have killed Steven Kelley?"

"He had the same opportunity as anybody else," I said. "The big crowd in the ballroom meant that anybody could have slipped in and out of the place with a good chance of not being noticed. And he would have known where to get that knife, too, since he lives here."

"Anybody could have gotten hold of that knife. I just work here, and I know where the kitchen is and where the knives are kept."

"Then maybe you killed Kelley."

I don't know why I said it. Sheer contrariness, maybe. I know I didn't mean it.

And yet when the words came out of my mouth, I felt a chill go through me. Despite the comfortable feeling between us that had been there right from the start, I didn't really know Will Burke. I didn't know what he was capable of doing. Maybe he was involved with some woman at the college, and Kelley had taken her away from him, just as Kelley had stolen Luke's girlfriend back in high school. Maybe Will wanted vengeance on Kelley for some other reason. As Will had just pointed out, he would have been able to get his hands on the murder weapon. I didn't know about motive, but that gave him means and opportunity.

Just like dozens of other folks, I reminded myself. Still, it was a little creepy to think that I was sitting on a dimly lit staircase with a man who was, at least within the realm of possibility, a murder suspect.

He might have been thinking the same thing about me, I reminded myself. And because of Kelley's improper advances toward my nieces, I had a motive, even if it wasn't a very strong one. So I was three-for-three on the whole means, motive, and opportunity business.

"I didn't kill him," Will said. "I'll admit, I didn't really like the guy, but I didn't kill him."

"I believe you," I said, and I did. "I didn't kill him, either."

"And I believe you. Now that we've got that established, what do we do?"

"We were going to talk to Lieutenant Farraday. I suppose we still can."

"Do we tell him about Ralston and Janice?"

I thought about that. I didn't want to cast any suspicion on innocent people . . . but I was beginning to doubt that anybody in this plantation house was really innocent. Put any group of people together, and chances are that quite a few of them will have secrets they don't want anybody else to know about. I knew that from working with tour groups in the past. Dig under the surface of anybody's life and you're liable to expose things that aren't meant for the light of day. Most of them don't have anything to do with murder, of course, but folks will go to surprising lengths sometimes to protect their privacy and that of their loved ones.

"I reckon we ought to," I said to Will. "The more information Farraday has, the better the chance that he'll be able to solve this murder."

"I was under the impression that *you* wanted to solve it."

"What gives you *that* idea?"

He smiled. "Oh, just the fact that we're sneaking around in the middle of the night and eavesdropping on other people's conversations to see if we can uncover some more motives and suspects. We've just found two more."

"Two?" I repeated. "Janice is just a kid. I could see her father killing Kelley to protect her from him, but why would she want to stab him?"

"Your daughter was a teenager once, and your nieces are now. They're not always capable of making rational decisions, especially where passion is concerned. Look at Romeo and Juliet. They didn't think things through."

He had a point there.

"Just because Janice plays Melanie doesn't mean that she's as sweet as Melanie was in the book," Will went on. "She has a temper. I've seen it. And I think she would have loved to take Rhett away from Scarlett."

"You're talking about Kelley and Maura."

Will nodded. "If Janice was having an affair with Kelley, she might have thought that sooner or later he'd leave his wife for her. Maybe they met in the garden tonight and Janice gave him an ultimatum. Kelley chose his wife and told Janice that he wasn't going to leave Maura." Will shrugged. "It holds together."

It did. It held together as well as any of the other theories I'd come up with. I wanted to groan in frustration but held it back. One thing you can say about a sleazy character like Steven Kelley, there was no shortage of people who might want to see him dead—and would be willing to stick a knife in his chest to bring that about.

"All right," I said, getting ready to rise to my feet. "Let's go find Lieutenant Farraday."

Will stood first and put a hand on my arm to help me up. A part of me wanted to pull away from him and tell him I didn't need any help. But a part of me enjoyed it, too, so I didn't say anything.

"We're going to get in trouble for not staying in our rooms, you know," Will said as we started down the staircase.

"What's he gonna do? Lock us up? Consider us murder suspects? I'm not scared of the lieutenant."

Farraday did make me a little nervous, though, with his bulldog determination. If I really was a criminal, I sure wouldn't want him on my trail. He might not be flashy about it, but he'd stick with it for however long it took, I sensed.

We were just about down to the second-floor landing again when I heard a door open and then close. Or one door open and another one close, it was impossible to make that distinction. Will heard the sounds, too, and put out a hand to stop me. He leaned toward me and whispered, "It didn't take people long to discover that there aren't any deputies up here after all, did it?"

Another door opened and closed. The noises were faint but audible—and unmistakable.

"This is startin' to remind me of one of those Bugs Bunny cartoons," I said, "where Bugs is being chased by Elmer Fudd or Yosemite Sam and they run in and out of all those different doors."

Will grinned at me. "You must've watched a lot of cartoons on TV when you were growing up, too."

"Everybody our age did."

"There was a Bugs Bunny cartoon that was a parody of *Gone With the Wind*, you know, called *Southern Fried Rabbit*. I referenced it in a paper I wrote on Mitchell's influence on popular culture. Bugs was Scarlett O'Hara."

"I remember it. I can still see Bugs in that long, curly wig. . . ." I started to laugh and had to hold my hand over my mouth to keep the sound in. I had been so long without sleep and had been under such a strain that I was getting giddy. Will was grinning, too, and that didn't help. Here we were faced with a serious, even deadly situation, and we were about to start giggling like a couple of eight-year-olds. I swatted Will lightly on the shoulder and told him, "Settle down now. We've got work to do."

"Yes, ma'am," he said, but that grin was still lurking around the corners of his mouth. "Things seem to have quieted down again. Do we try to make it to the first floor and find the lieutenant?"

"Yeah. Come on."

We went down the stairs to the second-floor landing, where we paused and peered both ways along the corridor. Nobody was tiptoeing in or out of any of the rooms. I wondered if what we had heard were the sounds of more romantic rendezvous being carried out. Probably not among the tourists—although such things weren't unheard of in my business—but with all those college kids working here, it stood to reason that there would be plenty of "hooking up," as they call it. I had already seen evidence of that in Lindsey Hoffman's visit to Perry Newton's room.

Will was about to move on down the stairs when I touched his arm and whispered, "Wait a minute."

"What is it?"

I had noticed something that wasn't quite right. One of the doors about halfway down the hall to the left was ajar. It was only open a couple of inches, but that was enough to make it stand out from all the other doors. I cast my mind back over the arrangements I had helped Edmond Ralston and Lieutenant Farraday make earlier.

That was Elliott Riley's room, I realized. He was by himself in there, because I'd figured that nobody would want to share the room with him and had warned Ralston and Farraday about that.

The thought that Riley was out and about somewhere in the house, long after midnight like this when all the other folks were supposed to be asleep—but obviously weren't—made my pulse jump a little. What was he up to? I was willing to bet that it wasn't anything good.

But if he wasn't in his room, that also gave me the opportunity to look around some in there. No telling what I might find, I thought.

I pointed out the open door to Will. "That's Elliot Riley's room," I told him.

"Who's Elliott Riley?"

It was too long a story to tell him all the details, so I just hit the highlights running. "I want to take a look in there," I finished.

A dubious frown creased Will's forehead. "I'm not sure that's such a good idea. If you're really suspicious of this guy Riley, let's go find Lieutenant Farraday and tell him that Riley's not in his room. Then Farraday and his men can search it if they want to, and look for Riley, too."

What he said made sense, but I shook my head anyway. I was a little like a bloodhound with a scent, I guess, unwilling to give it up. "Riley's been nothin' but trouble for me since this tour started. I think he's the strongest suspect in Kelley's murder, and I want to have a look for myself."

"It's a mistake," Will sighed. "But I've already learned that it's also a mistake to argue with you. Let's go."

"You don't have to," I told him. "You can stay in the hall and keep an eye out for Riley coming back."

"You don't know that he's actually gone," Will pointed out, and I realized he was right. "I'm not letting you go in there by yourself."

I liked the way he didn't try to stop me but insisted on going with me, instead. For some reason I liked the idea that he'd started to think of us as a team.

We moved as quietly as we could along the hall toward the door of Riley's room. As we got closer I could see some light coming through the narrow gap. It wasn't very bright, and I figured the lamp on the bedside table was on. That was good, because it would give me enough light to take a look around without being bright enough to draw any unwanted attention.

My nerves started jumping around. Even though I wanted to do this, it wasn't the sort of thing that I did every day, or ever. I had never searched a murder suspect's room. But even more undesirable was the feeling of being suspected of murder myself. If I could turn up some proof that Riley had killed Steven Kelley, then my name would be cleared, along with those of Luke and Mr. Cobb and everybody else who'd been unlucky enough to be on this plantation tonight. Mr. Cobb could go back to Betsy Blue, and the rest of us could go home, too. I wouldn't even wait for morning. I'd head back to Atlanta just as soon as Lieutenant Farraday said it was all right for us to go.

Despite those feelings, I still had the urge to turn and run, rather than going in there, and I was glad that I had Will with me so that I wouldn't chicken out. I wasn't sure why, but it was important to me that he didn't think I was a coward.

We paused outside the door and looked back and forth along the hall, just to make sure that no one was coming. Then I took a deep breath and reached out to push the door open.

Will's hand on my arm stopped me before I could touch the panel or the knob. Grim lines had appeared on his face. He leaned forward, putting his nose close to the opening, and sniffed. When he turned to look at me, I knew something was really wrong.

Smell that, he mouthed at me. At least, I think that's what he said. I put my nose closer to the gap and took a sniff anyway.

The smell was faint and reminded me of something. A second later I realized what it was: fire-crackers, like the ones we had popped on the Fourth of July when I was a kid.

Nobody had been setting off firecrackers inside Elliott Riley's room, though, and there was something else that smelled like that.

Gunpowder.

"Oh, Lord," I whispered. My heart started its hammering in my chest again. I hadn't heard a shot and it seemed impossible that somebody could have fired a gun here in the house without making a big racket, but that smell was unmistakable, even for somebody like me who normally didn't have anything to do with guns. "We better find the lieutenant right now."

A determined look had appeared on Will's face. "I'm going to have a look," he said.

"Dang it! Not without me, you're not."

If he could be stubborn, so could I. He looked like he wanted to chase me off, but he didn't try. Instead he used his foot to push the door open enough so that we could see into the bedroom.

I felt a little sick as I saw a pair of pale, bare feet sticking out on the floor past the end of the bed. Whoever they belonged to lay beyond the bed. The hem of a pair of pajama pants came down around the ankles of those feet. I had a feeling I knew who they belonged to.

Elliott Riley hadn't snuck out of his room after all, I thought. He was still here.

Will shuffled forward. Even though every instinct in my body was telling me to turn and run, I was right beside him, clutching his arm. I knew that I was holding on to him tightly enough that I might be hurting him, but I couldn't seem to let him go. My fingers dug in even more when I saw the ugly red splatters on the lampshade and the wall behind the lamp.

We reached the foot of the bed and both leaned forward, trying to see what was on the other side of it. The covers were pulled back, the sheets were rumpled, and there was a dent in one of the pillows caused by someone's head. Riley had put on his pajamas, turned in for the night, and evidently gone to sleep, before something had woken him up and caused him to get out of bed.

He would never go back to bed, but he wouldn't ever wake up again, either. He lay on his back, arms limp at his sides, the fingers of his right hand still partially curled around the butt of a small revolver. His eyes were wide, bugged out, staring without seeing anything. Blood hadn't just splattered on the lampshade and the wall, it had pooled under Riley's head, too. I knew without seeing it— I didn't *want* to see it—that the back of his head was probably a real mess, and he didn't even have his toupee to help cover it because the rug was on a stand on the dresser across the room.

Elliott Riley had blown his brains out.

CHAPTER 21

Well, I pretty much had two choices right then. I could get the fantods at the sight of the dead man and run screaming from the room . . . or I could suck it up and stay where I was and try to figure this out.

I managed not to scream and run. It was a few moments, though, before I could move on to the figuring-it-out part. I had to stuff my heart back down my throat first and wait for the anvil chorus in my head to settle down.

Will brought me back to something resembling coherent thought by saying, "He killed himself. Put the barrel in his mouth and pulled the trigger. That's why we didn't hear a shot. It was muffled by . . . by . . ."

Will looked about as sick as I felt. I swallowed hard and said, "By his head. I reckon you're right. But why would he do it?"

Will shook his head. "I don't know. Guilt?"

"Over being a thief?" Even knowing Riley as little as I did, that didn't seem very likely to me.

"Over killing Steven Kelley. You said that as far as you're concerned, he was the leading suspect."

"Oh. Yeah." I was still too shocked by this discovery to be thinking straight.

"He went to bed, but he couldn't sleep." Will gestured toward the tangled bedding. "He couldn't forget how he stabbed Kelley, and it gnawed at him until he got up and . . . well, did away with himself."

I looked around the room. "In that case, wouldn't there be a note?" I didn't see any pieces of paper on the bed or the table or anywhere else.

Will shrugged. "Maybe, maybe not. People who commit suicide don't always leave notes. Most do, I think, but not all."

He was probably right about that. Everything that had happened had gotten me in the habit of looking for complications where there might not really be any. It was pretty obvious that the gun was in Riley's hand and that it had been in his mouth when it went off. That spelled suicide, plain as day.

And being a murderer was sure a good enough reason for somebody to kill themselves. I wouldn't have been able to live with it, if it had been me.

Besides, this was what I'd been hoping for all evening: a solution to the case. Something that would let me call an end to this unmitigated disaster of a tour and hope that there wouldn't be a bunch of lawsuits that would put me out of business. Something that would let us all go home.

"By the way," Will went on, and his voice sounded a little pained now, "you might, uh, let go of my arm if you could."

I realized I was still latched onto his arm, with

both hands now. I must have grabbed him with the other one when we found the body. I forced my fingers to straighten out and let go, but it wasn't easy.

"We'd better go find Lieutenant Farraday," I said as I turned toward the doorway.

"You won't have to." The voice was hard and angry. "I'm right here."

I gasped as I saw the lieutenant standing there, just outside Riley's room. I wondered how long he had been there and how much of the conversation between Will and I he had heard.

Not much, evidently, because he continued, "What are you two doing out of your room? What's going on here?" His eyes went to the bare feet sticking out into view at the foot of the bed. "And who's *that*?"

As Farraday stalked forward so that he could see the body, I said, "That's Elliott Riley. You must remember him from earlier."

"Of course I remember him," Farraday practically growled at me. "What's he doing dead?" He motioned Will and me back away from the body and hunkered next to Riley. He didn't touch the body, but his eyes roved intently over it, taking in everything there was to see. After a few moments, he grunted and said, "Suicide."

"That's what we thought, too," Will said.

"The medical examiner will make the official determination. But with that blood spatter"—he gestured toward the stain—"and with the gun in his hand like that, there's not much doubt." With a groan of middle-aged effort, Farraday straightened from his crouching position and then ushered us back around to the other side of the bed, away from the body. "You still haven't told me what you're doing out of your rooms."

"We were about to come lookin' for you," I said, "to tell you about Riley."

"What happened? Did you hear the gunshot? If you did, you should have called one of the deputies."

"No, we didn't hear the shot," Will said, "but speaking of that, what happened to all the deputies? I thought they were going to be up here on guard duty all night."

"I pulled them off to help with the search of the garden," Farraday explained, confirming the guess I'd made earlier. His tone was caustic as he added, "I didn't know people were going to disregard my orders and start wandering around the halls."

"Did you find anything in the garden?" I asked. "Like all the stuff that was stolen earlier in the evening?"

"As a matter of fact, yes. It was hidden in a tool shed that the gardeners use—Wait just a minute! You two are supposed to be answering the questions here, not me. If you didn't hear the shot that killed Riley, what are you doing in his room?"

I glanced at Will. With Riley dead, I wasn't sure there was any point in telling Farraday what we had learned about Janice Ralston having an affair with Steven Kelley, or about the way Janice's father had said that whoever killed Kelley had done Janice a favor. That didn't amount to anything now except an argument between father and daughter, because for the life of me I couldn't see any reason for Riley to kill himself unless he was the murderer.

"I still thought Riley must've stolen all that stuff," I said. "I was going to try to get him to admit it. Will just came with me so I wouldn't have to confront Riley by myself."

Farraday looked from me to Will and back again. It was impossible to miss the fact that we were wearing pajamas and robes. "Are you two . . ." He held a hand out flat in front of him and wobbled it back and forth. "Like that?"

"What?" Will said in a tone of disbelief, at the same time as I exclaimed, "No! Not at all."

Will glanced over at me, and I wondered fleetingly if he was offended by my emphatic denial—or if, being an English professor, he thought maybe I doth protest too much.

"Ms. Dickinson's right, Lieutenant," he said. "We just met this evening. But I was happy to help her out with Riley. This has been quite an ordeal for her, you know."

Farraday looked like he wasn't sure if he believed Will or not, but he didn't press the issue. Instead he said, "So the two of you came over here and . . . what? Knocked on Riley's door?"

I was about to lie and say that we had, when I realized that if I kept piling on the untruths, our story was going to get so complicated that I couldn't keep up with it. So I said, "No, when we got here, the door was already open a couple of inches."

Farraday frowned. "Really? What did you do then?"

"Pushed it open and looked in."

"You didn't knock, or call out to see if Riley was here?"

Again I told the truth. "I thought that if he wasn't here for some reason, I'd take a look around and see if I could find anything to prove that he stole all those things."

"Then we saw the feet on the other side of the bed and smelled gunpowder," Will said.

"You should have gone for help right then."

"Probably," I agreed, "but whatever had happened in here was already over and done with. We didn't figure it would hurt anything to take a quick look around." I had to swallow again. "It nearly made me sick to my stomach, but that's all. We didn't touch anything, Lieutenant. Riley is just like we found him, and so is everything else in the room."

Farraday looked at us for a long moment and then finally nodded. "I'll get the ME and the crime scene people back out here, but I don't think they're going to find anything that isn't pretty obvious already. Scanlon's fingerprints were on some of those things hidden in the shed, so we know he put them there."

"Scanlon?" I repeated. "Who's Scanlon?"

Farraday waved a hand toward the body on the other side of the bed. "Ernest Scanlon, aka Elliott Riley, aka Peter Carlin, aka Jason Wilbur . . . you get the idea. The real Elliott Riley died of pneumonia at the age of seven in South Bend, Indiana, in 1959."

"So this Riley stole his identity?" Will said.

Farraday nodded. "That's right. It took us a while to wade through all the aliases and match up this guy's fingerprints with Ernest Scanlon, who had a record as a pickpocket and petty thief and low-level drug dealer in California back in the seventies. Then he dropped out of sight, and nobody knew whether he'd been killed or what had happened to him. Now we know. He continued being a professional thief; he just got better at it and started stealing people's identities, too. But he never broke the habit of picking pockets, looks like."

"He was hiding the loot in that tool shed," I said, "when Kelley came across him. Riley went after him, caught up to him closer to the house, and stabbed him."

Farraday nodded. "That's the way it looks to me. You had pretty much the same idea all along, didn't you, Ms. Dickinson?"

"It occurred to me," I admitted.

"I guess you have a detective's instincts, then. Don't know how much good that'll do you in the travel business, but I guess it can't hurt."

I still wondered about the knife, but Farraday could figure that one out. Or not. I supposed that in a lot of crimes, a few unanswered questions remained.

What was important was that this ordeal was over, and now I could get started on the important job of minimizing the damage it was going to do to my reputation.

Farraday shooed us out of the room and came out into the corridor himself. He pulled the door up but didn't close it all the way, gripping the edge of the door instead of the knob. I guess he wanted to make sure it could be dusted for prints, or whatever they do these days to check for fingerprints.

Something occurred to me, and I risked annoying the detective by asking, "Why were you coming up here, Lieutenant? To question Riley about those things y'all found in the shed?"

Farraday nodded. "Yeah, once I got the report linking Riley to Ernest Scanlon and all those other phony IDs, I figured I might be able to break him down on the murder, too. Too bad it didn't work out that way."

"You clear the case either way, though," Will said.

"Not the way I like to," Farraday said.

"Can we get out of here now?" I asked.

"Soon. When we get everything nailed down."

That wasn't the answer I'd been hoping to hear.

"If the investigation is over, there's no real reason to keep us here, is there?"

"The investigation isn't over," Farraday said. "I have to get the medical examiner and the crime scene people back out here. There's still work to be done before we can close everything out. Anyway, since most of the people here are in bed asleep, except the ones out wandering in the hallways"—he gave us a hard look as he said that—"we might as well not disturb them. Besides, you can't get all your clients back to Atlanta until morning anyway, because you'll have to get a bus out here to transport them."

I tried not to wince as I realized that he was right. Mr. Cobb was going to have to return to Atlanta, pick up the bus, and bring it back out here to the plantation. It did make more sense to let people get their rest, give them breakfast in the morning, and then take them back to Atlanta the way we would have if the murder had never happened. Summoning up a vestige of normalcy like that might even make folks a little less inclined to sue me later on.

I could hope, anyway.

"All right, Lieutenant," I said. "You need us for anything else right now?"

Farraday shook his head. "No, you can go back

to your rooms. In fact, I'd appreciate it. The more everybody stays out of our way, the faster we can wrap this up."

He used his radio to summon some deputies and then planted himself in front of the door to Riley's room. Obviously he wasn't going to let anybody else in there until he was good and ready, and I had no desire to enter the room again. I didn't need to look at Riley's body again. I had seen two corpses already tonight, and that was two too many, as far as I was concerned. I wasn't sure I would ever get those sights out of my brain.

Will walked with me to the room I was sharing with Augusta and Amelia. We paused in front of the door, and he said, "Well, that didn't work out exactly like we expected it to."

"This night's been so crazy, nothin' surprises me anymore," I said.

"Do you still want to discuss doing some more of these literary tours sometime?"

"Why wouldn't I?"

He laughed. "I don't know, I just thought maybe all the trouble had convinced you to forget the whole thing."

I thought about it for a second, then said, "No, I still think it's a good idea. Can I get in touch with you through the college?"

"Sure, but I'll give you my phone number and e-mail address in the morning before you leave, just to make sure you can contact me whenever you're ready."

"Thanks. That's a good idea. I'll give you my info, too."

He looked hesitant and uncomfortable, like he wanted to say or do something else, and suddenly my mind flashed all the way back to the time when I was a teenager, because at that moment Will Burke looked for all the world like a boy on a first date who couldn't decide whether he wanted to kiss the girl or not—or if he had the courage to do so, even if he wanted to.

But then he just smiled a little, lifted a hand in farewell, and said, "Well, good night . . . what's left of it, anyway."

He turned and started along the hall toward his own room. I didn't know whether to be disappointed or relieved. I decided on relieved. It really hadn't been long enough since the divorce to be thinking about getting involved with somebody. If I did, I would always wonder if it was real or just one of those rebound things.

I opened the door and slipped into the darkened room. The two sets of deep, regular breathing from the nearer of the beds told me that the girls had slept peacefully through the whole thing. I was glad of that. When they woke up in the morning, which was just a few hours away now, it would be to the welcome news that we could all go home.

I felt my way to my bed, took off the robe and dropped it on the foot, and crawled gratefully between the covers again. This time I was determined to go right to sleep and salvage what rest I could.

So wouldn't you know it? A little voice piped up in the back of my head, yammering insistently at me.

What it was saying was that something was still wrong. Something didn't make sense.

It wasn't over, no matter what Lieutenant Farraday said. No matter what Elliott Riley had done. Something didn't tie together just right.

And at that moment, I began to wonder if I was ever going to sleep again.

CHAPTER 22

I forced myself to close my eyes, but when I did I saw Bugs Bunny in a hoop skirt and a Scarlett O'Hara wig. I shook my head and tried to force that image out. Then I thought about the doors Will and I had heard opening and closing as we came down the stairs from the third floor. One of those doors could have been Riley's.

But Riley's door had been open when we found it, not closed. So that didn't work. I tried to reconstruct the sounds.

It was possible that someone had left one of the other rooms, opened Riley's door, seen the body, and then left without closing the door. I'd been wondering *why* the door was open and was leaning toward the explanation that Riley himself had left it open so that his body would be discovered sooner . . . but the theory that was forming in my head was just as plausible, maybe even more so. Anybody finding a body like that with the back of its head blown off might be so shaken that they would rush out and not pull the door all the way closed behind them.

It didn't matter, I told myself. Riley was dead either way, and it seemed obvious that he had killed himself because of guilt over Kelley's murder. Farraday was convinced of that.

But suddenly, I wasn't.

If we assumed that Kelley had discovered Riley hiding those stolen items in the gardener's shed, then there was a reasonable motive for Riley to kill him. Unfortunately, there was no way to *know* that was what had happened, because Riley and Kelley were both dead.

If that wasn't the case, then we were right back where we started, with numerous suspects under the roof of the plantation house who wouldn't have minded seeing Steven Kelley dead. We were worse off, actually, because now Elliott Riley's suicide complicated everything. If it *was* a suicide . . .

I rolled over, buried my face in the pillow, and tried not to groan in despair. Why couldn't I stop *thinking* about all of this? Why couldn't I just accept Riley as the murderer, as Lieutenant Farraday had done, and let it go at that? I wanted to get back to Atlanta with the tour group and not even think about plantations and Rhett Butler and Scarlett O'Hara for a while. I could think about it tomorrow, because after all, tomorrow was another—

Crap. The rug. That was what wasn't right.

I'd never seen Elliott Riley without his toupee. It was an expensive hairpiece, the kind that a man who was vain about his appearance would buy and wear. If he was going to kill himself, knowing that his body was going to be found, wouldn't he have taken the time to put on his toupee?

He hadn't been wearing it when he shot himself, because if he had been, even if it had flown off because of the shot, it would have landed on the bed or the floor close to him. Instead it had been on a stand on the other side of the bed, I recalled.

One part of my brain argued that even asking the question was too much of a stretch. A man on the verge of killing himself would have more important things to worry about than his appearance.

But that wasn't necessarily true. I didn't know a lot about suicide, but I recalled that even those people who committed the act on the spur of the moment often took the time to arrange the scene just the way they wanted it. A lot of them made sure they were dressed neatly, as if they wanted to make sure that they presented the best possible picture. It would have taken Riley only a couple of minutes to put on the toupee. I just couldn't see him not taking the time to do it.

Of course, if I tried to explain that to Lieutenant Farraday, I was sure he would laugh in my face. Well, maybe not laugh, because he wasn't the type to be easily amused . . . but he *would* think I was crazy, more than likely. He wouldn't throw out a reasonable solution to the case just on the basis of whether or not Riley had been wearing his rug.

So I was left to wonder: had Riley really committed suicide? Or had someone murdered him and made it look like Riley killed himself? Who would do such a twisted thing?

A lot of people were extremely upset because of the thefts. Would somebody really take a human life just because their pocket had been picked? I sure wouldn't have, but I've learned over the years that I can't judge everybody else's reactions to situations based on what my own would be. Everybody is different. There is no telling what people might do.

So it was possible, I decided, and it fit with those opening and closing doors Will and I had heard. Somebody could have gone to Riley's room, suspecting that he was the thief. The visitor could have tried to force Riley to confess, they could have gotten into an argument, Riley could have been hit on the head, or fallen and hit himself on the head, and died from the blow.

In that case, the visitor could have panicked, stuck the gun in Riley's mouth—using Riley's hand to do it because of the fingerprints—and pulled the trigger, again using Riley's hand. That would destroy the evidence of the blow to the back of the head. If the slug hadn't gone all the way through Riley's skull—if it had just bounced around in his brain—then that wouldn't have worked, but the killer could have been willing to take that chance. And of course, the way things had turned out, the bullet *had* blown out the back of Riley's head.

It made sense, as had so many other theories that had passed through my mind tonight. But if it was true, then that same pesky question remained: who could have done such a thing?

Most of the people on the tour had either witnessed first-hand or heard about the ruckus between Riley and Gerhard Mueller at the *Gone With the Wind* museum. Given everything that had happened since then, it seemed likely that Riley actually *had* tried to steal the German tourist's camera.

The man had been a pathological thief, a kleptomaniac who had turned his mania into a career as a professional criminal. So it could have been almost anybody who was convinced that Riley was the culprit and went to his room to confront him.

But I knew someone who had already demonstrated a violent reaction to Riley's attempt to steal something.

Gerhard Mueller.

Maybe it was because I just didn't like Mueller, but I could see him walloping Riley in the back of the head, knocking him to the floor, shattering his skull. And I could also see him coming up with the plan to conceal his crime by making it look as if Riley had killed himself. There were probably others in the group who could have done the same thing, but I definitely believed that Mueller was capable of it.

Like it or not—and I was pretty sure I didn't and he wouldn't—I had to talk to Lieutenant Farraday again.

Before I lost my nerve, I got out of bed, put on my robe, and went to the door. There would be deputies in the hallway for sure now since Riley's room was a crime scene, at least officially, and Farraday would want to protect it. I eased the door open so that I wouldn't disturb Augusta and Amelia, although it would probably take an earthquake that was at least a six on the Richter scale to disturb a couple of teenagers sleeping as soundly as they were, and stepped out into the hall.

Sure enough, a couple of deputies were standing in front of the door to Riley's room, which was closed at the moment. I thought they were the ones called Perkins and Morton. They turned toward me immediately and frowned as I started toward them.

"You're supposed to stay in your room, ma'am," Perkins said. "Lieutenant Farraday's orders—"

"It's the lieutenant I want to talk to, Deputy. You reckon you could get him out here for a second? I'm assumin' that he's in there." I nodded toward Riley's room.

"Yes, ma'am, but I'm not sure he wants to be disturbed."

"I'm pretty sure he *doesn't* want to be, but I'm gonna have to disturb him anyway." I wasn't looking forward to this. I figured that when Farraday heard my theory, he'd tell me that I'd gone nuts and order me back to my room. But I had to try to convince him anyway, since I knew I couldn't live with myself if I just ignored everything about the situation that was wrong.

Perkins and Morton hesitated and looked at each other. After a moment Morton nodded. "You might as well get the lieutenant," he told Perkins. "I don't think the lady's going away."

He was right about that. Crazy or not, I wasn't budging until I heard Farraday's reaction to the ideas I'd had.

Perkins opened the door—I guess they'd dusted the knob for fingerprints by then—and went inside, pulling it closed behind him. I wondered briefly if Riley's body was still in there. I wondered, too, how much trouble it was going to be to get his blood out of the carpet and the lampshade and off the wall. If it was me, I think I would have replaced the carpet and the lampshade and repainted the wall. Maybe even torn it out and replaced the sheetrock. The whole thing gave me the creeps.

A couple of minutes dragged by before the door opened again and Farraday came out into the hall, followed by Deputy Perkins. He didn't quite glare at me, but he came close as he said, "What is it, Ms. Dickinson? I thought you were going to get some sleep."

"I tried, but there's something bothering me about Riley's suicide, Lieutenant."

"What's that?" he asked through not quite gritted teeth. I could tell he was trying hard not to lose his temper with me.

"I'm not sure it *was* suicide."

His eyes narrowed, and he grunted. I had managed to surprise him. He took me down the hall, away from Riley's door and out of easy earshot of the two deputies.

"Is that so?" he said. "The gun was in Riley's hand, and the barrel was in his mouth when it went off. That's pretty doggone conclusive."

I stalled a little, unable to come right out with my theory just like that. "Whose gun was it?" I asked instead, not knowing if Farraday would tell me.

He did, though. "It's registered to Elliott Riley. The registration appears to be legitimate, even though Riley's identity was bogus, of course. He didn't have a permit to carry it here in Georgia, but it was definitely his gun. That's another thing indicating that he killed himself."

I took the plunge. "Yeah, but what about his toupee?"

This time the lieutenant's eyes widened, as if he couldn't believe what he was hearing. He struggled to get the words out as he said, "His . . . toupee?"

"Yeah." I gestured toward my head. "His hair-piece. His rug."

"I know what a toupee is, Ms. Dickinson." He scrubbed a hand over his face. "What does Riley's toupee have to do with whether or not he killed himself?"

"I think he would have put it on before he did it. You saw that bald dome of his. He wouldn't want to be found with that showing."

"If he was dead," Farraday grated, "what earthly difference would it make to him?"

"You've heard folks say that they wouldn't be caught dead doing so-and-so?"

Farraday nodded.

"Well, I think Riley was that way about not wearing his toupee whenever anybody could see him. He was pretty vain."

"You knew him, what, two days? That's not a very long time to make such a definitive judgment about somebody's personality."

"Maybe not, but I'm convinced that's the way Riley was. And there was no suicide note, either." I paused. "Unless you've found one since I was in here?"

Farraday shook his head, then grimaced. "Blast it, there you go again, getting me to tell you as much as you're telling me. Listen, Ms. Dickinson, I'm not saying that I believe what you're telling me about Riley and his toupee . . . but if he didn't shoot himself, then who shot him?"

"I've got an idea about that."

"I thought you would."

I considered being offended at his resigned tone of voice, then decided that it wasn't worth the effort. Instead I laid out my theory that someone who was upset about having their things stolen had come to Riley's room and confronted him, leading to a struggle, Riley's death, and the killer's attempt to make that death appear to be self-inflicted.

When I was finished, Farraday stood there frowning and nodding for a moment before saying, "Tell me, Ms. Dickinson, do you watch a lot of mystery shows on television? Read a lot of mystery novels?"

This time I *was* offended, and I didn't bother trying to hide it. "No more so than anybody else, Lieutenant, and I'm not just some crazy woman makin' things up, no matter what you think. I don't believe Elliott Riley killed himself, and what I just told you makes perfect sense."

"Maybe. It would also mean that Riley didn't commit suicide out of remorse over Steven Kelley's murder. It might even mean that Riley didn't kill Steven Kelley at all."

"Well . . . yeah." I had thought of that. I had even tried to consider all the implications of it, which weren't any too pleasant.

"Which means we would be right back where we started on Kelley's murder," Farraday went on, "and *that* means the killer is still on the loose. You'd still be under suspicion, along with your son-in-law and Wilson Cobb and who knows who else in this insane asylum of a plantation!"

I was shocked that Farraday raised his voice like that. It was the first sign I had seen of his self-control slipping since this whole thing began.

He paused, took a deep breath, and went on, "In that case, Ms. Dickinson, you and your group might not be returning to Atlanta in a few hours after all. Is that what you want?"

"You know it's not," I told him. "But if Riley didn't kill Steven Kelley and didn't commit suicide, then it wouldn't be justice to blame him for those things, would it? Do you want to close this case so much that you'd let a murderer go? I didn't think you were like that, Lieutenant Farraday."

I was getting a little hot under the collar myself now, even though the robe I was wearing didn't have a collar. Farraday and I stood there glaring at each other as a couple of long moments ticked by. Then he said, "Thank you for sharing your thoughts with me, Ms. Dickinson. I'll take your ideas under advisement and see if they warrant further investigation. I'd appreciate it if you'd go back to your room now and let us get on with our work."

"That's it, is it?" I demanded. "You're gonna just sweep everything under the rug and let a killer—or maybe two—get away with it."

"I'm going to forget that I heard you say that." He took hold of my arm, not roughly but firmly. "I'll escort you back to your room."

I was too mad to put up an argument, almost too mad to see straight. And I was shocked that Farraday had turned so lax in his determination to ferret out the truth. The bulldog had turned into one of those little Foo-Foo dogs that celebutantes carry around in their purses.

I had done all that I could, I told myself. It wasn't my job to solve murders. That was up to Farraday, and if he didn't want my help, then it was his own lookout.

We were almost back to the door of my room when rapid, heavy footsteps suddenly sounded on the staircase leading down from the third floor. Edmond Ralston appeared on the landing, looked around wildly, spotted us, and exclaimed, "There you are, Lieutenant! Thank God!"

Farraday let go of my arm and took a step toward the frantic plantation owner, asking, "What's wrong, Mr. Ralston?"

"You've got to come quick," Ralston gasped. His face was flushed with exertion, excitement, and possibly fear. "It's Maura Kelley. She's gone mad, and I think she's going to kill my daughter!"

CHAPTER 23

I was too surprised to do anything except stare at Ralston, but Lieutenant Farraday reacted like the professional he was. "Where is she?" he asked as he started swiftly toward the stairs.

"In Janice's suite," Ralston replied. "I heard them shouting at each other and went to see what was going on, and when I came out into the hall I saw Maura force her way into Janice's sitting room. She had a knife, Lieutenant! She's going to hurt Janice!"

Farraday was on his way up the stairs by now, with Ralston at his side. Farraday didn't look back to see whether I was following them.

What do you think I did? I was right behind them, of course.

Farraday jerked his radio off the clip on his belt and started barking orders into it. He called for some of the deputies to come up to the third floor, and since what was going on was basically a hostage situation, he ordered that the sheriff's department SWAT team and hostage negotiation team be alerted, too.

Maybe it wouldn't come to that, though, if he could get up there and talk some sense into Maura Kelley.

"Why would Ms. Kelley threaten your daughter, Ralston?" Farraday asked as they continued to hurry up the stairs.

"I . . . I don't know. I couldn't understand what they were arguing about."

Why, that was a bald-faced lie, I thought, and I almost blurted that out. The argument had to be over Janice's affair with Maura's husband, and Ralston knew that. If Maura was aware of the affair, that was one more reason to suspect her of murdering Kelley. She might be trying to finish the job now by going after Janice.

The two men reached the third-floor landing, and as they did, Farraday finally noticed that I was following them. "Ms. Dickinson!" he said. "Get back downstairs and into your room! Now!"

"I can help you, Lieutenant," I said, instead of following his orders. "I know why Maura Kelley's upset. Janice was having an affair with her husband."

Ralston let out a groan of dismay and shot me a look like I had just stabbed him in the heart. I couldn't believe he was more worried about keeping the affair a secret than he was about saving his daughter's life. Then I realized suddenly that he might be worried about more than that. He might believe that Janice had killed Kelley.

Will Burke and I had discussed that very possibility a while earlier. The meeting in the garden, the ultimatum, Kelley's refusal to leave his wife for Janice, an explosion of anger . . It sure as heck could have happened that way, and Ralston might have figured out the same thing. *That* was why he hadn't wanted Janice's involvement with Kelley to come out.

The secret had been revealed, though, and Farraday swung toward Ralston with a glare and demanded, "Is that true?"

"I . . . I don't know," Ralston stammered. "I don't know anything anymore except that Janice is in there with a crazy woman who has a knife! *Do* something, Lieutenant!"

Farraday didn't waste any more time trying to chase me off. He drew his gun, went to the door of Janice's suite, and called, "Ms. Kelley! This is Lieutenant Farraday! Come on out of there right now, please."

The only response from inside was a muffled scream. Farraday muttered a curse and grabbed the doorknob. It turned easily. Clearly, Maura hadn't bothered to lock the door, and Farraday shoved it open.

He went into the room swiftly but cautiously, the gun held in front of him. He didn't know where Maura was or if she might come at him with that knife Ralston said she had. As Farraday entered the room, I realized that we had only Ralston's word that Maura was even in there and that she was armed. Ralston hadn't seemed like he was faking his near-panic . . . but he *was* an actor as well as the owner of this plantation.

It occurred to me as well that if Ralston was

telling the truth and Maura had threatened Janice with a knife, that was another direct link to Kelley's murder, since he had been killed with a knife. *Either* of the women in that room could be a murderer. Before tonight, I would have thought that if I ever found myself in such circumstances, I would want to hightail it out of there as fast as I could.

Instead, I crowded forward right behind Farraday and Ralston, eager to see what was going on and what was going to happen. The strain of being mixed up in a murder investigation really *had* changed me.

Or maybe I'd been a little weird all along and just hadn't known it until now.

Either way, there I was, standing up on tiptoes and craning my neck, trying to see past the two men who were blocking the door. They moved farther into Janice Ralston's airy, lavishly furnished sitting room, and at last I could see the two women on the other side of the room.

Maura Kelley wore an old-fashioned pair of bloomers, probably what she normally wore under the corset and petticoats and hoop skirt of her Scarlett O'Hara role. I suspected that when she'd been put to bed following her collapse after seeing her husband's body, whoever had gotten her undressed had just taken off the cumbersome outer garments and left the underclothes on her.

The knife she had pressed to Janice Ralston's neck wasn't the sort of accessory you'd associate with the outfit, though.

Terror had drained Janice's face of color and put haggard lines on it. She was still wearing the nighgown I had seen her in earlier, when she was arguing with her father. Neither Ralston nor Farraday had thought to ask me just how I knew about the affair between Janice and Kelley. There would be time enough later to explain all that, although it would mean admitting to the lieutenant that Will and I had done more snooping and sneaking around than what we had told him about earlier.

All those thoughts flashed through my head in a matter of split seconds. We hadn't even been in the room long enough for Farraday to say anything else.

Maura beat him to it. She tightened the grip of her left arm around Janice's neck and cried, "Get out of here or I'll cut the little slut's throat!"

"Maura, p-please!" Ralston begged. "Please don't hurt her!"

"Why not?" Maura shot back. "She hurt me! She tried to steal my husband away from me!"

I wanted to say, *Honey, she was a long way from the first and she sure as heck wouldn't have been the last.*

But I didn't, of course. It wouldn't help anything at the moment for Maura to know that she never really had a husband to steal. With his history, it was obvious that their marriage meant nothing to Steven Kelley.

Or maybe it did. Danged if I know what's in the depths of somebody else's heart. I wasn't sure I even knew what was in my own anymore.

"Ms. Kelley," Farraday said in a firm, level voice, "if you'll just put the knife down and release Ms. Ralston, no one else has to get hurt here."

Maura let out a dramatic, scornful laugh worthy of Scarlett herself. "No one gets hurt but me, is that what you mean? I don't think so, Lieutenant. I'm not going to carry this pain alone. I lost my husband, so now Ralston can lose a daughter." She glared at the plantation owner. "And the little bitch can lose her life!"

I was vaguely aware of commotion behind me in the hall. The deputies would be out there by now, probably with some of the tour group and the other involuntary "guests" who had been awakened by the earlier argument between Janice and Maura. From what Ralston had said, it had gotten pretty loud before Maura forced her way into the suite.

Ralston took a faltering step forward, ignoring the warning look that Farraday gave him. He reached out his hand and said, "You're wrong, Maura, I swear you're wrong. Janice never had anything to do with Steven. They were just friends, that's all."

I knew that was a lie, but if Ralston could convince Maura it was the truth, he might be able to save his daughter's life. I kept my mouth shut, and so did Farraday, perhaps sensing that the best chance of ending this standoff without any more violence lay with Ralston's pleas.

Maura wasn't having any of it, though. "Shut up, you fat old fool!" she told Ralston. "I know they were having an affair. Steven boasted about it, threw it in my face! Told me all about his *young* lover!"

Well, shoot, I thought, that could've been a lot of people other than Janice Ralston.

"He said he always got what he wanted, always," Maura went on. "He said all he had to do was snap his fingers and she would come running back to him, no matter who else she'd taken up with. Even if Melanie married Ashley, he bragged, Captain Rhett Butler would never be denied what was his!"

Lord, things were getting jumbled up. In her grief, Maura was confusing Margaret Mitchell's novel with reality. In the book, Rhett hadn't been romantically involved with Melanie. Melanie had married Ashley Wilkes.

Real life didn't have to mirror Mitchell's fictional world exactly, though. Janice Ralston played Melanie in the re-creation, and her affair with the man who played Rhett had landed her in this moment of deadly danger, with a knife at her throat and a crazed, jealous woman ready to plunge that blade in.

"Please, Ms. Kelley," Farraday said again. "Let go of Ms. Ralston and put the knife down. Otherwise you're going to get hurt again, worse this time."

Maura shook her head. "Nothing could be worse than losing Steven."

She sounded like a woman gone mad with grief and anger, but not like one who had killed her own husband.

Suddenly, Ralston drew himself up straight, squaring his shoulders, and said in a voice thick with a Southern accent, "Scarlett, honey, I demand that y'all stop this nonsense this minute, you hear me? Put that knife down and let go o' that poor girl. That's jus' Melanie, sweet little Melanie. She wouldn't hurt a fly, honey, and y'all are scarin' her."

Maura blinked at him and looked confused. Was it possible that by falling back on his make-believe role as *her* father, rather than Janice's, he was getting through to her? It was a big gamble, but in Maura's precarious mental state, it might just work.

Ralston pushed the masquerade even further by stepping closer and extending his hand to her.

"Jus' gimme the knife now, child, 'fore you hurt yourself. You don't need to be handlin' knives. You're too genteel for that, Scarlett. You're made for dancin' at balls and breakin' the hearts of all the young men and livin' your life here at Tara, blessed Tara. Think about Tara, m'dear, think about all it means to you. This place, and the blood and sweat of all the cotton watered with the blood and sweat of all the O'Haras. You're home here. You'll always be home. Now gimme the knife . . ."

He got too close. Maura let out a strangled cry as the spell Ralston had woven with his words shattered. She lunged at him, slashing with the knife. Ralston yelled in pain as the blade sliced deeply across his outstretched palm.

But to do that Maura had to jerk the knife away from Janice's throat, and as soon as she did, Farraday leaped forward and chopped down at her wrist with the edge of his free hand. The blow connected solidly and knocked the knife out of Maura's grip. As it fell to the floor, Farraday tackled both young women. They toppled back on the big four-poster bed, pulling down the sheer drapes that hung around it. Ralston ignored the blood welling from his slashed palm to grab Janice and yank her free from the struggling Farraday and Maura.

Maura was a wildcat. I thought about trying to give Farraday a hand, but I figured I might get in the way more than I helped. Anyway, several of the deputies rushed into the room as Farraday managed to get Maura flipped over on her stomach. They grabbed her arms, pulled them behind her back, and in the blink of an eye some of those plastic restraints they use now instead of handcuffs were looped around her wrists, securing her. Farraday pushed himself up off the bed and said

in a slightly breathless voice, "Get her out of here."
Then he turned to Ralston, who had his arms
around Janice. "How bad are you hurt, Mr. Ralston?"

"I don't know and I don't care. Just as long as
Janice is safe."

I still didn't like Ralston very much, and I
thought Janice was a silly little fool for falling for
Kelley's smooth lines and letting him seduce her
into an affair. But at that moment, watching the
burly plantation owner cradle her in his arms as
she sobbed against his chest, my heart went out to
them. I was glad that Janice hadn't gotten hurt.
Maybe she was heartbroken over Kelley, but that
would go away, just like the gash on Ralston's hand
would heal.

Maura had been half led, half carried out of the
room by the deputies. She would be in custody for
the foreseeable future. A couple of the deputies
took Ralston and Janice downstairs, too, at Farraday's order. The lieutenant told his men to see to
it that Ralston's wound received medical attention.

That left Farraday and me by ourselves in Janice's sitting room. He looked at me and shook his
head. "I don't think I've ever seen a civilian who
manages to stick her nose in where it doesn't belong
as much as you do, Ms. Dickinson."

"Heck, Lieutenant," I said, "I'll take that as a
compliment. And as much as we've been through
together tonight, maybe you ought to call me
Delilah."

I wasn't sure why I said that. I was still mad at
Farraday, too, but I admired the way he had acted
so swiftly and decisively to save Janice's life.

I couldn't forget, though, that he was willing to

let the blame for Steven Kelley's murder fall on Elliott Riley, and even though I had considered Riley the leading suspect, I no longer believed he was guilty. I thought he was probably a murder victim himself."

Farraday frowned and said, "I don't think it would be proper for me to call you by your given name, Ms. Dickinson. I may not sound like it most of the time, but I'm a Southern gentleman myself."

He didn't sound like it at all. His accent was about as neutral as it could be. And at times tonight he hadn't acted like much of a gentleman, either, although to be fair I supposed that his job made that difficult.

I changed the subject by saying, "I don't think Maura Kelley killed her husband, do you?"

Farraday shook his head. "Despite the fact that she threatened Ms. Ralston with a knife . . . no, she certainly didn't sound like she killed Kelley. Of course, we'll question her again, just to make sure, but my gut never did think she was much of a suspect."

"And yet your gut doesn't understand that Elliott Riley would've put that toupee on before he killed himself."

Farraday's eyes rolled in their sockets. "Let's don't start *that* again. Tell you what. I'm sure the whole house is awake by now, and since it's"—he checked his watch—"only an hour or so until dawn, why don't I go ahead and send Mr. Cobb back to Atlanta to fetch that bus? You and your people can get an early start, as soon as he gets back."

"Sounds good to me," I said. "The sooner we all

get out of here, the better, and if I never see another plantation, that'll be just fine with me."

"Sho' nuff." He flashed an unexpected grin at
me. "See? I told you I was Southern, too."

CHAPTER 24

When I finally came out of Janice's suite with Lieutenant Farraday, I found Luke, Augusta, Amelia, Will Burke, and Wilson Cobb among the crowd in the third-floor hallway, waiting for us. The girls threw their arms around me, and then Luke enveloped us all in a relieved group hug.

Will looked a little like he wanted to get in on that hug, too, but he hung back with a smile on his face. I reckon he was just a little too shy to demonstrate how glad he was to see that I was okay.

After a minute or so the hug broke up, and suddenly everybody was full of questions.

"Did somebody else get killed?" Luke asked.

"Has the murder been solved?" Amelia asked.

"When can we go home?" Augusta asked.

"Soon," I said, answering the last question first. "Nobody else was hurt too bad in there just now, although Mr. Ralston got a nasty cut on his hand. And yeah, Lieutenant Farraday is in the process of closin' the case, even as we speak."

"So who did it?" Luke asked. "Who killed Steven Kelley?"

The words tried to stick in my throat, but I was able to force them out. "The lieutenant thinks Elliott Riley did."

"Riley?" Augusta said. "That creepy old guy with the toup?"

"You could be a little more respectful than that, young lady. The man's dead."

"Dead?" The surprised exclamation came in unison from Augusta, Amelia, Luke, and Mr. Cobb.

But not from Will Burke, since he already knew about Riley's so-called "suicide." He didn't know I had come to doubt that Riley actually killed himself, though, because I hadn't had a chance to talk about that with him yet. Will might not believe my theory, either, since he hadn't known Riley at all, and didn't even have the limited acquaintance that I had with the man.

Quite a crowd gathered around me as I explained about finding Riley's body earlier. Farraday hadn't instructed me not to talk about it, so I figured there was no reason to keep any of it a secret now. I told them about how the stolen items had been found hidden in the tool shed in the garden, too, and how Riley had been identified as a professional thief with a long criminal record and several phony identities.

"I told you so!" Gerhard Mueller practically crowed when he heard that. "The man tried to steal my camera while we were at the museum, just as I said!"

"Yeah, Mr. Mueller, he probably did," I said with a weary sigh.

"There is no 'probably' about it, as you Americans say." He pounded a fist against his pajama-clad thigh. "There is no doubt!"

"Sure, whatever you say."

Mueller sneered, seemingly determined to be as arrogant and unlikable as possible. "If you ask me, this man Riley got what was coming to him. I am glad that he is dead."

His wife finally spoke up, for one of the few times on the whole tour. "Gerhard!" she scolded. "You should not say such things."

"Why not? It is true."

Why not? Because if Lieutenant Farraday hadn't been so willing to accept the idea of Riley killing himself because he was guilty of Kelley's murder, comments like that might make somebody start wondering whether or not Mueller had something to do with Riley's death.

Somebody besides me, that is.

Perry Newton pushed his way to the front of the crowd. "You said this man Riley killed Steven, Ms. Dickinson?" he asked.

"That's what Lieutenant Farraday believes, yes. That's why he's releasing all of us. The investigation into Kelley's murder is wrapping up now."

Perry frowned. "But why would Riley do that? He never even met Steven until yesterday during the tour. He didn't have any motive."

"Kelley must have found Riley hiding those stolen items in the shed, and Riley killed him to keep him from telling anybody about it." As I repeated the lieutenant's theory, I knew that the words had the ring of truth to them. Things could have happened just that way. They surely could have.

So why was I so reluctant to accept all of it? Just because of a wig that was on a stand instead of its owner's head? That *was* crazy.

Or was there something else, I suddenly asked myself. Something I had seen or heard and not fully understood, just sensed that it was wrong somehow, that everybody, myself included, was looking at things from the wrong angle?

Perry Newton had begun to nod as if what he'd heard had made sense to him, though. He said, "Yeah, it could have happened like that. Since that guy Riley killed himself, I guess there's not much doubt that it really did."

His girlfriend, Lindsey, had come up beside him. She nodded and muttered agreement, and other people in the crowd did, too. Acceptance of Riley's guilt was beginning to spread, and I had a feeling there was nothing I could do to stop it, no matter what I believed.

And it sure as heck wasn't my job to be the defender of Elliott Riley's reputation now that the man was gone. He'd been a slimy thief, and *that* I didn't doubt at all.

Of course, there was a difference between being a thief and being a murderer. A big difference.

A feeling of utter weariness swept over me. I hadn't slept for nearly twenty-four hours, because excitement and anticipation had woken me up early the day before. At the time I had expected the plantation tour to go just fine and had no idea that before it was over I'd be dealing with a murder or two, a bunch of stolen stuff, and a mob of angry clients.

I guess you never really know what to expect when you get up in the morning, do you?

"What about our valuables?" Mueller asked. "You say that the police discovered the place where they were hidden?"

I didn't want to deal with this annoying man anymore, but it was a legitimate question. I nodded and said, "Yes, they did."

"When will they be returned to us?"

And that was a good question, one that I didn't have the answer to. Farraday hadn't said anything about returning the stolen items to their rightful owners.

I still had a responsibility to my clients, no matter how worn out I was. "I'm not sure, but I'll try to find out," I told them. "There's a chance the authorities may have to hold those items as evidence, so you may not get them back right away."

That news brought a fresh wave of angry muttering. I held up my hands to quiet it and went on, "I'll check with the lieutenant, and you have my word that I'll stay on top of this situation until everybody gets their stuff back and gets what's comin' to 'em."

I don't know why I phrased it exactly that way; wishful thinking, maybe. I wished I could see to it that everybody got what was coming to them, including me.

But then, there's an old Chinese saying: *May you get what you deserve.*

It's a curse for one's enemies, not a blessing for friends.

The members of the tour group were excited that they were going to get to leave right after breakfast, or as soon as Mr. Cobb got back to the plantation with the bus, anyway. The actors who worked here wanted to head for home right away, but Farraday nixed that, explaining that everyone would be released at the same time.

"Just so we can keep things straight," he said.

A few people wandered back to their beds to get another hour or so of sleep, while others stayed up to get their things packed. It didn't matter to me what people did; I was too tired to care anymore.

Mr. Cobb hunted me up to have a private word with me before he left to get the bus. "I just want to thank you, Miz Dickinson, for believing in me. When you found out about what happened all those years ago, you could've turned on me and figured I was guilty of killin' that fella Kelley, too."

"I never thought that, Mr. Cobb. And as far as I'm concerned, what's past is past. It sounded to me like you had a good reason for doing what you did . . . some of it, anyway."

"Yes, ma'am. But if I could change it, I reckon I would. It's hard to live with knowin' that you killed a man, even an animal like Chantry who didn't even deserve to be called a man."

I didn't know if he would answer me or not, but I risked one more question. "If you had known about Steven Kelley, about the kind of man he was . . . if he had made advances to your grand-daughter, say . . . what would you have done?"

His eyebrows lifted in surprise. "You don't still think I'm a suspect, do you?"

"No, of course not," I said quickly. "And you don't have to answer. I was out of line to even ask."

He smiled, showing that he wasn't offended. "Can't blame a person for bein' curious, I reckon.

If *I'd* known about Kelley, *I* wouldn't have killed him. Might've taken a swing at him—*not* with an iron pipe—but with my fists and that's about all."

Luke had said just about the same thing. I believed Mr. Cobb, just like I believed my son-in-law. Because when I'd heard about the things Kelley had said to Augusta and Amelia, *I* felt like punching him, too. That was a normal, common reaction when you found out somebody was a sleazy, disgusting son of a gun like Kelley.

Murder was different. The stakes had to be higher to provoke murder, I thought, at least in most people.

Like preventing exposure as a professional thief? Maybe. It stood to reason that Riley wouldn't want to go to jail. If the only way to prevent that was to kill Kelley, I supposed he might have done it.

Dad gummit, I thought. I was starting to accept the theory that Riley was the murderer and had committed suicide because of it, too. It made too much sense, and I was too tired to keep on being stubborn.

Go home, I told myself. Go home and forget all about it . . .

"I'd best be headin' for Atlanta," Mr. Cobb said, "before the lieutenant changes his mind about lettin' me out of here. I'll be back in a couple hours or so with the bus."

"Thanks, Mr. Cobb." I risked giving him a hug, hoping that he wouldn't mind the familiarity. "You go ahead and drop by your place to check on your little Betsy Blue before getting the bus. We can wait that long. I'll see you later."

He returned the hug briefly, giving me an awkward pat on the back, then turned and started down the curving staircase from the second-floor landing where we'd been talking.

I went back to the room and found that Augusta and Amelia were awake and talking as they got dressed and packed their bags. "This was a really exciting tour, Aunt Delilah," Augusta said. "Are they all going to be like this?"

"Lord, I hope not! Have you forgotten that two people *died* here?"

"No," Augusta said, "but you've got to admit that just touring the plantation and going to a dance would have been more boring."

Amelia stared at her. "You're setting a new standard for callousness, you know that, don't you?"

"No, I'm not," Augusta protested. "I'm just saying what everybody knows already. Murder is interesting. If it wasn't, there wouldn't be so many books written about it."

Maybe she was right, but at that moment, as far as I was concerned, murder was just exhausting. I got my clothes and went in the bathroom to get dressed. I thought I could manage to keep going until the bus returned to Atlanta and I had seen all my clients delivered back safely to their hotels.

But after that I was headed home, and when I got there I was gonna crash. Boy, was I gonna crash. I thought I might sleep for a week. Around the clock, at the very least.

When I came out of the bathroom wearing slacks, blouse, and blazer, the girls were gone, although their bags were still on the bed. I went looking for them and found them downstairs in the big dining room, where people were starting to congregate even though it would be a while before Ralston's kitchen staff had breakfast ready. Augusta and Amelia were talking to the two college boys who played the Tarleton twins. E-mail addresses were being exchanged, I suspected.

I didn't want to interrupt their flirting, so I looked around the room. I saw Gerhard Mueller sitting with his wife and looking sour. I sure didn't want to talk to him. I wasn't totally convinced that Mueller hadn't had something to do with Elliott Riley's death . . . although if that was the case, he'd been pretty blatant in his satisfaction when he heard about the way Will and I had discovered Riley's body. I had to admit that crowing about it didn't seem like the reaction of a guilty man, unless Mueller was really tricky and was trying to throw everybody off his trail by acting that way. I didn't believe he was that cunning. He was just a natural-born jackass.

Perry Newton and Lindsey Hoffman were sitting at one of the tables with some of the other kids from the college. They were pretty subdued, and I reminded myself that they had lost their mentor. Sure, Steven Kelley had been pretty much of a scumbag where women were concerned, but he had also been a decent drama teacher, from what I had seen, and he had gotten all of them acting jobs here on the plantation for the summer. Most college kids always needed extra money, and this would be a professional acting credit they could put on their resumé, too. It couldn't hurt when they went on auditions in the future.

Edmond Ralston wandered into the dining room. He had finally changed out of his Thomas Mitchell outfit and now wore jeans and a polo shirt. A white bandage was wrapped around his hand where Maura Kelley had cut him.

He spotted me and came toward me. I summoned up a smile and asked, "How's your hand?"

He lifted it and looked at the bandage as if he had forgotten it was there. "Hurts like the dickens," he said. "I'll be going to the doctor later this morning to get some stitches taken in it. But I think it'll heal up nicely in time."

"I hope so. That was mighty brave of you, trying to get the knife from Mrs. Kelley like that."

Ralston shrugged. "I had to do something. My daughter's life was at stake. And I thought Maura might respond if I acted like Scarlett's father. Steven was a believer in the method school of acting, you know. He liked to immerse himself in a character, and he demanded that all the other actors do so as well. That's the way he taught them in their drama classes."

"So you thought that a part of Maura might still be so wrapped up in playing Scarlett that she would react like Scarlett."

He nodded. "That's right. It almost worked, too. But at least Janice is all right. That's all that really matters to me."

"Where is she now?"

"Upstairs, sleeping. She has a prescription for sedatives, and she took one of them. What she needs to do now is rest and forget all about everything that's happened."

I understood that feeling. That was exactly what I wanted to do. I didn't think I would need a sedative, though. Sheer exhaustion was going to take care of the problem for me.

"I'm going to go out to the kitchen and see how breakfast is coming along," Ralston said. He started in that direction and then paused to look back at me. "I hope all this unpleasantness won't keep you from bringing some of your tours back here in the future, Ms. Dickinson."

"You're going to continue with the *Gone With the Wind* re-creations?"

"Of course. Perry's already agreed to take over as creative director on an interim basis, and if he does a good job, I'll keep him on. He knows all the actors, of course. With a wig and a mustache, he can even take over as Rhett . . . although he won't be as good in the role as Steven was." Ralston sighed. "For all his faults, that young man made a really good Rhett Butler. Sometimes I thought he believed that he really was Rhett."

With that, Ralston lifted his uninjured hand in farewell and went on to the kitchen. I strolled around the room for a few more minutes, then finally realized that I was looking for Will Burke. He'd said that we would exchange contact info this morning, and I didn't want to miss him before the bus left.

But I didn't see him anywhere in the dining room. He was probably still upstairs. He might even be getting a last-minute nap before breakfast. I knew which room he was in because I'd been part of the arrangements with Ralston and Lieutenant Farraday, but I couldn't bring myself to go up there and knock on his door. Despite the friendship that had sprung up quickly between us and a few intimate feelings that had cropped up here and there, I figured it would be too forward to go calling on him in his bedroom before dawn.

So I left the dining room instead and wandered down the hall, looking idly at the antique furniture and the paintings on the walls. I came to a partially open door, pushed it back further, and looked into the big library. It was a beautiful room with several mahogany tables and chairs, some comfortable armchairs, and built-in bookshelves on three walls. The other wall was a sort of *Gone With the Wind* shrine. It was hung with framed photographs of scenes from the movie and of the actors who had played in it, of various editions of the novel, and of Margaret Mitchell herself.

I went in and walked slowly around the room, looking at everything. A valuable first-edition copy of the novel, signed by Mitchell, was safely locked up behind glass, but there were numerous other editions on the shelves. I ran my fingers over their bindings, then selected one and carried it to a table and sat down.

I wasn't going to read the book, but I felt a certain sense of peace steal over me as I sat there slowly turning the pages of the most popular novel of all time. The wall of photos was behind me, and it seemed almost like Clark Gable, Vivien Leigh, Olivia de Havilland, Leslie Howard, Thomas Mitchell, Hattie McDaniel, Butterfly McQueen, and even poor, doomed George Reeves were looking over my shoulder at the words that had given birth to the characters they played. All of them rose up from those pages, figments of one woman's imagination, phantoms who had taken on life and become real in the minds of millions of people.

I looked up suddenly from the book on the table in front of me, then twisted in the chair to peer up at the photographs on the wall. Things started coming together in my brain with dizzying speed, so fast that they took my breath away. Because of that, it was several moments before I could put into words some of what was filling my head.

"Son of a gun," I said. "Ashley Wilkes."

CHAPTER 25

"**W**hat?" Will Burke asked from the doorway. I was so deep in thought that his voice surprised me and made me jump a little. I stood up and turned toward him.

As he stepped into the library, Will went on, "I'm sorry, Delilah. I didn't mean to scare you. I was just going past in the hall and happened to see you sitting in here. I was about to say hello when you said something about Ashley Wilkes."

My heart was doing that trip-hammer thing in my head again. I saw now that I might have misinterpreted something I had heard earlier. That was understandable, because I had been under a considerable strain at the time, wondering whether or not Maura Kelley was going to cut Janice Ralston's throat.

Despite the early hour and the long night that had preceded it, Will looked good, very professorlike in jeans and a corduroy jacket, but I was barely aware of that. My head was still filled with new con-

nections and speculations. He probably thought
I'd completely lost my mind, the way I was staring
and maybe even muttering to myself. I'm not sure
what I said, if anything. But after a moment he
took a card from his shirt pocket and held it out
toward me.

"Here's my phone number and e-mail at school,
and I wrote my home phone and e-mail on the
back."

I took the card without really thinking about it
and slipped it into the pocket of my blazer. I did
manage to mumble, "Thanks."

Will's eyes narrowed. "I assume you still want to
keep in touch . . . ?"

"Yeah, sure."

He definitely looked a little hurt by my lack of
interest now. I remember it plain as day, but there
was nothing I could do about it at the time.

"You were going to give me your contact
info . . ."

"Yeah, I'll do that before we leave," I rushed on,
"I've gotta ask you a question."

Obviously, he wasn't so offended that he wasn't
going to answer, because he said, "Sure, go ahead."

"All the college kids who work here as actors,
they were in Kelley's classes? Every single one?"

"That's right. Well, except for Janice Ralston,
who just graduated from high school. But she's already enrolled and signed up for Kelley's fresh-
man class in the fall." Will shook his head. "They'll
have to find somebody to replace him."

"Kelley wouldn't like that. He was Rhett Butler.
He couldn't stand to have Ashley Wilkes get the
better of him."

Will frowned. "What are you talking about, Delilah?"

I didn't answer. I just said, "I've got to go. Got to find somebody."

Then I rushed out of the library, leaving Will there staring after me in confusion.

I headed straight back to the dining room and looked around, not spotting the people I was looking for. I turned around, thinking frantically about where else they could be. I headed for the ballroom, knowing that was a longshot.

Now, of course, it seems obvious even to me that I should have gone looking for Lieutenant Farraday and told him what I had figured out in the library. But my brain wasn't working along those lines at the time, and besides, Farraday was hung up on the idea that Riley had killed Steven Kelley.

I knew that wasn't true. I didn't have any proof, but I knew it anyway.

I pushed one of the doors to the ballroom open and saw that it was dark inside. I was about to turn away when I caught a glimpse of one of the French doors swinging shut on the other side of the room. Somebody had just gone out into the garden. Dawn was less than an hour away, but shadows still covered everything under the magnolia trees outside.

I'd like to think that my mama didn't raise any fools, but she did raise one stubborn, redheaded daughter. I hurried across the ballroom and slipped out through the same door, easing it closed behind me without making any noise.

This early in the morning, there was a faint hint of coolness in the magnolia-scented air. It might have been pleasant if there had been even a breath of a breeze, but there wasn't. A humid stillness hung over the place. Since it was a garden, full of growing things, it should have seemed like a place full of life.

Instead I seemed to smell decay and death. The garden had lost its beauty and was just a murder scene to me now.

The two people I was following must have slipped out here to make one last check to be sure there was nothing left behind to tie them to Steven Kelley's murder. Crime scene tape was still strung up around the place on the path where Kelley's body had been found, but there were no deputies guarding it. The three of us were alone in the garden.

I guess I wasn't as stealthy as I thought I was. Lindsey must have heard my foot scrape on the gravel or something, because she whirled halfway around, grabbed Perry's arm, and said, "There's somebody out here."

The beam from a small flashlight lanced out and caught me. "Ms. Dickinson!" Perry exclaimed. "What are you doing out here?"

I swallowed hard. "Just thought I'd come out for one last bit of moonlight and magnolias before we leave after a while." I managed to chuckle. "Sorry I interrupted you lovebirds. I'll let you get back to whatever you were doin'." I knew it was a mistake, but I couldn't resist asking, "Did you two get engaged out here?"

Perry turned the flashlight beam down toward the path so that it wasn't in my eyes anymore. As they started to adjust, I saw him smiling. He said,

"That's right. How did you know we were going to get married, Ms. Dickinson?"

Before I could answer, Lindsey tightened her grip on Perry's arm and said in a horrified voice, "She knows, Perry. Just look at her. She knows!"

I started backing up. "Yeah, and so does Lieutenant Farraday," I said with a show of bravado. "He'll be out here in just a minute with some deputies—"

"That's a lie," Perry said. He took a step toward me. "Farraday wouldn't have let you come out here after us by yourself if he knew anything about this."

"Get her," Lindsey urged.

I wondered if she had urged Perry to stick the knife in Kelley's chest or if Perry had come up with that idea on his own. Heck, Lindsey might even be the one who had stabbed Kelley. I was pretty sure, though, that it was Perry who had struggled with Elliott Riley, either knocking him out or maybe even killing him with a blow to the head, then staging things to make Riley's death look like suicide.

"It won't be near as easy to get away with killin' me as it was with Kelley," I said as I continued to back away. "You won't have a fall guy for this murder who serves himself up to you on a silver platter the way Riley did." The words bubbled out of my mouth, giving voice to the theory that had begun to form in the library. The picture was becoming clearer all the time. "What did he do, tell you to come to his room so you could talk about the blackmail money you were going to pay him?"

Perry wasn't giving up on the idea of talking their way out of this. He said, "Ms. Dickinson, I don't have any idea what you're going on about. Lindsey and I didn't hurt anybody, and we certainly weren't being blackmailed by that poor Mr. Riley. He's the one who killed Steven, remember?"

"He didn't have near as good a motive as you did. Kelley was going to ruin everything for you, wasn't he? He was your boss, both at the college and here in this show on the plantation. He was gonna fire you from both jobs unless you broke off your engagement with Lindsey, because he wanted her back. He'd been involved with her before, but she dumped him for you, and then when the two of you got engaged, it was more than Kelley could stand. He always had to win. He'd been like that since he was a kid. And he sure as heck wasn't gonna let Ashley Wilkes take a woman he wanted away from him."

Yeah, a lot of it was guesswork, but it jibed with everything I knew about these people. And it fit with what Maura had said earlier about her husband. When Steven Kelley had ranted about not allowing Melanie to marry Ashley Wilkes, he hadn't been talking about Janice Ralston at all. He was talking about "Ashley Wilkes"—*his teaching assistant, Perry Newton.*

That meant the "Melanie" he'd been referring to was Lindsey, Perry's girlfriend and—I now knew—fiancée. Sure, Lindsey didn't play Melanie, but that hadn't mattered to Kelley. What was important to him was not letting "Ashley" take the girl away from "Rhett." To Kelley, that was just wrong on more than one level. He was the one who was supposed to steal the ladies from other men, not vice versa.

But in his determination to force Lindsey back

into his arms, he had pushed Perry too far. With Kelley dead, not only could the two of them go ahead and get married, but Perry would also take over as creative director of the troupe that worked on the plantation. His position at the college would be secure. He might even win some sympathy because the professor he worked for had been murdered. Heck, he was even going to play Rhett Butler!

Yeah, Perry Newton had the starring role in "The Revenge of Ashley Wilkes," all right.

But now I stood between him and that goal, and he must have been able to tell from my face that no matter what he said, I could never be persuaded that I was wrong about him.

So at that moment he leaped forward, breaking into a run toward me. Lindsey was right behind him.

I spun around and tried to run, but they were too close. And too blasted young, to boot. Perry grabbed the collar of my blazer and slung me to the ground. I rolled over the flagstones on the path. Lindsey tried to kick me, but I got out of the way just in time.

I don't know what they thought they were going to do with me. Pry up one of those flagstones and beat me to death with it, maybe. Then they could've hidden my body in that shed or somewhere else and slipped back into the house. When the bus got here and I didn't show up, there would be a search for me, of course, but that would be a whole lot too late to do me any good. I'd already be dead.

And with some luck, the two of them might get away with that murder, too.

I wasn't going to let that happen. Anger mixed

with self-preservation sent me scrambling off the path and into the shrubs and flower beds that bordered it. I knew I couldn't outrun them to the house, so my only chance was to give them the slip in the still-dark garden.

They came after me, of course. They couldn't afford to let me go now. I could hear them crashing through the brush—but they could hear me as I tried to get away from them, too. I darted around a magnolia tree and then pressed my back against the trunk, standing stock-still in hopes that they would go on past me. I forced myself to hold my breath so they wouldn't hear me gasping for air, but my pulse was thundering so loud inside my head that it seemed inevitable they would hear it and know I was there.

"Where the hell did she go?" Perry whispered. He wasn't more than ten feet away from me. He had turned the flashlight off, and I figured he didn't want to go flashing the beam around for fear of attracting attention inside the house.

"We have to find her," Lindsey said. "She'll ruin everything, and then it'll all be for nothing."

Perry was silent for a moment, like he was trying to figure out what to do next. Finally he said, "All right. She can't have gone very far. We'll split up. If you find her, grab her and hang on. I'll be right there."

"We need to hurry. What if she starts screaming?"

As a matter of fact, I had thought about doing just that. Perry's answer was the reason I hadn't.

"If she does, we'll get to her first and shut her up. Nobody else knows we're out here." He gave a curt laugh. "Who knows, maybe we could even pretend to find her and start yelling for help because there's been another murder."

The little weasel, I thought. It was high time I stopped feeling even a little bit sorry for those two. Sure, Kelley had put them in a bad spot. That didn't justify anything that they had done.

I'd been holding my breath for about as long as I could. I tried to take a shallow, silent breath, but it still sounded loud to me. I heard movement in the shrubs nearby, then Lindsey muttered a curse.

She was almost right on top of me. I could have reached out and touched her.

Instead I stayed frozen, my back pressed against the tree trunk. I'm convinced she would have gone on past without noticing me, too, if she hadn't stumbled on a root just then and put out a hand to brace herself. Instead of leaning against the tree, her hand went right into my shoulder.

"Perry!" she cried in a low, urgent voice. "She's here!"

She grabbed at me, trying to tie me up and pin me against the magnolia. I planted my hands on her chest and shoved hard, sending her stumbling away from me. She tripped over a low stone wall covered with honeysuckle and toppled backward.

I broke into a run. I knew that Perry was somewhere close by and just wanted to get away from him. I didn't know if I was going toward the house or deeper into the garden. Fear and the shadows that still cloaked everything had disoriented me.

Noises of pursuit came from behind me and made me run even harder. Suddenly, something loomed up in front of me, and I just managed to stop before I ran full tilt into a stone wall that would have knocked me silly. I had reached a small building of some sort, and even without seeing it before, I was convinced this was the tool shed where Elliott Riley had hidden his loot.

It was after leaving the shed and starting back to the house that Riley had come across Steven Kelley and witnessed either Perry or Lindsey shoving that knife into Kelley's chest. Riley was no murderer, but he *was* a career criminal who certainly wasn't above attempting a little blackmail. How much he thought he could collect from a couple of young actors like Perry and Lindsey was a good question. Unless they came from wealthy families—which was a possibility, I guess—they wouldn't have much money.

Riley had tried to cash in anyway and gotten killed for his trouble. I wasn't going to mourn him. Not too much, anyway.

Right now I was more worried about saving my own life. I felt around to the front of the tool shed. There might be something inside that I could use as a weapon to fight off the two people who wanted to kill me, I thought. I found the door. It was closed and latched, but not locked. As quietly as possible, I unfastened the latch and swung the door open.

A few strands of pinkish light had begun to filter down through the leafy branches above me, signifying the approach of dawn. But it was still pitch-black inside the shed. I had to feel my way around. After a minute my fingers brushed against what felt like the wooden handle of a shovel or a hoe or something like that. I clutched it and lifted it carefully, then ran the fingers of one hand along the handle. It was a shovel, all right. That would go a long way toward evening the odds for me against Perry and Lindsey, I thought. Even if they had another knife like the one they had used to kill Steven Kelley, the shovel was a lot longer. I thought I could keep them at bay with it while I yelled for help.

That was the plan as I stepped out of the tool shed. Unfortunately, Perry was waiting right outside the door.

I didn't know he was there until he grabbed the shovel with one hand, ripping it out of my grasp, and swung the other against my head in a punch that knocked me to the ground. Stars seemed to burst in front of my eyes. I knew I had to get up and that there was no time to waste. But my muscles didn't want to work and all I could do was lie there.

"I'm sorry, Ms. Dickinson," he said. "I really am. But you shouldn't have tried to play detective."

He didn't understand. I hadn't been trying to play detective. Things had just sort of worked out that way.

But now it was too late to explain. Perry shifted his grip on the shovel handle and lifted it so that the head was poised above him, ready to come slashing down and crush my skull. It was light enough now in the garden for me to see him. I would be able to see my own death descending on me.

Then flame spurted in the shadows near the tool shed and the loudest thunderclap I'd ever heard slammed through the early morning air and Perry went flying backward to land on the flagstone path in a moaning heap. Lieutenant Farraday rushed out from under the magnolia trees with his gun in one hand. He kicked the shovel well out of Perry's reach, then holstered the service revolver, rolled Perry over, dug a knee into the small of his back, and slipped the restraints on his wrists.

While Farraday was doing that, Will Burke appeared beside me and knelt to put his arms around me and help me up. "Are you all right?" he asked, and when I nodded he pulled me against him and wrapped his arms around me.

Maybe I was just a little loopy from getting punched in the head, but him holding me like that felt pretty darned good. A heck of a lot better than getting my brains beaten out with a shovel would have, I'll bet.

Deputies showed up, a couple of them with Lindsey Hoffman in tow. Two more lifted Perry to his feet. He was pale and only half conscious. Blood welled from the bullet wound in his right shoulder where Farraday had shot him. The lieutenant told his men to take Perry and Lindsey away, then turned to me.

"Well, you almost got yourself killed," he said to me. "Are you satisfied now?"

I was still a little out of breath. "You know that . . . Perry and Lindsey . . . killed Kelley and Riley? I don't know who did what, but they were in it together . . . I reckon."

"We'll sort that out, don't worry. They'll probably be testifying against each other before we even get them locked up. That's pretty much what I had in mind when I let everybody think I was blaming Riley for Kelley's murder."

"You knew Riley wasn't guilty?" Will said.

Farraday made a face. "Please. I know a phony suicide when I see one." He glared at me. "I was hoping that would make you stop poking around, though, and lull the real killer into making a mistake. I realize now the mistake was mine, thinking that a redheaded bulldog like Ms. Dickinson here would ever let go once she sunk her teeth into something."

I started to sputter. "Redheaded bulldog? *You're* the bulldog, you . . . you . . . ."

Farraday grinned. "Take it easy, Red. You don't want to bust a blood vessel."

Will tightened his arms around me. "You just made another mistake, Lieutenant," he said. "I'll hang on to her. You'd better run while you've got the chance."

I have to admit, I wanted to give Farraday a good piece of my mind right about then.

But what the heck. I liked the sound of Will Burke hanging on to me even better.

CHAPTER 26

"**I** don't understand," Augusta said. "Ashley Wilkes killed Rhett Butler? That's just wrong."

"They weren't really Ashley and Rhett, Augusta," Amelia said. "They were just actors."

"I *know* that! You don't have to act like I'm an idiot or something."

"Well, I don't see why you don't understand. Aunt Delilah explained everything perfectly clearly."

I was glad Amelia thought everything was perfectly clear. I was so tired, I wasn't really sure of anything anymore, plus I had a little headache, probably from getting punched.

But at least this time it actually was over. With Mr. Cobb at the wheel, the bus full of my clients had pulled out of the plantation driveway past all the TV news trucks and the reporters clamoring for exclusive statements. The trip back to Atlanta had gone off without a hitch and everybody was back where they were supposed to be, including the girls and Luke and me. I sat in my office along with Melissa. She had wanted to know everything that had happened, of course, so I had just gone through all of it again.

Now she shook her head and said, "I was so worried when I heard that there was some sort of trouble at the plantation. I couldn't reach any of you on your cell phones, and I didn't know what was going on. I started to drive out there, but then I thought you might need me to hold down the fort here this morning."

"You did exactly the right thing," I told her. "There was nothing you could have done to help, anyway."

"I dunno, Miz D," Luke said. "We could've used a hand with all our detective work."

Augusta laughed. " 'Our' detective work? I don't remember you doing anything to help Aunt Delilah solve the murders, Luke."

"Well . . . I would have. I sure wouldn't have let her go out there into that garden by herself and nearly get killed."

That comment sobered the place up real quick. Now that it was all over, it was easy to get caught up in the solution to the mystery and forget about how close I had come to dying.

Easy for the rest of them, maybe, I should say. I wasn't sure I'd ever forget what it had felt like to lie there on the ground and watch Perry Newton get ready to kill me.

But it was over and done with now, and I said, "Here's something you can do for me, Luke. You and Melissa take the girls back to my house, okay?"

"Sure. What are you gonna do, Miz D?"

"I thought I'd just sit here for a while. You know, decompress." As exhausted as I was, I still wasn't sure I could sleep.

"Are you sure you'll be all right, Mom?" Melissa asked. "You've been through a lot, and you're not as young as you used to be."

"I'm not as old as I'm gonna be, either," I said, flaring up a little. "Now go on, all of you. Git, and let me have a little peace and quiet for a change. Just turn on the answerin' machine on your way out."

They all stood up to leave. Augusta said, "I still want to talk to you sometime about getting my belly button pierced, Aunt Delilah."

"Augusta!" Amelia, Melissa, and Luke all said at once.

Finally, they were gone and I was alone with my thoughts. I was still worried about what this mess was going to do to the reputation of my business, not to mention the possibility of lawsuits and things like that, but I would deal with all that when the time came. I pushed all of that out of my mind and tried to think about the future instead. My hand stole into the pocket of my blazer and found the card Will Burke had given me.

If I was still in the business of setting up literary-oriented tours when all the hoopla from this one blew over, I would definitely need to call Will and get his advice. I was already thinking about other Southern authors. There were plenty of 'em: Tennessee Williams, William Faulkner, Harper Lee, Truman Capote, even old Mark Twain himself. We just might be on to something here, I thought.

I went to sleep right there in my office chair, with Will Burke's card still in my hand and a smile on my face.

Gone With the Wind Tours

Experience the legendary land of *Gone With the Wind*:

- Margaret Mitchell House & Museum, birthplace of *Gone With the Wind*, where Margaret Mitchell penned the world's best-selling novel
- Lunch at Mary Mac's Tea Room, authentic Southern hospitality and cuisine

And in nearby Clayton County:

- Stately Oaks Plantation, antebellum plantation home

Margaret Mitchell House & Museum
990 Peachtree Street
Atlanta, Georgia 30309
404-249-7015

The Visitors Center, located next to the house on the corner of Peachtree Street and Peachtree Place, includes the ticket counter, a small theater, and a visual arts exhibit gallery. Exclusive photographs and exhibits tell the story of Margaret Mitchell before, during, and after *Gone With the*

Wind made her a household name. The tour starts in the Visitors Center with "Before Scarlett: The Writings of Margaret Mitchell" and continues into the house, through her apartment where she wrote *Gone With the Wind*, and finally to the *Gone With the Wind* Movie Museum, which includes objects such as the legendary doorway to Tara from the movie set. The museum shop offers unique gifts, souvenirs, and *Gone With The Wind* collectibles and memorabilia.

Margaret Mitchell and her husband, John Marsh, moved into the house in 1925, when the building was known as the Crescent Apartments. Apartment #1 is the only interior space of the restored house that is preserved as an apartment. Architectural features include the famous leaded glass window out of which Margaret looked while writing the book, and tile in the foyer of her apartment. All furnishings are of the period.

Moving on to the *Gone With the Wind* Movie Museum, attractions include the front door of the Tara Plantation house and the portrait of Scarlett from the Butler house, both taken from the actual movie sets. The portrait still bears a liquor stain from a drink Clark Gable's Rhett Butler threw at it. Other original materials on display include storyboards from the film studio's art department created to choreograph movie scenes, and costume sketches by Walter Plunkett. The exhibition also features Margaret Mitchell's original correspondence from 1938 and 1939, discussing her hopes that the novel over which she had labored so long would be portrayed accurately in the film version.

Mary Mac's Tea Room

Not far from the Margaret Mitchell House, Mary Mac's Tea Room opened in 1945. Over the years a series of hard-working proprietors developed it into one of the South's best-known restaurants with a great tradition of Southern cuisine and hospitality. Still in the same place it has always been, the Tea Room offers a menu that remains very similar to what it was when the restaurant was founded all those years ago.

Plantation Tours—While Tara Plantation in this novel is fictional, there are many plantations to visit like Stately Oaks.

Experience history and genuine Southern hospitality when you visit the historic 1839 Greek Revival Antebellum plantation home, Stately Oaks. Stately Oaks is a beautifully restored home with the original log kitchen and other historic outbuildings located in Jonesboro, Georgia. Nineteenth-century, authentically costumed docents provide guided tours depicting the rural South during the mid-1800s. Recapture the past with a visit to Stately Oaks!

For more information about Gone With The Wind and for tour information check out the website **http://www.gwtw.org.**

Turn the page for a preview of

HUCKLEBERRY FINISHED

The second in the Delilah Dickinson

Literary Tour Mystery series

by Livia J. Washburn!

Coming in November 2009!

CHAPTER 1

Mark Twain once wrote, "I can picture that old time to myself now, just as it was then ... the great Mississippi, the majestic, the magnificent Mississippi, rolling its mile-wide tide along, shining in the sun."

As I stood at the railing of the *Southern Belle*, I knew what he meant. I had seldom seen anything quite so beautiful and serene as the great river. Sure, the scenery along the banks wasn't as pristine and unspoiled as it was back in Twain's day. I could see tall fast-food signs and electrical lines and jets winging across the blue summer sky. But out here in the middle of the river all I could hear were the gentle rumble of the boat's engines and the splashing of the paddle-wheels as they propelled us through the water at a sedate pace. I felt the faint vibrations of the engine through the deck, and the sun was warm on my face. If you closed your eyes, I thought, it would almost seem like you were really back there and Sam Clemens himself was up in the pilothouse, guiding the riverboat toward the next quaint little river town where it would dock.

And then somebody's dadgum cell phone rang.

"Yellll-o!"

That's the way he said it, swear to God.

"Yeah, guess where we are? . . . We're on a riverboat! . . . Yeah, on the Mississippi. Helen wanted to come. But it's so freakin' slow, I think I could walk faster! Haw, haw!"

My hands tightened on the smooth, polished wood of the railing. I figured I'd better hold on, because a good travel agent never punches her clients. That's one of the first rules they teach you.

"What? . . . No, damn it, I told him those reports had to be finished by yesterday . . . What's he been doing this whole time, sitting around with his thumb up his—"

I couldn't let him go on. I turned around and said, "Sir!"

He looked surprised at the interruption. He was a big guy, balding, with the beginnings of a beer gut in a polo shirt. Played college football, from the looks of him, but that was more than twenty years in the past. Beside him, wearing a visor, sunglasses, a sleeveless blue blouse, and baggy white shorts, was a blond woman carrying a big straw purse and a long-suffering look. She was married to the loudmouth, more than likely.

He said, "Hold on, Larry," into the cell phone, then took it away from his ear. "Yeah? What can I do for you?"

About a dozen other members of my tour group had lined up along the railing. I gestured vaguely toward them and said, "These folks are tryin' to, you know, soak up the ambience of the river, and your business conversation is a little jarring."

"I'm sorry"—he didn't sound like he meant it—"but I got a crisis on my hands here."

"I understand that. Maybe you could go inside to talk to your associate."

He shook his head. "My crappy phone won't work in there. I'm barely getting any reception out here." He put the crappy phone back to his ear and went on, "Larry, you still there? You tell that worthless little weasel to get those reports done by the end of the day or he's fired! You got that? And if any of this comes back on *my* head, he ain't gonna be the only one, *capeesh?*"

I didn't know whether to be mad at him for ignoring me or flabbergasted at the guy's language. I couldn't remember the last time I'd heard anybody say "Capeesh?"

"Yeah, yeah, you and Holloway both know where you can put your excuses. Just take care of it."

He snapped the phone closed, looked at me, raised his eyebrows, and shrugged his shoulders as if to say, *Now are you satisfied, lady?*

I managed to say, "Thank you."

He rolled his eyes, shook his head, and moved off down the railing toward the stern.

His wife lingered long enough to say, "I'm sorry, Ms. Dickinson. Eddie's just very devoted to his business."

"That's all right, Mrs. Kramer," I told her. I had finally remembered their names. "I understand."

I didn't, not really, but that's what you tell people anyway. I didn't understand why people would pay good money to take a vacation and then bring their work with them. I was devoted to my business, too, but if I were getting away from it, I'd get as far away as I could and stay there until it was time to go home.

Louise Kramer smiled at me and then followed her husband along the deck. He had already opened his phone and was talking on it again, but at least he wasn't disturbing the other members of the group as much.

The *Southern Belle* had started upriver from St. Louis about an hour earlier, after the forty members of my tour group had gotten together for lunch at a restaurant not far from the riverfront. I had booked a private room so that we could eat together, and then everyone had gotten up and introduced himself or herself. I don't think that everybody who goes on one of my tours has to be all buddy-buddy with the other clients, but since we were all going to be together on a relatively small boat for the next twenty-four hours I didn't think it would hurt for them to get to know each other. After all, some people go on vacation tours *hoping* that they'll meet someone who'll turn out to be special in their lives.

Most folks, though, just want the scenery and the history. And, in the case of the *Southern Belle*, the gambling. The side-wheeler was a floating casino.

Casino gambling is legal in most places up and down the Mississippi River, and there are numerous riverboats devoted to that purpose. Most of them are permanently docked, however. Some even have the engines gutted out so that they'll never move again, at least not under their own power.

The *Southern Belle* was a little different. Built in the late nineteenth century, it had been lovingly restored and refurbished under the supervision of its current owner, a real estate mogul named

Charles Gallister. From what I'd heard, he owned half the shopping centers in the greater St. Louis area.

In addition to being a very successful businessman, he was a Mark Twain buff. Because of his interest in the man some consider to be the greatest American author, Gallister had bought the riverboat and set up these overnight cruises to Hannibal, Missouri, the town where young Sam Clemens had grown up.

Gallister had the golden touch in more than real estate, too. Rumor had it that he was making a small fortune from the gambling that took place on the *Southern Belle.*

All I knew for sure was that it was a powerful draw. When I decided to add the riverboat cruise to the list of literary-oriented tours that my little agency in Atlanta books, I hadn't had any trouble filling it up. This was the first time my clients had gone on the tour, so I figured I'd better come along, too, just to make sure there were no glitches. I had flown to St. Louis, leaving my daughter and son-in-law back in Atlanta to hold down the fort at the office.

I had been running tours like this for nearly a year. Thanks to a suggestion from a friend of mine, an English professor named Will Burke, I had concentrated on tours with some sort of literary angle. The *Gone With the Wind* tour, which included an overnight stay at a working plantation designed to resemble Tara from the book and the movie, was the most popular. Which sort of surprised me considering the fact that there had been a couple of murders on the plantation the very first time I ran the tour.

Since then I'd been a little leery of trouble every time I added a new tour to my list, but so far everything had gone smoothly. I didn't have any reason to expect that this riverboat cruise would be any different.

Laughter from the tourists attracted my attention. I turned to see a man in a rumpled white suit ambling along the deck. He had a shock of white hair, a bushy white mustache, and carried an unlit cigar in his hand. He nodded to the tourists and said, "It could probably be shown by facts and figures that there is no distinctly native American criminal class . . . except Congress."

That brought more laughter and applause. The white-suited man waved his cigar in acknowledgment and went on, "I'll be dispensing more of the wit and wisdom of the immortal Mark Twain tonight in the salon, at eight o'clock. Thank you."

The tourists applauded again. The Twain impersonator continued along the deck, coming toward me. He stayed in character for the most part, stooping over, shuffling his feet, and walking like an old man.

He greeted me with a nod and said in his gruff Twain voice, "Good afternoon, young lady."

"Hello, Mr. Twain," I said. I held out my hand to him. "I'm Delilah Dickinson. I put together one of the tour groups on the boat."

He took my hand. His hand was a giveaway that he wasn't as old as the character he was playing. His grip was that of a much younger man.

"Very pleased to meet you, Ms. Dickinson. I quite fancy redheaded women, you know. I'm Samuel Langhorne Clemens."

"You know, I can almost believe that," I told him

with a smile. "You've got the look and the voice down."

He waved the cigar. "Thank you, thank you." He leaned closer and half whispered, "You can't tell that I'm new at the job?"

That took me by surprise. He looked and sounded like he'd been playing Mark Twain for a long time.

"Not at all," I told him. "You must be a quick study."

He shrugged. "I have some acting experience." His real voice was also that of a younger man. "My name actually is Mark . . . Mark Lansing."

"I'm pleased to meet Mr. Lansing as well as Mr. Twain."

I was happy that he'd referred to me as a young lady, too. When you get to be my age, which I refer to as the late mumbly-mumblies, and you're divorced and have a grown, married daughter, you don't often feel all that young. I was just vain enough to enjoy the attention from Mark Lansing, even though in reality he might be younger than me.

"Will you be attending my performance tonight?" he asked.

"I hadn't really thought about it—"

"I'd appreciate it if you would. I could use a friendly face in the audience. Like I said, I'm new at this."

"Well, all right, sure. I'll be there," I promised.

"I hope you won't be disappointed." He lifted a hand in farewell. "I have to circulate among the other decks and the casino. See you later."

He shuffled off—not to Buffalo—and I went over to the members of my tour group who had gathered along the rail to ask them if anybody had any questions or needed any help with anything. Nobody did.

That gave me a chance to go back to my cabin for a few minutes and call the office. Unlike Eddie Kramer's cell phone, mine worked just fine inside the boat.

Luke Edwards, my son-in-law, answered. "Dickinson Literary Tours."

"Hey, Luke, it's me."

"Miz D! Are you on the riverboat?"

"I sure am. Everything's going just fine, too. I met Mark Twain a few minutes ago."

"Really? The guy who wrote *Huckleberry Finn*?" Luke hesitated. "Wait a minute. He's dead. He can't be on that riverboat."

"No, but an actor playing him is."

"Oh. That makes sense, I guess."

"Is Melissa there?" Luke is big and handsome and charming as all get-out with the clients, but Melissa has a lot better head for business.

"No, she's gone to the office supply place to pick up some stuff."

"Any problems since I've been gone?"

"Uh, Miz D, you only left this morning. We've been able to manage just fine for the past five hours."

"I know, I know. Anybody else sign up for that New Orleans tour yet?"

"Nope. Of course, I haven't checked the Web site in the past five minutes. Somebody could've e-mailed us about it."

"Why don't you do that?"

"Right now? Really?"

I sighed. "No, you're right. I need to just relax

and enjoy this tour I'm on. What's the point in being a travel agent if you can't get some fun out of it yourself?"

"That's it exactly. Just relax and let us take care of everything here. It'll be fine. You'll see."

"All right. Tell Melissa I called, okay?"

"Will do. Don't worry about a thing."

"I won't. Love ya both."

"Love you, too," he told me. I knew he meant it. They were good kids, both of them.

I closed my cell phone and slipped it back in the pocket of my blazer. Real estate agents and tour guide leaders would be lost without blazers. And everything was going along so smoothly that I was sort of at a loss to know what to do next.

I know, I know. I couldn't have jinxed myself any worse than by thinking such a thing. That realization occurred to me just as somebody knocked on the door of my cabin.

CHAPTER 2

I was muttering something to myself about being nine different kinds of darned fool when I opened the door and saw one of the riverboat's stewards standing just outside my cabin, which opened onto the deck.

"Ms. Dickinson, ma'am?"

"That's right."

"There's a, uh, problem with one of the members of your tour group in the casino's main room. Could you come with me?"

"Sure," I said. "Lead the way." As we hurried along the deck I asked, "What sort of trouble?" I had visions of somebody winning a jackpot and having a heart attack, or something like that.

"I couldn't really say, ma'am. Mr. Rafferty just asked me to see if I could find you. One of the members of your group told me you'd gone to your cabin."

He wasn't claiming not to know what the

trouble was; he just wasn't allowed to tell me. That's what it sounded like, anyway.

"Who's this fella Rafferty?"

"Mr. Rafferty's the head of security for the *Southern Belle.*"

Uh-oh. There went the hope that this was something minor and easily brushed aside. The head of security didn't get involved unless the problem was an important one.

We came to a set of fancy double doors with lots of gleaming wood, gilt curlicues, and stained glass. They opened into a foyer with parquet flooring and several windows where pretty girls sat at cash registers. Gamblers bought chips there for the various games and cashed them in when they were done. If they were lucky enough to have any winnings, that is. The unlucky ones just came back and bought more chips.

On the other side of the foyer was the casino's main room. It looked just like what you'd see in a Vegas casino, only on a smaller scale. A couple dozen slot machines instead of hundreds. Poker tables, roulette wheels, faro layouts. Garish lighting. Music blaring from concealed speakers. Laughter, smoke, the *chunk-chunk-chunk* of slot machine wheels turning over, the clicking of the little white ball dancing merrily around the roulette wheel, the occasional whoop of triumph or groan of despair . . . It was a seductive atmosphere, all right, but it seemed as far removed from the sedate and stately Mississippi as if it had been on the moon.

The steward nervously touched my arm to guide me across the room. "This way, ma'am."

"Where are we going?"

"The security office, ma'am."

That's what I had figured. Somebody was being detained. One of my clients, more than likely. I hoped they weren't about to boot whoever it was off the boat.

The steward took me to a nondescript metal door. The short hallway behind it was strictly functional. It ended at some carpeted stairs that led up to the next deck. At the top of the stairs was a large open area equipped with numerous computers and monitors. A low, almost inaudible hum filled the air. The feeds from all the security cameras on board wound up here, I assumed. None of the men and women sitting at the monitors looked around as the steward took me to another door. He knocked on this one.

"Come in," a man called.

The office on the other side of the door was spacious and comfortably furnished with a big desk, a leather-covered sofa, a plasma TV hanging on the wall, and a window that looked out on the river. Two men waited in the office, one on the sofa, the other behind the desk. Both of them stood up when I came in. The one behind the desk was deliberate about it. The one on the sofa jumped to his feet.

"Ms. Dickinson," the one from the sofa said. "I'm sorry. I didn't mean to cause trouble."

I remembered him from the luncheon in St. Louis earlier that afternoon. "What's happened here, Mr. Webster?" I asked him.

His name was Ben Webster. He was in his mid to late twenties, I'd say, with fairly close-cropped dark hair and what seemed to be a perpetually solemn expression. His age and the fact that he was traveling alone made him a little unusual for one of my clients. I get a lot of families and middle-aged and older couples. Not to overgeneralize, but most young men these days aren't that interested in seeing where Mark Twain or Margaret Mitchell or Tennessee Williams lived and worked.

Which meant that Ben Webster was probably here for the gambling, so I wasn't particularly surprised to find him in the casino. I was surprised that he seemed to be in trouble, though. He had seemed like a nice, polite young man in the short time we had talked together at lunch. He even reminded me a little of Luke.

"I'm sorry, but I couldn't let it pass," he said now. "That roulette wheel is rigged. I saw the man working it run his finger over the same little mark on the table several times while it was spinning, and then all the big bets lost. There must be a pressure switch of some sort there, or maybe an optical one built into the table."

The man behind the desk let Webster get his complaint out without saying anything. But he wore a tolerant smile and shook his head slowly while the young man spoke.

When Webster was finished, the man stepped out from behind the desk and extended a big hand toward me. "Ms. Dickinson, I'm Logan Rafferty, the head of security for the *Southern Belle*. I'm sorry we couldn't meet under more pleasant circumstances."

Like his hand, which pretty much swallowed mine whole, the rest of Logan Rafferty was big. He was about forty, with a brown brush cut, and although he wore an expensive suit, he looked like he'd be just as much at home working as a bouncer in a roadhouse somewhere. The afternoon sunlight that came in through the window winked on a heavy ring he wore.

"What seems to be the trouble here, Mr. Rafferty?" He inclined his head toward Ben Webster. "As you just heard, a member of your tour group has a complaint about the way the games are run in the casino. I assure you, all our games are conducted in an honest, legitimate manner," A faint smile appeared on his face. "As you may know, the odds always favor the house to start with. We see no need to tilt them even more."

"No offense, but I would think you'd be used to folks complaining when they lose. It's sort of human nature, after all," I said.

"Complaints we don't mind," Rafferty said with a shrug of his big shoulders. "We don't like it when passengers try to slug one of our employees, though."

I frowned at Ben Webster. "You *didn't*?"

He hung his head and didn't say anything.

I turned back to Rafferty. "I'm sorry," I began. "I hope there wasn't too much of a ruckus. I didn't see any signs of trouble while we were coming through the casino."

"No, things got back to normal quickly once the commotion was over," Rafferty admitted. "And there wasn't much commotion to start with. My security personnel were on the scene before Mr. Webster here could do any real damage."

"I'm sorry," I said again. "What do we need to do to put this matter behind us?"

"The man who operates the roulette wheel could press charges, you know."

I wasn't sure what law enforcement agency had jurisdiction over the Mississippi River. There was bound to be one, though. I said, "Do we really have to get the law involved in this? I was hopin'," we could sort it out amongst ourselves, you know?"

"Webster gets off the boat in Hannibal and doesn't get back aboard." The words came out of Rafferty's mouth hard and flat, like there was no room for negotiation. That suited him more. He just wasn't the affable type, no matter how hard he tried.

Webster's head came up. "You can't do that," he said. "I paid for a round-trip. And my car's in St. Louis."

"You can rent a car in Hannibal and drive back down to St. Louis," Rafferty said. "As for what you paid, that's between you and Ms. Dickinson. But as far as the *Southern Belle* is concerned, you're not welcome on board." He went behind his desk and leaned forward, resting his knuckles on the glass top. "Or I can make a phone call and have the authorities waiting when we dock in Hannibal to *take* you off the boat."

"I'm sure that won't be necessary," I said. I turned to look at Ben Webster. "Will it?"

I don't know if he saw the pleading in my eyes, but after a second he shrugged and said, "No, it won't be necessary. I'll leave the boat. It's not fair, though. That guy really was cheating."

Rafferty's mouth tightened into a thin line. I thought Webster had pushed him too far. But all he said was, "You can go back to your cabin now, Mr. Webster, and stay there. The casino is off limits to you."

"Fine," Webster muttered. "I don't want to lose any more money to your crooked games anyway."

It was all I could do not to grab him by the collar and shake him. Either that or smack him on the back of the head. Didn't he know he was getting off easy? They send people to jail for attacking other people.

I took hold of his arm and steered him toward the door. "Let's go, Mr. Webster."

Behind us, Rafferty said, "I hope to see you again during the cruise, Ms. Dickinson. Do you need someone to show you out?"

"No, thanks. I remember the way I came in."

"Very well, then. Good afternoon."

I figured out then who he reminded me of. With his overly polite demeanor, coupled with the air of violence and menace that hung around him, he was like the movie and TV gangsters played by Sheldon Leonard, the character actor and producer. I had a feeling Rafferty's civilized veneer was pretty thin.

Nobody followed us as we went down the stairs and back out through the security office and the casino. Ben Webster trudged along beside me without saying anything until we reached the deck.

Then he said quietly, "They really were cheating, you know. I'm not just a sore loser."

"I wouldn't know about that," I told him. "I wasn't there, and even if I had been, I don't know anything about how a roulette wheel could be rigged. I think you'd be smart to just let it go."

"What about the money I paid for a round-trip?"

I thought about it. Since he had brought the trouble down on himself, I figured I'd be within my rights to keep his money. But since I like to be accommodating, I said, "I'll refund you, say, thirty percent. But you'll have to wait and let me send you a check."

"I'll be out whatever a rental car costs me, too."

"Should've thought of that before you took a swing at that guy."

"Yeah, I guess so." He nodded, glum as ever. "All right. Thanks. I know you could've told me it was my own fault and to go to hell."

"That's right," I said. "I could have."

He stopped in front of a door with metal numerals 1 and 7 nailed to it. "This is my cabin."

"I'm sorry this happened. You'd better stay in there, like Mr. Rafferty told you. I got the feeling he was pretty mad. He'll call the cops if you give him any more trouble."

"He looked to me more like he wanted to break my neck."

"Yeah, well, he might do that, too."

I left Ben Webster at the door and headed back to my cabin. I got out my laptop and wrote an e-mail to Melissa, telling her to pull the file for Ben Webster and send a check for 30 percent of the money he had paid us to his home address. That was another big difference since Mark Twain's time: The riverboats hadn't been equipped with wireless Internet service back then. They didn't even have dial-up.

The cruise from St. Louis to Hannibal takes a couple of hours. The boat docks in Hannibal early enough so that folks can get some sightseeing done before dark. Then they have dinner on the boat and enjoy an evening of gambling and other entertainment, including Mark Lansing's performance as Mark Twain. More sightseeing the next morning rounds out the trip, and then the boat cruises back downriver to St. Louis that afternoon, so the whole trip takes about twenty-seven hours.

That's long enough to give the passengers the authentic flavor of a Mississippi River voyage without causing a problem for modern-day attention spans.

I didn't have much interest in gambling. I own a small business; that's enough of a gamble for me. I didn't intend to spend the evening boozing it up like some of the passengers would, either. My hope was that nobody would get drunk and cause trouble. The incident with Ben Webster was more than enough of a ruckus for this trip.

So my plan was to take in the Mark Twain show in the salon. Mark Lansing had struck me as a nice guy, and I couldn't help but wonder what he looked like without the wig and the fake mustache and the old-man make-up.

I hoped the wild white hair and the big mustache really were fake. You never know, though, with actors. Some of them really get into the parts they play.

First, though, there were sights to see, and a little later, as the riverboat's steam whistle let out several shrill blasts, I knew we were about to dock at Hannibal, Missouri, boyhood home of Mr. Samuel Langhorne Clemens himself.

CHAPTER 3

I'd never been to Hannibal before. As I walked toward the front of the boat, I saw the town sprawled on the western bank of the river with rolling green hills behind it. Since tourism was an important industry here, it was deliberately picturesque. Oh, there were plenty of modern touches visible, but many of the buildings really were old and had been restored to look like they had in Mark Twain's time, like the riverboat itself.

Quite a few of the passengers had gathered on the bow to watch the approach to the dock. I saw about half the members of my group among them. The others were still in the casino, I supposed. I noticed Eddie and Louise Kramer at the railing. She was snapping pictures with a digital camera. I was sort of surprised to see that he wasn't talking on his cell phone but was resting his hands on the railing instead and looking at Hannibal with what appeared to be genuine interest. Maybe his wife had read him the riot act about actually enjoying this vacation of theirs, even though she didn't seem the type to do such a thing.

I didn't see Ben Webster anywhere. I supposed he was still holed up in his cabin. That was good. Once we docked he could come out and get off the boat.

The whistle blew again. Several people strolled out onto the dock and waved enthusiastically at the passengers as the riverboat approached. The women wore bonnets and long skirts and carried parasols. The men were in old-fashioned suits and beaver hats. One young couple wore the sort of period clothing that youngsters would have in Mark Twain's time. I knew from the Internet research I'd done before the trip that they were supposed to be Tom Sawyer and Becky Thatcher. Folks in Hannibal played up its literary heritage for all it was worth, and I didn't blame them a bit for doing so. The tourists would have been disappointed if it wasn't that way.

The captain, or whoever was at the wheel of the *Southern Belle*, maneuvered the boat next to the dock and brought it to a stop with a smooth, graceful touch. The big paddlewheels on the sides stopped turning. Water sluiced off the paddles and sloshed against the pilings that supported the dock. Members of the crew hurried to extend a railed gangway from the main deck to the dock so that the passengers could disembark.

I didn't have any group activities planned for the afternoon or evening, although I had a table reserved in the riverboat's dining room so anyone who wanted to eat together could. My clients were free to take in whatever sights they wanted to, and there were plenty of dinner theaters and restaurants in Hannibal where they could eat if they chose. Or they could continue gambling in the boat's casino if that was what they wanted to do. The more informal tours like this were welcome breaks from having to herd groups of tourists around from one attraction to another.

People began disembarking from the boat as soon as the gangway was in place, among them the Kramers. I lingered there along the rail, waiting to make sure that Ben Webster got off the boat. I could see the door to Cabin 17 from where I was and expected to see it open any minute now.

But it didn't.

I waited some more. Still no sign of Ben Webster. He couldn't have gotten off the boat without me seeing him, I thought. I'd been close to the gangway ever since the boat docked.

If Webster didn't leave, like Logan Rafferty had told him to, Rafferty might call the cops and have him arrested. That would lead to bad publicity for my tour. Webster seemed like a pretty good kid overall, so that was another reason to avoid bringing the law into this. I walked along the deck to Cabin 17 and knocked on the door.

No one answered. I knocked harder and called, "Mr. Webster!" When he still didn't respond I added, "This is Ms. Dickinson. We've docked at Hannibal. You need to get off the boat now, Mr. Webster."

Nothing.

I was starting to get mad now. Rafferty had offered Webster a way to smooth this over with a minimum of fuss and no legal involvement. Sure, he'd lose a little money and have his trip ruined, but that was his own fault. Now, by refusing to come out of his cabin, he was causing more trouble for me.

Assuming, of course, that he was actually *in* his cabin, I suddenly thought. I hadn't been keeping an eye on Cabin 17 ever since the incident. He could have slipped out of it almost anytime. He could be anywhere on the boat's three decks by now. I didn't relish the idea of having to search the entire *Southern Belle* for him.

So much for him being a good kid. Maybe he really was a troublemaker.

I wanted to find him myself. I could go to Rafferty and get his security personnel involved in the search, but if I did that, Rafferty would likely call the police because Webster had reneged on the agreement to leave the boat. I wished Luke were here so I could split up the chore with him.

But he was back in Atlanta, so it was up to me to locate Ben Webster on my own. I started by making a circuit of the main deck.

This deck had passenger cabins, the casino, and the dining room. On the second deck were offices, the salon, and more passenger cabins. The third deck was off limits to passengers except for observation areas at bow and stern; crew quarters were up there, as well as more offices. The pilothouse that sat on the very top of the boat was off limits as well except for scheduled tours that let passengers see the river from the vantage point of the captain and the pilot.

It took me an hour to cover all the areas where passengers were permitted. Since Ben Webster was already in trouble, I figured it wasn't very likely he would venture into the off-limits areas. But nothing was impossible. If I didn't find him in any of the public areas, I'd have to consider asking Rafferty for help in searching the other parts of the boat.

When I had looked everywhere I could look and still hadn't found any trace of Ben Webster, I went back down to the main deck. I was getting pretty hot under the collar. I'd wanted to see some of the sights in Hannibal myself, and I couldn't do it as long as he was missing. This time I didn't just knock on the door of his cabin—I pounded on that sucker.

While I was doing that, somebody came up behind me and said, "Excuse me? Can I help you?"

I turned around to see a tall young man with blond hair standing there. He looked familiar, and I realized after a second that he was another member of the tour group. I had met him at the luncheon earlier that day. I'm usually pretty good with names, but I was upset enough right then that I couldn't come up with his.

He knew me, though. He smiled in recognition and went on, "Ms. Dickinson, right? I'm Vince Mallory. I'm a member of your tour."

"Of course, I remember you, Mr. Mallory," I told him. "I was just looking for another member of the tour."

A slight frown of confusion appeared on his face. "Then, uh, why are you pounding on the door of my cabin like you're trying to knock it down?"

"Your cabin?" I blinked. "This isn't Ben Webster's cabin?"

"Who?"

"Ben Webster," I repeated. "About your age, six feet tall, dark hair . . ."

Vince Mallory was shaking his head before I finished describing Webster. He said, "I'm sorry, I don't know the guy. But I'm sure this is my cabin." He reached into the pocket of his jeans and brought out a key. "See, here's the key to this door."

He slipped the key into the lock, turned it, and sure enough, the door opened. I looked into the room. It was empty.

I closed my eyes for a second and told myself that I was a darned fool. I had walked off and left Ben Webster standing in front of the door like he was about to go in, but I hadn't actually seen him enter the cabin. He'd waited until I was gone, then headed for somewhere else on the boat!

"Is there a problem?" Vince Mallory asked.

"No, not at all," I lied. I had an unaccounted for rogue tourist with a grudge, that was all. Ben Webster had to be hiding somewhere on the riverboat, and the only reason for him to do that would be if he wanted to cause trouble of some sort. To avenge his losses in the casino that he thought were caused by a rigged roulette wheel. To get back at Rafferty for threatening him. Heck, who knew what was going on in Ben Webster's mind. All I knew was that it couldn't be anything good.

"I'd be glad to give you a hand if there's anything I can do," Vince Mallory said.

"No, everything's fine," I said. I had thought of something else I could check. But first I forced myself back into tour director mode. "Are you heading into Hannibal to see some of the sights this afternoon?"

"Yeah, I thought I would. I've been in the casino, but you can't just gamble away the whole trip, now can you?" He waved a hand toward Hannibal. "Not with all this history waiting to be seen and experienced."

"You're a history buff, are you?"

"I had a double major in college: history and American literature. That was before I sort of got sidetracked into the military."

He had sort of a military look about him, all right. Probably the short hair and the fact that he was in really good shape. He didn't really seem like the academic type, but he went on, "Mark Twain has always been a particular interest of mine. When I was doing graduate work I planned to write my doctoral thesis on him."

"But you got sidetracked," I said.

He grinned. "Yeah. Wound up an MP instead of a PhD. Funny how life works out sometimes, isn't it?"

"It sure is. Are you still in the army?"

"No, I've been out for a while. I've been trying to decide whether to go back to school or maybe get into the security field."

He was a likable young guy, but I had a potential crisis on my hands. I had chatted long enough to do my duty as the tour director, so I said, "Well, I'll see you later, more than likely. Enjoy your cruise, Mr. Mallory."

"Thank you." He looked concerned. "You're sure there's nothing I can do to help you?"

"No, thanks." I smiled and turned to head for my cabin.

When I got there I opened my laptop and called up the records for this cruise. I had a copy of the passenger manifest that someone in Charles Gallister's office had e-mailed to me earlier in the day. In addition to giving me something to check against my own records, it provided the numbers of the cabins assigned to my clients. It took me only a second to scroll down the list to Ben Webster's name and see that he was supposed to be in Cabin 135.

That was on the second deck. The son of a gun had lied to me. He had picked Vince Mallory's cabin at random and claimed it was his so he could get away from me and do whatever it was he planned to do—which couldn't be anything good. Now I was stuck with not knowing where he was or what he was up to.

I still had one thing I could check before giving up and going to Rafferty, though. I left my cabin and hurried up to the second deck again. Earlier I had walked all around it looking for Webster, but I hadn't knocked on the door to Cabin 135. That's what I did now.

Somehow, I wasn't the least bit surprised when there was no answer.

I tried the knob, not expecting the door to be unlocked. But it was. I confess, I jumped a little in surprise when the knob turned in my hand. I didn't know whether to open the door or not. It had occurred suddenly to me that I might not like what I found in there.

But I had gone too far to back out now, I figured, so I eased the door open a couple of inches and knocked on it again, just in case. I even called out, "Mr. Webster? Ben? Are you in there?"

When there was no answer, I really thought about closing the door and going for help, so I wouldn't have to go in there by myself. I sort of wished now that I'd asked Vince Mallory to come with me. Having a big, strapping former MP with me would have done wonders for my confidence right then.

It seemed like I stood there, torn by indecision, a lot longer than I actually did. Probably not more than a couple of seconds went by after I called out before I pushed the door all the way open and stepped into the cabin with my heart pounding.

Nobody was in there.

Unless they were in the bathroom, my nervous brain reminded me. The closed door loomed ominously in a corner of the room.

I took a better look around first. There had been a suitcase sitting on the bed in Vince Mallory's cabin, as there probably was in most of the passenger cabins on the boat. Not here, though. I didn't see a bag anywhere. I opened the door to the tiny closet. No suitcase, no clothes hanging up, nothing. By the looks of the cabin, it could have been unoccupied.

That left the bathroom. There's an old saying in the South about being as nervous as a cat on a porch full of rocking chairs. That's how I felt as I approached the bathroom door. I was ready to jump.

I knocked on it first. "Mr. Webster? Are you in there?"

Either he wasn't, or he couldn't answer.

"Stop that," I told myself out loud as that thought went through my head. "Just because you found a dead body that other time doesn't mean you're gonna find one now."

I knew that made sense, but I still felt a whole cloud of butterflies in my stomach as I reached out and grasped the knob. I swallowed hard and then turned it. I pushed the door open, halfway expecting to bump up against a corpse.

Instead the door opened all the way, revealing a bathroom with a toilet, a tiny vanity, and a shower, just like the one in my cabin. The shower curtain was pulled across the opening. I started to push it back, then hesitated. I didn't think the shower was big enough for a body to be hidden in it. The only way that would be possible would be if the body was stiff enough so it could be propped up against the wall and stay there.

With a rasp of curtain rings on the rod, I shoved the curtain back.

Then blew out a long breath because the shower was empty. Not just empty, but also dry, as if no one had used it since the passengers came on board.

I looked around the bathroom. It didn't take long. No shaving kit or anything else personal. The hand towel beside the vanity was damp, the only sign that this cabin had been occupied anytime recently. If not for that, it would have been like Ben Webster had never been here.

So he had come to his cabin and cleaned it out after leaving me down on the main deck, I thought. Why? It made sense if he'd been planning to get off the boat at Hannibal, as he'd agreed to do. But he hadn't gotten off. At least, I hadn't seen him if he had.

So where the heck was my missing tourist?

**Check out the
Mysteries of
Laura Levine!**

Death by Pantyhose
0-7582-0786-7 $6.99US/$8.49CAN

Killer Blonde
0-7582-3547-X $6.99US/$8.49CAN

Killing Bridezilla
0-7582-2044-8 $6.99US/$8.49CAN

Last Writes
0-7582-0161-3 $5.99US/$7.99CAN

PMS Murder
0-7582-0784-0 $6.99US/$9.99CAN

Shoes to Die For
0-7582-0782-4 $6.99US/$9.99CAN

This Pen for Hire
0-7582-0159-1 $5.99US/$7.99CAN

Available Wherever Books Are Sold!
Visit our website at www.kensingtonbooks.com

More Mischief, Murder, & Mayhem in These Kensington Mysteries

Grab these
Kensington Mysteries

A Catered Valentine's Day 0-7582-0690-9	Isis Crawford $6.99US/$9.99CAN
Remains to Be Scene 0-7582-1281-X	R.T. Jordan $6.99US/$9.99CAN
Knock Off 0-7582-1558-4	Rhonda Pollero $6.99US/$9.99CAN
Staying Home Is a Killer 0-7582-1339-5	Sara Rosett $6.99US/$8.49CAN
Streets of Fire 0-7582-0625-9	Troy Soos $6.99US/$8.49CAN
Ham Bones 0-7582-1093-0	Carolyn Haines $6.99US/$8.49CAN
Kilt Dead 0-7582-1644-0	Kaitlyn Dunnett $6.99US/$8.49CAN

Available Wherever Books Are Sold!
Visit our website at www.kensingtonbooks.com